# 2026

E. COMPTON LEE

BLUE FORTUNE ENTERPRISES LLC

*Lavender Press*
an imprint of Blue Fortune Enterprises LLC

2026
Copyright © 2024 by E. Compton Lee



This book is a work of fiction. Names, characters, businesses, organizations, places, events and incidents either are the product of the author's imagination or are used fictitiously. Any resemblance to actual persons, living or dead, events, or locales is entirely coincidental.

For information contact :
Blue Fortune Enterprises, LLC
Lavender Press
P.O. Box 554
Yorktown, VA 23690
http://blue-fortune.com


Cover design by BFELLC

ISBN: 978-1-961548-10-7
First Edition: May 2024

*I dedicate this book to
my sister Denny*

## Acknowledgements

I would like to thank my publisher Narielle Living; my friend and support system, Alma Kendall; the members of the Silver Quill and the Williamsburg critique groups. Their input was invaluable.

*Elizabeth*

# CHAPTER ONE

**H**er mother looked the same as she had when Sloan left home six years ago. Same unkempt black hair untouched by gray, same high flat cheekbones, and almond-shaped eyes. Same way of watching her: enigmatic, waiting. She was thinner, of course, but then so were they all.

"I know what you're thinking," Sloan said.

Clare didn't take the bait.

Sloan waited, then impatient, continued. "You think once we get really, really hungry, I'm going to fillet the horses. Well, I'm not."

Her mother looked away with a wry smile. "That's a relief."

They stood in front of the barn with its familiar musky, slightly acrid odor, a smell Sloan suddenly realized she had missed.

Clare looked at her daughter. "I seen the story about you in that magazine, what's it called, *Food and Beer*? John brought it from town. It said you was a marvel being so successful in the Big Apple and only twenty-four." Then she surprised Sloan by adding, "I'm glad you're here. I was scared you wouldn't get out."

Sloan looked past her mother's shoulder at the half-empty stable. "New York's not so big anymore," she said quietly. "There are places to slip through. And the magazine's called *Food and Wine*."

"I know that. I was just teasing. How'd you get out?"

"A friend of a friend. Tallest man I ever saw up close. With a neon orange afro."

"Didn't that make him kind of noticeable? And how'd you know you could trust him?"

"Cause of the 'fro.' Diamond wouldn't have a man with hair like that in his army. Especially a Black man. Anyway, he stuffed his hair under a baseball cap once we were on the street."

Clare nodded. "He didn't bring you straight here, did he?"

"No, he dropped me in Hagerstown where an ordinary-looking guy picked me up and drove me to Coleton. I walked the rest of the way." They stood contemplating each other in the hot, damp air. Sloan hadn't wanted to return, but the space around the illusive Clare Raffienne seemed the safest place to hide. Finally, her mother changed the mood and asked if Sloan wanted something to eat.

In fact, Sloan was starving. "Do you have food? Enough to share?"

"We killed a bear about a week ago. There's plenty. Come on, John's cooking some right now."

Walking behind her, Sloan studied Clare's broad shoulders, her easy stride and how the thick, loosely braided hair swung down her back. She thought of catching up to her and telling her how hard it had been to get hooked up with the man she thought of as Orange. The constant no shows, false leads, the final meeting when she almost changed her mind and said no, because the strange hair put her off. Instead, she'd silently gotten in the front seat beside him. During the over four-hour drive, they had spoken once when the man asked, "Do you need to pull over for a pit stop?" They had taken the back roads.

"Yes, please."

The man pulled to the side of the road and Sloan slipped into the woods. "What about you?" she asked when she returned. He shook his head. Sloan appreciated his silence. These days, the less you said to anyone, the better.

Unlike Orange, the man who picked her up in Hagerstown worried her from start to finish. His manner was too familiar. He didn't exactly make small talk, but he did ask how long it had taken to get from New York City to where they were now. He wanted to know how they'd managed to find him. Sloan ignored him, didn't answer any of his questions until finally he muttered, "Have it your way, bitch." When they reached Coleton, Sloan told him to stop and let her out. As far as she was concerned, even fifteen miles from her old home was too close. She just hoped he wasn't familiar with these parts.

Those were the words she wanted to tell her mother, but familial patterns die hard.

She followed her mother into the woods bordering the yard, where there was a small clearing with a fire pit in the ground. John was flipping slabs of meat, and the slightly sweet, charcoal smell filled her mouth with saliva. Once, at the restaurant, one of the cooks prepared bear steaks for staff dinner. Sloan couldn't bring herself to eat it. She had a history with bears, one in particular. She had called her Sister. John looked up and smiled at Clare, who sat close to him and picked up a plate. He forked a slab for her. Clare handed it to Sloan, who held onto the plate and lowered herself awkwardly to the ground. She didn't see any knives or forks, so she figured she was meant to eat with her fingers. She blew on the steaming meat.

"Did you bring any luggage?" John asked.

"I'm wearing it."

Clare rolled her eyes, smiled, and fluffed John's hair. "Luggage. I love your positive thinking, sweetie." Still smiling at him, she said to her daughter, "Don't worry, I kept a few things of yours. T-shirts, jeans. Maybe even some sneakers."

For a horrifying instant, Sloan thought they might kiss. Instead, John shook his head and smiled back at Clare. He had loved and left her mother when Sloan was eight. Six years later, he returned to the farm for good.

Sloan tried to pick up the meat, but it was still too hot. Bear meat in the middle of summer. A little lean but a gold mine nonetheless. She didn't want to think of her mother killing another bear. Maybe John had done it. Maybe with a knife, but that was pushing it. "You use a gun, a knife, or what?"

"I used the rifle," he said.

"How do you get bullets?"

"The underground." John put another piece of meat on a plate for Clare. "There's an active resistance here."

Sloan looked up, following the smoke.

Her mother noticed and said, "You can't see it from the road."

Sloan touched the meat, but it was still too hot. She blew on it some more and finally took a bite, barely able to swallow. She gulped it untasted as fast as possible. She was starving. When she had licked the last morsel off her fingers, Sloan put down the plate and asked how they were surviving. "Have any of you had Hepatic 26? What about electricity? And water?"

Clare chewed her steak for a few seconds before she swallowed it and said, "Colleen was pretty sick. We thought we might lose her. The spring's still workin' and Crab's eddy runs fast, though I wouldn't drink it. Just use it for washing. Water ain't no problem. We only use electricity for the fridge and freezer. I'm thinking the tiny amount of juice we use won't be noticed. And by the way, we got someone quarantined in the shed. A Whitbeck."

Sloan's eyes popped open. "A Whitbeck!?"

The Whitbecks were one of the richest families in the country, possibly the world. They had migrated from New York to Pennsylvania for reasons no one knew. They ignored the locals. Even the staff was imported from France, Italy, or Mexico.

"Yes, a Whitbeck. A young girl. Showed up high in the mountain on horseback. Beautiful animal. I'll show him to you." Clare said this casually, as though she didn't know how deadly it was to have a Whitbeck here at the farm.

John swallowed the last of his steak. "She's been here five days. It's hard to get her story. Shy or still in shock from what happened at the estate— whatever that might be. Maybe Jamie will know when we see him."

The Whitbecks owned a large section of the Alleghenies where they raised horses but didn't do much else as far as anyone could tell. "Maybe she'll be more talkative when she's out of quarantine in nine days." John stood and stretched, lifted the grate off the fire with a stick and stamped at the coals with his boots. He glanced up the mountain. "It's cooling off. Think I'll go fishing."

Sloan took stock of her new life; a fire pit in the ground, hungry horses, hungry—possibly sick—people, a mother who still scared her, a Whitbeck in the shed, and her with not a clue what she would do here.

She'd been a top-of-the-line chef in New York City, and top-of-the-line chefs in New York City spent evenings and most of the night filled with adrenaline and blazing on all cylinders. In the wee small hours, they went to the markets for fresh fish, meats, and vegetables. They caught a few hours of sleep in the middle of the day, then it started all over again. Sloan thrived on the pace.

Almost two years into the Diamond presidency, all the energy, initiative, creativity, and nerve were driven out of the city. Only Nationalized restaurants were allowed open, and Sloan's wasn't one of them. Fear replaced optimism. She closed shop and spent a week moving from one hiding place to another, sleeping on bare floors, in closets, starving and going from contact to contact, trying to find her way out of the city. Her adrenaline pumped and her parasympathetic nervous system worked on high alert. She'd left her mother's farm at eighteen because it was in a backwater only the locals cared about, and Sloan needed so much more. Now its remoteness was its virtue, but Sloan still didn't know if she could stand the slow pace, the predictable rhythm. But then, there was no such thing as predictable anymore.

Clare finished tamping out the last ember. "Have you had the virus?"

"No."

Her mother continued making sure no live coals were left. "There're empty stalls. We can fix one up, so you'll be comfortable. After two weeks, you can sleep in the house. Don't get too close to no one in the meantime."

# CHAPTER TWO

**N**ot only was the dining room empty for breakfast, but the dinner dishes were still on the table and food on the sideboard. Rosemary wandered to the stables. Large sliding doors flew open before she reached it. Pedro's brown, creased face appeared between them. "Thank God you come. I was afraid to go to the big house and get you. I have Wilson saddled and ready."

"What are you talking about?"

By holding his hand six inches from her back, he guided Rosemary to a stall where a seventeen-hand gleaming copper-colored horse stood tossing his head and fidgeting.

"You must leave now, Miss Rosemary." Pedro opened the stall door, unhooked the horse's lead shank from a ring on the wall and led him into the aisle where he jigged in place. Rosemary noted in a bemused, distracted way, the halter was under the bridle. The Whitbecks never put a halter under a bridle. They considered it unprofessional and a sign of laziness. She also noted the small, elegant, perfectly proportioned leather bag attached to the saddle; the kind used when riding to hounds. Being a jumper not a hunter, Wilson had never carried one before.

Pedro unsnapped the lead shank from the halter and put it in the diminutive saddle bag. "You'll need that," he said.

He had been running the stables for as long as Rosemary had been alive. She grew up following him around, getting in the way until she turned five and could be of some help. He put her to work filling water buckets and pouring grain into feed dishes.

She didn't think to ask him questions about his past. He had always been there, and as soon as she was old enough, she slipped away from the house and came to the stables and stayed as long as she could. She had seen horses come into the barn ready to kill something or someone, but they gave Pedro little trouble. He moved among them like a slow-moving shadow, touching them here and there so softly they barely felt it. Today, he wore an expression she'd never seen before—a mixture of wild concern turning into terror.

"Pedro… tell me what's going on… please!"

"Your parents are gone. Your brothers are gone. The servants are gone. I am the only one left. Now mount up and ride away from here as fast as you can."

Stunned into obedience, Rosemary put her foot into a stirrup and swung into the saddle. "How long must I stay away?"

"Forever."

"Where should I go?"

"Deep into the mountains. Find someone to help you."

The girl's pupils dilated, making her eyes darker than ever. "What about you?"

"The helicopter landed in a far pasture late last night," he said. "I'm ready to go. Don't worry about me. I have connections." Without further ado, he led horse and rider out of the barn.

Wilson snatched at the bit, pulling Rosemary forward. She regained her seat, gave the horse his head, and as he burst into a gallop, she called goodbye to the person she loved most on this earth.

The horse's back hooves landed ahead of his front ones as he tore through the manicured lawn of the big house and up the mountain. Even when he entered the dense woods it seemed he would never tire, but at last he did, his shoulders and flanks covered in foaming sweat. His gallop dropped to a canter, his canter to a trot. He slowed, slowed some more, then walked a few paces, set his four feet and remained there, his sides heaving. Rosemary patted his wet, sleek neck. She slipped off her horse and sat hopelessly against a tree, noticing for the first time they had come to a patch of sunlight where grass grew. Wilson nibbled at it until Rosemary hauled herself upright and onto her horse's back and nudged him with her heels. His breath back and his legs rested, Wilson began a steady walk as he carried his weeping rider farther from home.

Rosemary had not heard the helicopter landing or lifting off. She had not heard footsteps running up and down the stairs, the occasional shouts and doors slamming.

The tension in the house yesterday had been profound. Rosemary avoided all tension when she could, so she had spent the morning and early afternoon in the barn with Pedro: bathing horses, shampooing their tales, combing them out strand by strand with her fingers, polishing hooves, filling stalls with clean, sharp-smelling wood shavings.

In the afternoon, she had gone to the man-made lake to skinny dip. The water, always brisk, flowed over her skin, across her breasts, which were the size of grapefruits, along her belly and between her legs. She swam across the lake and back, then did it again. She did the backstroke and dove under water, going down as far as possible. She swam until the sun told her it was time to dress for dinner. Dinner at the Whitbecks' was at 8:30, and no one was ever late.

Rosemary put on a white frock that flowed from her shoulders to her knees. Feeling clean, refreshed and especially thin after her swim, she walked into the dining room. All her family were seated at the table. Her father looked at his watch but said nothing. In fact, no one had much to say throughout the meal and when they did speak, their voices were brittle and made no sense to the girl. She noticed a few furtive glances and then shortly after the entrée had been served, she became aware the servants were gone. The servants were never gone before the end of the meal. No one spoke of their absence so neither did Rosemary.

The family retired to the parlor where her father and brothers paced, and her mother sat still on the couch clutching her long sapphire necklace. Rosemary kissed them all goodnight, went upstairs to her bedroom, and fell asleep as soon as her head hit the pillow.

This morning when she walked into the dining room, the tension was gone and only a dull silence remained.

Now, terrified and detached from the world around her, Rosemary focused on the push of Wilson's haunches, one then the other, and the careful way he placed his front feet among the rocks. Sometimes, when his shoe hit one, a small spark flashed. He didn't spook. He didn't attempt to turn around and go back to the barn as many horses would. "You're such a good boy," Rosemary said and patted his now dry neck. The hair was stiff with salt. As she did this, the image of the day he arrived at the estate rolled unbidden into her mind.

The horse had walked off the trailer with his neck arched, eyes huge, ears ramrod straight, and nostrils flaring. Nothing unusual for a horse arriving for the first time. But the sun turned his copper-colored hair to fire. He danced around, pulling the groom's lead shank as taught as it would go then leaned back on his hocks, taking weight off his front legs. Rosemary waited for him to paw the air with his front hooves, but he didn't. Instead, he equalized his weight, took a small step toward the groom, stretched his neck as far as it would go, and shook himself from nose tip to tail tip. Once he was satisfied, he looked around, his eyes alert and demanding, as though to say, "All right, I'm here. Now what?" Rosemary thought he was the most beautiful horse she had ever seen, and she'd seen many beautiful horses. She wanted him to be hers more than anything. She took great care not to show this to her father.

As it turned out, she was the first to ride Wilson Elliott the Third and in not too long a time, her father allowed her to be the only one to ride him. Mr. Whitbeck had never done this sort of thing before. Normally, he watched one of his trainers ride a new horse, thought over what he had seen, and then decided what to do with it. Never before had he assigned a horse to be in the sole charge of his daughter.

Wilson was a good mover but not good enough to go on the hunter circuit. Rosemary talked this over with her father, and they decided he should be a jumper. The horse used his size and athleticism to his advantage and at times was brilliant, clearing jumps with more than a foot to spare. However, other days, he decided he wasn't interested and dropped his hind legs, bringing down three rails or dangled his knees knocking down the top rail. Rosemary lived in terror her father would hand him over to a professional to teach him how to behave or, worse, sell him. Her father always wanted his horses to be the ones to beat at any event he entered, and he only entered the best. Luckily, for reasons Rosemary couldn't figure out, he didn't take the horse's training away from her.

Now, as Wilson picked his way up the mountain, the events of the day pushed into Rosemary's awareness with brutal clarity. Her stomach clenched as if she had swallowed glass. Why did they leave her behind? They could have woken her, gathered her up and taken her with them. How could they have left her alone in that house? What were they running from? She bent at the waist, loosened the reins, and laid her head on the horse's mane. She wrapped her arms around his rhythmically bobbing neck and fell asleep. Rosemary was a frequent sleeper. She tended to nap when things got edgy on the estate and today, events had gone light years beyond edgy.

As the sun headed toward its zenith, the horse continued his steady ascent up the mountain. When the flies bit Wilson's neck, instead of throwing his head around and stamping his feet as he normally would do, he shivered his skin and the base of his mane so as not to disturb the balance of the weight he carried. A light sweat broke out along his body. The air did not grow cooler the higher they traveled, and his pace slowed.

After three hours the sun bore down on horse and rider from straight overhead. When Wilson reached the pinnacle, he shifted his power from behind to his front legs for the descent. Rosemary felt the change and woke up. She was at once aware of a terrible thirst. Looking around, she recognized nothing, but then why would she? She had never been in these woods. In fact, she hadn't gone anywhere off the estate except to school and riding events.

"I don't know what to do," she told Wilson. In response, he stopped with his head hanging below his withers. Rosemary ran her fingers through his mane, which was sticky with sweat. "You're exhausted too," she said. There is a common folklore that horses can smell water from miles away. Rosemary touched Wilson with both heels, leaving the reins lying loose on his neck. "You're in charge now," she said, as though he hadn't been in charge all along. "Find us something to drink."

Wilson didn't move.

"Go on. Find water."

Wilson sighed and walked on.

Rosemary's thirst robbed her of all sense of time. All she could think about was water. Wilson's head drooped; Rosemary's head drooped. The horse picked his way through the rocky terrain. Eventually, he stopped again. Rosemary sat mutely on his back. She didn't have the heart to make him keep going. If I'm going to die, she thought, there is no creature I would rather have with me. She began to doze in the heat, but Wilson's body suddenly tensed. His ears twitched this way and that and he chortled deep in his throat. Rosemary looked around then heard something sounding like hoof beats. She forced herself fully awake and paid attention. Yes, it was definitely a horse, and it was coming close. Her back straightened, pushing her deeper in the saddle. Wilson turned his head and nickered. A tall, thin woman on a tall, thin horse rode out of the woods and stopped to stare at them.

"Help," Rosemary whispered, desperate, her throat raw from thirst.

"Who are you?"

"Rosemary Whitbeck. I think I'm lost."

When Clare first saw the girl through the trees, she should have slipped past her unseen, but curiosity had taken over. Now she was face to face with a Whitbeck. "What are you doing way over here?" she said, her voice deceptively casual.

"You know where I live?"

"Everyone knows where you live."

"They've all gone."

"Who's all gone?"

"My family. The servants. Except Pedro. He was still there when I left."

Clare sat still, letting this information fill her. She took her time looking the girl over: Huge dark eyes, fluffy brown hair matted around her face, vacant expression, narrow body. She looked to be in her late teens and dumb as a box of rocks. Perhaps it was just fatigue. Or shock. She didn't appear threatening, but, still, if she really was a Whitbeck, that would bring nothing but trouble. The horse was magnificent and must have cost a fortune. A Whitbeck sort of fortune. Clare rested her folded hands on the front of her saddle. "If they all left, how come you're still here?"

"I don't know." The girl stopped gaping at Clare and stared into the distance with such dignity the woman could only feel admiration. Despite all the reasons this was a bad idea, she said, "Follow me. You look like you could use some food and water."

# CHAPTER THREE

After leaving the firepit, Sloan watched her mother wrestle a twin mattress out the kitchen door. Its dead weight reminded her of a body before rigor mortis sets in. Clare wouldn't let her near enough to help. Once her mother had it in the yard, it was easier to tug and drag to the stable. Still, sweat ran along the sides of Clare's face, under her chin and down her neck. Her t-shirt clung to her skin, wet and transparent by the time she dropped the mattress into an empty stall. A light skim of wood shavings kept it off the ground which was hard packed crush-and-run, a mixture of shale and dirt that packed perfectly for a horse stall.

"I'll get some sheets," Clare said while Sloan stood the required ten feet away.

After dropping the sheets along with a pillow and pillowcase on the mattress, Clare brought a gray horse from one of the stalls. Thin gray horses look more wretched than chestnuts or bays. The points of their hip bones are more noticeable, their ribs more countable. Their lackluster coats seem drier and more brittle. Clare threw a lightweight racing saddle over his back and slipped a one-ear-loop bridle onto his head.

"Where you going?"

"Up the mountain."

"Is he going to make it up the mountain?" Sloan asked.

"This is his last trip for a while. The grass is good up there. Maybe he'll pick up some weight. If he'll stay there. Last time I tried to do this, he ran back to the barn the minute he was loose." She lifted herself into the saddle. The horse raised his head. "I'd like to fence that field off but don't have any wire left. It's been a life saver, that place. Lucky we found it."

"How many horses are out there?"

"Four. That new chestnut and this gray make six all together. Too many. Go look at him. He's a beauty."

The chestnut whinnied as Clare rode away. Sloan leaned over the bottom door of his stall. The horse twirled around, stuck his head out the back window, and whinnied again. "Come here, boy." Sloan held out her hand. The horse turned to sniff it and licked off the salt. His eyes looked bewildered, the sharp edge of fear just beginning to show. Sloan guessed he'd never been hungry before. He was tucked up underneath, but his coat still shone, and his muscles stood out, toned and fully formed. What would he look like in a week or a month?

Sloan went back to her stall and spread the sheets loosely on the mattress, then walked to the springhouse for some water. On the way, she passed the shed with the Whitbeck girl in it. It was eerily quiet. She thought about knocking on the door and saying hello but suddenly felt too tired to do even that.

Back at the barn she put the enamel cup of water in a corner, squatted down on her mattress, and wrapped her arm around her raised knees. Well, she thought. She felt a little dizzy. Too many questions unanswered. And the bear meat made her stomach sick. She laid down on her back, then sat up and pulled the sheet to her chin even though at this time of day the barn was filled with sunlight and warmth. What the hell, she thought. A fly flew through a path of sunlight, buzzed around the stall, and flew out. Sloan watched the dust motes and wondered if she was going to vomit. Why did her mother have to be so efficient? She could have hung around for a while. Help Sloan get the lay of the land. Like where was Colleen? And Annie? She and John could have elaborated a little. The horses could wait. The fish could wait. Her eyes closed. Sloan was used to sleeping at this time of day and the barn felt familiar, maybe even safe. The horse snuffled around his stall looking for something to eat. Sloan wondered why her mother was taking horses up the mountain when they had pasture right here. She rolled on her side and closed her eyes again then rolled over to the other side. Her legs wouldn't stop moving. She sighed and decided to get up and take a look at the nearby pastures. She pushed away the sheet covering her. The slight puff of air it made as she flicked it blew shavings away and it landed on the bare stall floor. The sight of the sheet, rumpled and now lying on dirt, reminded Sloan of an afternoon three years ago.

She was standing in what passed for a bathroom in the apartment she shared with four others. She had run her hands over her head, pulled back her red-gold hair, and forced it into a rubber band. At the restaurant, she would fold a white linen napkin into a triangle, cover her hair and the tips of her ears and tie it into a tight knot at the nape of her neck. At *Sally's Sauce* one did not allow stray hairs to drop into a bowl of soup to be plucked out just before the waiter sailed through the swinging doors separating the kitchen from the dining room. On Sloan's way up the ladder, she had witnessed hair picked out of soups, salads, pot au creme, off the tops of flame broiled rib-eyes, and Quiche Lorraine. Never at *Sally's Sauce*, however. Her first big break came when the owner of an Upper West Side restaurant was scouting for a new chef and fell in love with her simplest dish. May, a friend of her mother and a mainstay at the farm, had created it in her food truck and passed it along to Sloan. Made with spaghetti, cubes of cheddar cheese and milk, a humbler dish would be hard to find. After eating his second portion, the owner of the prestigious restaurant interviewed Sloan. When she gave him the "recipe," he said, "Anyone can make a good dish copying a delicate or exotic recipe, but it takes a real chef to make something this good from such simple ingredients. The reason I chose this to test was its simple name. Spaghetti and Cheese.

What chef puts just the words, 'Spaghetti and Cheese' on the menu? When you work for me, don't change it." He offered her a job as Chef de Cuisine at *Sally's Sauce* where the cooks she supervised were so carefully covered in sparkling white cotton they could have performed surgery. One reviewer said her restaurant had the cleanest kitchen in New York. Sloan's pay was good enough to share a three-bedroom apartment in Manhattan.

As she continued trying to find something to control her hair, Sloan looked around for a bottle of hair spray in the mass of detritus on the tiny countertop alongside the rusted sink. She found instead a navy-blue book trimmed in gold entitled *Make Your Bed*. She picked up the book. It was written by four-star Admiral H. McRaven, who had spent thirty-seven years as a Navy Seal. She turned the book over and read the words on the back. They started with, "If you want to change the world, START OFF BY MAKING YOUR BED." A short paragraph followed, explaining why this was so.

Sloan thought of the dirty laundry, dirty dishes, empty beer cans and pizza cartons, overflowing garbage bags, bowls of sour corn flakes, and whatever else the frenetic twenty-year-olds living in this apartment left lying around the place. She promptly went into her corner of a bedroom and made her bed with military precision and continued to do so every day she had a bed to make.

✶━✶━✶

Now, she picked up the sheets from her bed in a stall, shook them with enough force to make them snap, and tucked them in square corners around the narrow mattress. She placed the pillow at the head, squarely in the middle and turned down a corner of the top sheet. She stood, hands on hips, staring at her first completed task since returning to the farm. As always, it set the tone.

Walking through the nearby pastures, she saw clearly why no horses grazed these fields. The grass had been nibbled down to the dirt, leaving just enough to hold the soil in place and feed the roots. Any farther and it would turn dry and crisp and die. The pastures would be irretrievably lost, something Clare Raffienne in a normal world would never let happen.

Sloan tilted her head back and smelled deeply the moist, soft air, then leaned forward, her head spinning. She suddenly felt exhausted to her bones, tired in a way that no amount of sleep could cure.

Back in the barn she sat on her bed, slipped carefully under the top sheet, tucked it close to her body, and laid her head against the pillow with her arm over her forehead.

She hadn't said goodbye to anyone.

A week ago, when she arrived at work and saw the sign "CLOSED" in the window, she was not surprised. Once it had taken weeks to get a reservation at *Sally's Sauce*. Lately, vast glacial spaces separated the few diners brave enough to eat there. The virus was partly to blame. Vaccines were scarce and only those connected to the government had access. But even more importantly, food could only be bought in government run stores—which were risky to enter—or off vans in back alleys. The menu shrank and shrank. Sloan had been expecting the owner to close for weeks. The sign, when she first saw it, was almost a relief. Then with an alarm so sharp she felt electrocuted, she noticed the small smiley face with stars for eyes in the bottom right corner. In code, it meant, "run like hell."

Now she was here, in her mother's stable. A swallow with a worm in its mouth flew in through an open Dutch door. Sloan watched it land on a nest in a rafter just below the peaked roof. She liked her staff. Most of them had been with her since the beginning.

Her sous-chef was her best friend.

Blond, blue-eyed, beautifully built with hair like straw and an open friendly expression, Luther Hinkien looked like he had just stepped out of a corn field in Idaho. Which he had. Seven years ago. At fifteen, he started working after school in a small local restaurant near the farm. At eighteen he moved to Boise, leaving (in the normal, cold-hearted way of eighteen-year-olds) his parents on the front porch, blinking tears and waving at the back of his retreating, banged-up Jeep.

Luther did well enough in Boise to move from prep cook to line cook to head chef in one of those joints that serve over a hundred different burgers.

Bored and ambitious, he decided, at twenty-two, to move to the Big Apple and happened to walk into Sloan's restaurant when she was desperate for a sous-chef. Hers had run off to God knew where.

"This is just until I find someone with bona fide experience," Sloan told him. "And real talent. Just a few days, a week at most."

A week came and went. Then another. The thing about Luther Hinkien was, this man from the land of Jell-O salads, hamburger helper, hummingbird cakes, corn on the cob and mayonnaise, had a finely tuned and delicate palette. One night when they were slammed, Sloan told him to make the brandy cream sauce for the pork medallions. One of her secret recipes, it required many spices, including the priceless saffron, to be added in very precise amounts.

Sloan suspected Luther might be a better chef than she was. She should have felt threatened, but how could she when he so obviously worshipped her. During slow times, he looked over her shoulder, with always a slice of air between them, and nearly vibrated with anticipation of what magic she would conjure.

The young man from Idaho told anyone who would listen to the story of how Lady Luck had blessed him the day she put him next to Sloan Raffienne, "the best chef in New York City."

There was another thing about Luther. He never touched her. When it was slow, captivated by her skill, he would lean over her shoulder and stare. But he always left a space of air between them. During the busiest time of service, when everyone dashed around the kitchen, he never bumped into or brushed against her. Instead, he danced a few steps away, as though she were made of Venetian glass. She felt a strange mixture of relief and disappointment at his caution.

Now he was a world away and she hadn't said goodbye. No one carried cell phones anymore or used email. You might as well go on Fox News and announce to the world your whereabouts and intentions. Those Americans not connected to the government returned to snail mail. The Nationalists apparently weren't interested enough to bother opening actual envelopes. For one thing, the postal system was so under-funded and backlogged there was no telling when mail would arrive at its destination, if it reached it at all. Still, a few weeks before they'd all had to scatter, Sloan made sure to obtain the address of the corn field from which Luther had stepped. Now, in her mind, she began to compose the letter she would write to him. Before she produced two sentences, she fell asleep.

Dusk had arrived when Sloan woke. Four more horses were in the barn. She smelled rather than heard them, that distinct odor of dry leaves, musk, and yeast with a hint of molasses underneath. She sat up, ran her fingers through her hair, which had come undone. It was greasy and snarled into clumps her fingers couldn't break loose. She felt disgusting: dried stress sweat, grime, food stains, stinking underwear. I'll go to the eddy, she decided.

Across the road from the house and barn, Will's Creek made a forty-five degree turn against the rocks supporting the mountain on its right. Slowed and distorted, the water dug down into the earth and rocks below, swirled in circles, ate the land on the other side, and formed a pool wide and deep enough to swim in before it found its way free and continued toward Coleton.

The path through the woods between the road and the creek had narrowed since Sloan's move to New York, but still existed, leaf covered and easy to walk on. She shivered briefly at the anticipation of the creek's current removing the filth on her skin and in her hair. When she was a few feet away from the eddy, she heard a sound above the burble of water flowing over rocks. She stopped. Silence. She stepped behind a tree. She could see the black surface of the swimming hole. In the middle of the eddy, the water up to their chests, John and Clare stood leaning into each other, her mother's arms draped on his shoulders, her forehead touching his. From their position it was obvious he was holding her, probably his arms wrapped under her bottom. Clare's head dropped so that her mouth touched him where his neck met his shoulder. A ripple of water formed and then another moved slowly outward into Will's Creek. Clare made a sound deep in her throat, a cross between a gasp and a moan. She moved her arms, so they crossed over John's back and even in the dim light, the force with which she pulled him against her was obvious.

Sloan froze. She stopped breathing. No one wants to see their parents making love, but Sloan's horror was fueled by a truth she couldn't hide from, couldn't run from, couldn't cure. She carried the shame of it with her wherever she went and whatever she was doing.

She was frigid. She was frigid and still a virgin, no matter how many times she had tried to remedy the situation.

She liked men, found some of them attractive. A few were so attractive she dreamed about them, followed them with her eyes around a room, blushed to her hair when they looked up and caught her. If they asked, she went gladly to their apartments, her arms around their waists, aware of the moist and eager tug between her legs, sure this would be the time that broke the curse.

But the moment he stepped out of his pants, his readiness popping forth in salute to his ardor, a tsunami of panic crashed over her, turning her witless. Visions formed, all of them ugly: hips slamming against her, contorted faces, thighs pushed out of the way, shouts, blood and pain. A roar filled her ears. Helpless against this force, unable even to make an excuse, she would run out into the street. After three or four blocks she would stop, catch her breath, so filled with relief she felt no remorse for the poor man she had left stunned and aching.

The shame and guilt developed while she slept and the following afternoon, her cheeks flaming, Sloan would creep to work.

Naturally, she became known as a cock tease. Her staff treated her with a sullen, guarded obedience until gradually they unanimously decided her behavior was so extreme, so bizarrely consistent, she must have survived something awful, and their distrust turned to a careful respect.

Now, Sloan stood paralyzed as she watched the ripples forming and sliding away from her mother and John. She watched as they slowly grew bigger and faster. The couple rocked back and forth, moved like dancers. A tender mist, undisturbed by their movement, rose from the water and disappeared into the descending night.

When the couple finally ended, it was so dark Sloan could only make out their silhouette as they walked side by side out of the water, their bodies touching from shoulder to foot. They picked towels off tree branches and dried each other. John lifted Clare's hair from where it spread across her shoulders, gathered it together and squeezed out most of the water. Even in the dark he managed to twist it into a loose braid and laid it over her breast.

They wrapped the towels modestly around themselves and, holding hands, walked onto the path toward the road.

The word *beautiful* filled Sloan's mind, followed by a voice from the dark alleys of her being. *They were underwater, you idiot. On dry land it would be as ugly as you always imagine.*

## CHAPTER FOUR

**C**rabb's eddy always ran cold. Sloan didn't allow herself to think as she waded in up to her hips, dove, touched the bottom with her fingertips, rolled a full turn then kicked to the surface. She shivered a little as she made her way to the bank. Picking up sand and tiny pebbles in her fists, she rubbed the mixture into her hair. She scrubbed her scalp, then the length of her hair to its tip, holding her hands in the prayer position and forcing grit into it. Her coarse, wavy hair took well to the scrubbing. When Sloan was satisfied, she began on her body, starting under her chin, down and around her neck, across her shoulders, down her arms, torso, buttocks, thighs, calves, even the bottoms of her feet. The pebbles pricked here and there, and the coarse sand felt abrasive enough to do some good.

She walked into the water, laid on her back, letting her hair hang straight down, flutter kicking to stay in place. She stared at the darkening sky where a half-moon shed a thin light. Full moon. Crescent moon. Sloan wondered why you seldom heard of the poor half-moon. The stars were beginning to show themselves, but they were blurry, unimpressive. She stayed on her back, running her hands through her hair until she began to shiver. She turned over to swim free style; crossed the eddy, reversed, and returned to the beach, turned again and swam back across. Returning to the middle, Sloan stood, dunked her head under water and tossed it this way and that. Finally, she walked to the shore, gathered her t-shirt, panties, and jeans, took them to the place where the water ran over rocks as it left the eddy. She scrubbed and slapped her clothes over the edges until goosebumps covered her skin.

The wet jeans would be unbearable to wear, but Sloan pulled on her panties and t-shirt, which came down just far enough.

Instead of going straight across to the driveway, she turned left and walked along a two-lane undivided macadam road until she came to a narrow, rocky, rutted stretch of hostile terrain on the right. Meant to be a single lane road, it ended at her mother's old farm, the one where Clare had grown up and ran a horse business with her pap. After he died and she and Annie became partners, they left the mountain and bought the Norton farm, located a mile below. Directly off the macadam, it would make better access for customers and be easier on their trucks and horse trailer.

The climb to her mother's abandoned old place took Sloan longer than normal, for she wore no shoes. Ouching and gimping, with tree branches leaning into the road, she eventually came to the woods in front of the house. The woods from where Colleen, her almost-sister, had been kidnapped when she was only five and Sloan eight.

Sloan touched one of the trees. She could just make out their forms. Carefully, she walked until she stood in front of the house. The collapsed roof had taken down the outside wall of the bedroom she and Colleen had shared, leaving it exposed to the elements. Boards hung from the opening at awkward angles as though flung there. It was too dark to see inside.

Sickened by the sight, Sloan spun around and ran, stumbling, falling and sliding down the mountain, cutting the bottoms of her feet, grabbing trees to keep from falling until she reached the gently rolling valley. She stood still, allowing her breathing to become normal again, then ducked under fencing, jumped across a small swift stream, and circled around the back of the barn into a twenty-acre pasture. It ran from the bottom of the mountain to the road. She stopped and gazed into the dark, picturing horses standing in this now empty place, slowly swishing their tails, noses to the ground, nibbling the succulent grass. Funny, she thought, she had never loved them as much as Colleen had. She was John's sister. He'd brought her to Clare when she was five. She'd never spoken a word until she matter-of-factly said goodbye to the pony Clare had given her. Unlike Sloan, she never left the farm, wanted only to stay there with Clare and the horses.

Colleen spent every free moment with them, riding, grooming, training, becoming crazed if they were sick or lame. It was Colleen who never missed a horse show, spending days before, cleaning tack, washing her horse, braiding its mane and tail, preparing her riding clothes. She would never become the rider Sloan was, but she became damn good.

Sloan, on the other hand, discovered in her early teens she preferred riding with May in her food truck, making both plain and haute cuisine to sell at affordable prices to the poor. She loved the organized, sweaty rush to fill plates as a line of at least ten waited to be served, the precise preparation needed to make it possible to work so efficiently. She even liked the disasters—milk gone sour, strawberries forgotten and left in the farm sink—and the improvisation that followed. She watched the loving care May used to make complicated dishes like Peking duck, the easy, off-handed way she threw together a dish like spaghetti and cheese. Sloan didn't mind getting up before dawn to help her mother's friend prepare the food and put it with scientific care in the truck's small refrigerator. Watching May work her magic in such delicate and varying ways, along with Sloan's dread of living and dying in these remote mountains where the days and weeks were frozen in time, swept her off to the Big Apple, the mecca of diversity and wonderful food.

Now, she was back where she began. With no routine at all, no idea what the future or the next day would bring. Or even the present. Where was Colleen? Or Annie? What would become of any of them? How were they to survive?

Wide awake, Sloan walked the sixty acres of the farm that night even though the moon gave off no light. She knew this land like she knew the back of her hand. Toward dawn she felt tired enough to try to sleep. She slipped into her neatly made bed and turned onto her side, her right arm under the pillow.

*   *   *

Bright, unforgiving sunlight filled the stall, forcing Sloan's eyes open. She rolled onto her back, looked at the rafters then out the stall door. There, smiling at her, was the strangest looking human being she had ever seen. Male, with a mop of black curls falling across his forehead, merry, almost black eyes, and brown skin covered all over in golden speckles. She snapped to a sitting position, holding the sheet under her arms. "What…ah, who are you?" Her mind was fuzzy, still half asleep. She rubbed her eyes.

"I'm Jamie." The young man placed his forearms on the top of the stall door. "And you are Sloan, daughter of the mighty Clare." He looked her up and down, smiling. "You look like her, except of course the wrong color. Must be from your father."

Sloan had never seen her father. When she'd asked her mother about him, Clare had simply lied. "Your father died before you were born, but he would have adored you if he had known you." Sloan, having lived apart from normal society and its customs, never gave the absent parent another thought.

Jamie opened the stall door and stepped inside. Sloan scooched back toward the edge of her mattress. "Don't… you can't come in here… I mean, what are doing?"

Jamie sat on the edge of her bed. "Yes, I can see her in you but not so strong. Or maybe you are strong in a different way."

Sloan stared at him.

"It should not have taken you so long to come back. But I can understand that you were busy. And it's possible you would not have noticed the way Diamond sent the National Guard, armed to the teeth, to surround the schools after the last mass murder in Texas. That was just the beginning, of course." He rolled his eyes. "Just an excuse. You could not have been too busy to notice the rest. Closing of businesses, people disappearing. Why did you stay so long in that city? You had to know how easy it would be for Diamond to declare martial law. All those crazy republicans in the Supreme Court and congress. Just waiting for a takeover. They have TV where you were, no?"

"Actually, no, we didn't."

Jamie patted his knees. "But you are here now. That is the important thing." He smiled at her.

Sloan pulled the sheet higher. "And who are you to be commenting on my behavior?"

"A friend." Jamie stood and retrieved her jeans from the stall door where she had left them to dry and handed them to her. "Now, get dressed. I have big surprise for you."

Sloan had noticed his accent right away but couldn't place it. She pulled her jeans on under the sheet. "How do you know my mother?"

"Is a long story. I will tell you later. Now come and see your surprise." Jamie took her hand, pulled her to her feet and outside.

Sloan pulled away from him and stopped. "I have to make my bed."

Jamie's pointed black eyebrows drew together. He lifted his hands palms up. "What? You need to make your bed? You live in a barn."

"Doesn't matter." Sloan returned to her stall with Jamie close behind her. He helped her put the bottom sheet on the mattress, then lifted his side of the top sheet, and together they flapped it up and down until it was taut and straight. They lowered it over the mattress. Jamie watched Sloan make a square corner then tried to imitate her. "Your mother says you used to be a bobcat in a former life. You know, a fiery bad ass, won't back down. Sounds like you, no?" Jamie pulled his corner of the sheet out from under the mattress and started again.

Sloan watched him. "You and my mother talk about me? You don't even know me."

"I feel like I do."

"That's ridiculous. We've never met. How much has my mother said about me?" Sloan had stopped with the sheet and was sitting back on her heels.

"Is nothing to worry about. I have nothing but admiration for you. I think she misses you. She says because they are small and secretive and adaptable, they will survive human encroachment."

"Because what is?"

"The bobcat." Jamie was shoving the sheet into place. "It's lonely out here. We sit around and talk sometimes. Not often but sometimes. Your name comes up now and then, is all."

Sloan leaned across the mattress. "Not like that. Here, you must fold the bottom corner as sharply as the top of it."

Jamie stepped back. "Is okay now? Yes. Good. Now follow me."

In the bright light, the yellow specks on his brown skin sparkled.

Shimmer, Sloan almost said out loud.

As they walked across the yard to the house, Sloan could just make out a figure sitting on the stump of a large oak tree next to the door to the kitchen. Several smaller trees surrounded it, creating enough shade to make it difficult to tell if it was a man or a woman.

When they drew closer, Sloan's arms began to prickle. The closer they got, the more the prickling spread. She and Jamie stopped three or four yards from the figure, who seemed to be waiting for them. This close, ambiguity vanished and the person sitting so still in front of them was clearly a woman even though her hair was so short it looked merely a shadow. Her blue eyes stood out against the white skin stretched over her gaunt face.

Sloan stared, and the gaunt woman stared back at her for an unbearably long time. Finally, the woman lifted a thin black eyebrow and said, "I guess you don't recognize me."

Sloan recognized her all right but couldn't believe it.

People had said of Colleen she was the most beautiful child they had ever seen. Black hair, white porcelain skin, corn flower blue eyes and a naturally rosy mouth. She'd never used her looks or shown any pride in them. Her disposition was naturally cheerful and friendly. She loved people and people loved her.

While Sloan tried to reconcile the changes, Colleen turned to Jamie. "Help her, will you? She's freaking me out. I haven't changed that much, I hope."

"I recognize you." Sloan walked deliberately closer. "Have you been sick?"

Jamie followed her. "Well, of course she's been sick. Is obvious. So have I.

Obviously. We caught the plague. We fought the plague, and we won. We are now safe and a danger to no one. Come sit. Is rude to stand over someone you are talking to." He settled himself comfortably against a tree, smiled, and patted the ground next to him.

Sloan wondered if she should offer to hug Colleen, but the woman sat so stolidly on her stump she decided to sit on the ground next to Jamie. Her friend, who was more of a sister than friend, had been a joyous child. Hepatic 26 had transformed her into something brittle, grim, and a little frightening.

"Is all right to be shy," said Jamie. "It has been years, right? Go ahead, sit here and stare at each other as long as you like." He cleared his throat. "Let's start with how you got here. Tell us about your escape."

"How about we start with what you, a total stranger, are doing here."

"I am here to help. To help Clare and John grow their vegetables and kill their food and then I take these foods to Coleton to feed people and bring back supplies to the farm."

"In other words, he's a runner."

Jamie sat up straighter. "I am not." Running was the most dangerous job in the resistance. "Anyway, so are you."

Colleen shrugged one shoulder.

"Where do you come from? I've never heard your sort of accent before," Sloan asked.

Jamie turned away, lifted his eyebrows, and gazed straight ahead. "Am citizen of the world."

Colleen rolled her eyes. "Don't bother. He'll never tell you anything about where he was before he showed up here."

"That is false. I tell you everything about my life before I came here. I tell you I knew as soon as Diamond became president the second time, the world as we know it is over. I knew soon we would have martial law. I told everyone, but no one listened. So, I move."

Sloan looked him over. He had a narrow, tidy body with hard, round muscles. "Where were you when you started prophesying?"

Jamie shifted his eyes. "Here and there. What does it matter?"

"What brought you to Coleton?"

"As good a place as any. Remote, good land, mountains. Anyway, I started telling everyone here what would happen. That they should spend all their monies on non-perishable food and guns with bullets. And hide them. No one listens. I get a job at Southern States and tell all the customers to buy all the provisions for their animals they can afford. Bales of hay, bags of corn, oats, sweet feed. Buy it all. They don't. Look at me as though I might be crazy. I almost get fired. Then in comes Colleen. I tell her the same thing, only she believes me. She takes a wallet out of her jeans and counts all the monies she has. We load up her truck so full of bags of grain and bales of hay we must tie a net of clothesline over it to keep it from falling off. When she drives away, she looks like the Okies going to California."

"When was this?"

"Before the National Guard became the Nationalists, otherwise known as Nazis. Now they own Southern States." The sun had moved just enough to shine through the trees onto his skin, turning his speckles to gold. *The Happy Prince,* thought Sloan. Would he turn into a statue of gold leaf and give himself to the poor, piece by piece? She squared her shoulders. "Where's Annie?"

Colleen and Jamie glanced at each other. Jamie waited for Colleen to answer. "In Coleton. With Marshall."

"Does she ever come to the farm?"

"Yes, sure."

"How often?"

"As often as she can. She's busy. She helps with the… people." Jamie kept his voice light.

Sloan knew he had started to say the resistance but had stopped himself. He looked around. "Speaking of where is, where is Clare?"

Sloan realized he was talking to her. "You woke me up, remember? I don't know anything."

"Figures," Colleen said. "We never see her. Not since she found religion."

Sloan crinkled her eyebrows in disbelief. "What? No way."

Colleen shifted forward on her stump, her expression one of exasperation mixed with a perverse pride. "Yup, she did. Well, she didn't find it so much as invent it. A few years ago, it came to her in a dream that the reason Adam and Eve were thrown out of the garden of Eden had nothing to do with an apple or snake or even Eve. It was because Adam decided to build a shed."

When Colleen paused to watch Sloan's expression, Jamie seized the moment and jumped in. "Apparently, what Clare decided was, here they were, those two, in paradise. God had provided everything they needed. Trees laden with fruit. Veggies growing wild. Nuts, seeds of all manner. Perfect weather. Only rains at night, was never too hot or too cold. Plenty of comfy caves to sleep in. But then one day a tree fell over. Adam looked and looked at it. His mind began to hum. He found a suitable rock and broke that dead tree into pieces he could use to make shed." Jamie produced a philosophical shrug. "Perhaps he was bored. Who knows? Well, God looking down could not believe it. Here he created an absolute paradise where all possible needs are met and instead of being grateful, Adam decides to improve it. Takes time away from loving Eve in the proper way." He lifted his eyebrows for emphasis. "All God had ever asked was that these two go forth and multiply. And here was Adam laboring away at something totally unnecessary. So… naturally, God cast him out of Eden and Eve had to go with him. Am not sure why, but Clare thinks it has to do with sex. You know. Making babies."

Sloan's face was the picture of gleeful astonishment. "The Sufis believe the highest form of spirituality is sexual love because you lose yourself completely to the other."

Colleen scowled. "Where'd you hear that?"

Sloan strongly suspected her mother was mocking them with this story of a Godly reason for her behavior. Sloan had been twelve when she heard the rumors about Clare, how comfortable she was with her own body, how willing to share. Her mother was discreet, though. Protective in her own way. She never brought a man to the farm and the relationship never lasted long, a blip on the radar screen. This Garden of Eden story was undoubtedly Clare's sly way of explaining her love of "biblical" unions. What Sloan really wondered was how John continued to hold her in such a thrall. She shook her head, tried to keep a straight face. "I'm not so sure about that go forth and multiply thing. How would Mother even know those words? And I think they were in a different part of the bible."

"She went to school," said Colleen.

"They don't teach religion in school."

"You don't think there's a lot of religious mumbo jumbo going on in school? Anyway, since Clare's conversion she spends all her free time 'praying' with John."

Sloan ducked her head to hide her smile. When they were children, Colleen's love of Clare was second only to her love of horses. Maybe she even loved her more than the horses. She went riding with her, cleaned her tack, even happily mucked out stalls. It was Clare, after all, who teased out the first words she ever spoke. Colleen had been five. Selectively mute was the diagnosis.

Now she stretched out her legs. "Clare does her jobs. No one works harder. But every free moment is spent in a 'prayer meeting.'"

"Well," said Sloan reasonably, "why aren't there a passel of babies running around here then?"

"She had two miscarriages. After that, she took herbs she found in the woods to prevent pregnancy. And she's pretty old, you know."

Jamie stood and stretched. "We should be going. Can't wait till dark this time. I've got shit to do in Coleton. Let's give Sloan the stuff, switch trucks, and go." The runners didn't drive the same truck twice in a row if they could help it. They drove at night when possible and when they couldn't, they switched their route even if it meant going miles out of their way.

Colleen rose and then Sloan. She desperately wanted them to stay but wouldn't risk asking. Standing, Colleen was all angles, boney wrists and knuckles. This, more than anything, brought home what their lives had become. Sloan suddenly felt hollow, afraid for the future. "What stuff?"

"Bullets and salt. We'll just get some squash and dried meat." Jamie frowned, stepped close to her and peered. He reached for a strand of hair and rubbed it between his fingers. "You've got sand in your hair. Lots of it."

Colleen shook her head. "Jesus, Shimmer, I swear you were raised by wolves."

"Shimmer?"

"I call him that cause of the way his spots sparkle sometimes."

"That's the exact word I thought when I saw him. So, we've still got it?"

Colleen smiled for the first time and put an arm around Sloan's neck. "Yes, we do."

Even with the burst of relief at having her oldest friend back, Sloan could feel the unrelenting hardness of that arm.

# CHAPTER FIVE

The roll of barbed wire was too big to fit in the bed of Jack's truck. He had to tie it onto the steel rings on the side and still it teetered this way and that. Fortunately, he didn't have far to go. He pulled the pickup in front of Clare's stable, stepped out, and looked around. Not a soul in sight. He had come from Hozelroad Holler located across the road and a few miles back from Clare's farm. He never showed his face when Annie was here. He'd worked for her one summer when he was sixteen, and she ran this place on her own. She'd been a good boss and he thought of her as a friend until the last night when in a drunken, jealous rage, he'd assaulted her young horse trainer.

He'd never seen Annie since. In the course of time, Clare and Annie became partners and Clare moved her business to Valley Farm. After a few years, Annie spent more and more time in Coleton and Jack began showing up, testing the waters. Clare seemed willing to do business with him, which was handy because the farm was so close. This meant low-risk bartering.

It helped that the Holler existed apart from the world, its own hostile denizen. A two-mile stretch of land completely taken over by the detritus of humanity, it remained closed to anyone who didn't live there. No flora existed within those two miles. Burned out school busses, trucks, cars, RVs, motorcycles, rusting enamel refrigerators, stoves, dishwashers, decayed storage sheds, shacks covered in tar paper, porches listing away from scoured buildings, their windows covered in black plastic, every conceivable form of junk and garbage covered the earth. Those who dared drive the narrow road into the Holler were watched by gray men, rifles at their sides, motionless except for the small movement of their heads as their cold, flat eyes watched the cars with their locked doors slide by. If Coleton and its environs were a blip on the map, the Holler was a world so foreign it remained impenetrable to the laws of the rest of the country. The inhabitants were all thieves who made invisible forays into yards, barns, and unlocked houses to keep themselves supplied. Inbred, they looked surprisingly alike: dark hair, pale skin, and rangy bodies.

Jack had grown up on the edge of Hozelroad Holler, in a single wide detached from the mass of fused metal by a patch of weeds and a driveway. When his mother died, the Holler spread toward his trailer slowly, steadily, surrounding it until only a thin driveway leading to the cinder block front steps remained open.

Having lived on the outskirts, Jack was a hybrid. In his youth, he enjoyed working for people in the outside world. Liked the money in his pockets. Even more, he enjoyed the conversations, the exchange of ideas.

The people from the Holler hunted or trapped their food. There was no room for even a sliver of vegetable garden. Unlike his neighbors, Jack minded his teeth falling out. He'd lost a back molar and didn't intend to lose another. In his time in the outside world, he had acquired a taste for fruits and vegetables. So, he drove across the road to Clare's and bartered tools for apples, tomatoes, squash, any other veggie she might have and the occasional fish.

There was another reason Jack showed up so often. Ever since his last night at Valley Farm, he'd felt an urge to go back. Before the Nationalists forced free people to go into hiding and Annie still lived there, every time Jack turned onto the road that led to the Holler, he looked over his shoulder at the tidy fields with regret and loss.

Today, as he surveyed the stable yard, he heard a woman's voice. It didn't sound like Clare. He assumed it was Sloan. He called out hello, walked into the cool building, and saw a woman who was definitely not Sloan standing inside a stall with a large chestnut horse. She turned from leaning her head on her horse's neck to stare at Jack. He had never seen her before, or anyone remotely like her. Brown curly hair stuck out from her head, framing the largest, darkest, most terrified eyes he had ever seen.

"Hi," he said. "I'm Jack."

The girl didn't answer.

Jack stepped closer. "I'm a friend of Clare's. I've brought her something she'll love. Know where she is?"

The girl shook her head.

"What's your name?"

"Rosemary."

Jack nodded toward the horse. "He's new. Big too."

"He's mine. His name is Wilson."

"Oh, he's yours, is he? Well, hello, Wilson." Jack moved closer. "You're new here, Wilson. And so is your owner. Clare generally don't let strangers come here anymore."

When Rosemary didn't respond, he continued, his tone just a shade less friendly. "So, why are you here? Rosemary? With your own horse?"

"Clare brought me here."

"What? Why?"

Rosemary opened the stall door and stepped into the aisle.

Jack opened his mouth, but whatever he meant to say vanished. He'd never seen anyone so narrow. Long, thin limbs, long neck and jaw, no hips, straight up and down except for breasts that had to be a D cup or bigger. He'd seen big-busted women before, but the rest of them had bodies that went along with the picture; their wide hips and asses balanced the helium balloons. He became acutely aware of his own looks. Hepatic 26 had turned his black hair the color of driven snow. The unhealthy pallor of the Holler people had turned dead white in Jack. His skeleton remained intact, if a little stiff, and provided him with excellent posture. From a distance he looked like an elder statesman. Up close his facial bone structure and a spray of unevenly sized freckles across his cheeks and nose made him appear younger. He was thirty-nine. He'd survived H26 relatively unscathed and to his mind continued to still be handsome. He wondered if Rosemary had had the disease and that was why she looked so odd, but he doubted it. H26 turned people into skeletons, burned away their hair, which often didn't come back and left them with strange shades and shapes of yellow on their skin. It bent their bones, deadened their extremities, causing gangrene followed by amputation if they were unlucky. Rosemary didn't display any of these disfigurements.

Recovering himself, he said, "Clare don't let just anyone on her land. Where'd she get you from? And why?"

Rosemary said nothing.

"I'd speak up if I was you. Clare and me are partners, and I need to know what's goin' on."

"I don't know where she got me from. The top of some mountain. She brought me down cause I was lost and put me in the shed for two weeks for quarantine. I don't know how many days it's been, but I'm going crazy in there. I just snuck out to see Wilson."

"She locked you in the shed for two weeks?" Jack drew his shoulders back in disbelief.

"I didn't say she locked me. She wants me to stay there two weeks to make sure I don't have the virus."

"You can't stay there for two weeks. Clare's strange, some say a witch, but she ain't cruel. I'll talk to her." Jack's eyes drifted to the girl's chest and lingered. "What's this shed like? Is it comfortable?"

"I have food and water. A blanket."

"Come on, show it to me. We'll talk some more. Figure stuff out."

Rosemary shook her head abruptly.

"What? Don't be afraid. Just want to help you out. Clare and me… we got an understanding. You tell me everything that happened, and I'll talk to her."

Rosemary stood still, a statue of misery.

Jack made a sound of disgust. "Okay, stand here if you want to. Fine by me. But if Clare catches you, and me here with you, they'll be hell to pay."

Rosemary nodded, and the two walked across the yard to the shed. Inside, the floor was covered in pine boughs with a blanket and sheet in the middle. An old-fashioned glass milk bottle and plastic plate lay in the corner. There were no windows. The only light came through the spaces between the boards. The air was stale and funky, an animal in a small place smell, with a faint background scent of pine coming through.

Jack sat amidst the pine with his knees bent and his arms around his legs. He motioned Rosemary to sit, which she did, facing him.

"Now tell me the whole story."

"I'm not sure."

"What do you mean you're not sure? How can you not be sure?" Jack let out an exasperated sigh. "Where exactly did Clare find you?"

"I told you. On the top of a mountain."

"What mountain?"

"I don't know. I'd been riding for hours and hours and Wilson was so good, but finally we couldn't go any farther. And he and I were just there. Unable to take another step. Doing nothing. I was so thirsty I thought I'd die. And then Clare comes riding out of the woods, and I guess she felt sorry for us because she brought us here."

The girl looked terrified. She leaned forward. "See, when I got up that morning everyone was gone. My whole family. All the servants. Except Pedro. He was still in the barn. He had Wilson saddled up, and he told me to ride away as fast as I could and never come back."

"Huh." Her story was so weird it just might be true. Especially in these times. People disappeared all the time. "What's your name?"

"Rosemary. I told you."

"Just Rosemary? You ain't got no last name?"

"Whitbeck."

Jack thought the name sounded familiar. He'd heard of some rich family living in the mountains not too far from here, but too far to be of use to folks from the Holler, so he never thought about them. "Go on. Your family leaves you stranded, some man puts you on a horse and you ride away without knowing where your family's gone. Or why. Or why they left you behind."

"His name is Pedro. He ran the stables. He's not just 'some man.'" Tears sparkled in the corners of her eyes.

"Where's Pedro now?"

"I told you; I don't know. He told me to leave and not come back," Rosemary's voice cracked.

Jack stretched his legs out. "Rosemary, that's the strangest story I ever heard, and I've heard a fair few. Why'd your parents leave you behind?"

She hung her head and mumbled, "I don't know."

Jack looked around. "So, this is it. You've been livin' in here for days with just this."

"They bring me food and water. Leave it outside the door."

"Is that so? They bring you food and water. Well, bully for them. And what about…?" Jack blushed.

"I can go in the woods when no one's around."

"Well, hell, that's special." He stared at her for a while. Her white shirt and breeches were stained and dusty. She had yellow sweat circles under her arms. Her hair amazed him with its uneven, matted bunches. "Do you ever get to wash yourself?"

Rosemary shook her head.

Jack jumped to his feet. "Look, I'm gonna find a bucket and bring you some water so you can wash your hair. Looks pretty bad. Jesus Christ," he muttered as he ducked out the door.

When Jack returned, he brought a large bucket of water and a bar of soap which, smiling, he waved in front of Rosemary. "I snuck in the house and snitched it." He cleared away some pine boughs and put the bucket down so it wouldn't tip. "Now just lean over it and I'll help you."

Rosemary moaned when he rubbed her soapy scalp. "Now hold your breath," he said. "I'm going to put your head in for a few seconds to rinse it."

When she came up for air, Rosemary shook her head like a wet dog. She sighed and smiled.

Jack pulled off his t-shirt and handed it to her. "Use this to dry it."

Rosemary toweled her hair then handed his shirt back. 'It's wet now. I'm sorry."

The two looked at each other for a long time. Jack never took his eyes from hers. Finally, he untied her paddock boots and slipped them off.

Rosemary trembled like a leaf in a hailstorm. "Stop it," she said.

"What, you ain't afraid, are you?" Jack reached for the buttons of her shirt. "Don't be afraid. I'll just help you get clean. Like wash your back. Places you can't reach."

"No."

He sat back on his heels. "Okay. I thought you might like it, is all. You ever been with a man?"

The girl shook her head, though she'd been with two different men at horse shows. The first was older, experienced, and knew how to take a girl's virginity with the least amount of trauma. He had an accent, probably Spanish, and Rosemary thought he rode beautifully. After the painful first time, he'd shown her how to enjoy sex, and it surprised her when the next man was rough and careless.

"How old are you?"

"Seventeen."

Jack had a tough time not looking at her breasts. "Most girls start having sex around fourteen or fifteen. But that's okay. There's time." He smiled. "Tell you what. I'm real tight with Clare. I'll get her to let you out of this shed. I've had the virus. So, we can be friends. We can go for walks." Rosemary's expression didn't change. He continued quickly, "I'll help you with your horse. We could take him to find some grass. I'm real good with horses."

Clare rode with Jack as far as the truck would go, helped him pull the roll of wire off the back then sent him to pick vegetables, as many as he could. "Tomatoes are coming on real good. Take as many as you want. And thanks for this. I mean it."

"I guess there's some girl livin' in the shed back there. She poked her head out when she heard the truck."

Clare said nothing.

"We talked for a bit. Said you had her in quarantine. I've had the virus so I'm safe. You wouldn't mind if I visited her once in a while, would you?"

Clare eyed him for a few moments. "Don't get any ideas about her, Jack. She's just a kid."

"She's seventeen."

Clare narrowed her eyes.

"But I know. She's real innocent. I wouldn't take advantage."

Two days later, Jack found Clare working in the stables. When he asked, she told him Rosemary wasn't there. She'd taken Wilson for a ride.

"Good. Good. She needs that." He stood with his hands at his sides.

Clare stopped raking the aisle. "You got any business to take care of?"

"Um, no, not really."

"Best be going home then."

When Rosemary and Wilson returned, Clare was still in the barn. She watched the girl untack, being sure to stand ten feet away. "That man, name's Jack, the one with the white hair. He ever bother you?"

"No. He came and talked to me once. That's all."

"Be careful around him. He's got history."

"It was nice to talk to him." Instinctively, Rosemary knew not to say he'd been in the shed, washing her hair.

"Look, I know this is awful for you. As soon as the two weeks is up, you can do what you want. Maybe we can even go look for your folks."

"No! Please. Pedro told me not to, and he knows everything. He said I can't ever go back."

"Pedro must be very important."

"I've known him all my life."

# CHAPTER SIX

**S**loan stared at the vegetable garden. She shifted her weight from one leg to the other. She recognized the tallest weeds: thistle and milkweed. She didn't know the names of the shorter ones. Tangled among them, the vegetables fought for survival. The tomato vines crawled over the ground, twisting and turning, looping over themselves to find space. The over ripe tomatoes stood out, a burst of red begging to be eaten right there and then. The squashes looked like they could be used as weapons. Pole beans, bright green and turgid, hung from stakes. Sloan was astounded by the fact that all this decent food would go to waste if someone didn't get in there and clean things up. Her mother must be overwhelmed to have let this happen.

Sloan put her hands on her hips. She wasn't one of those cooks who grew herbs and veggies on roof tops. Fresh produce was precious to her but let someone else grow it. She'd gladly pay them. Now, this was her assigned task.

She was on her knees weeding when Shimmer and Colleen arrived in a truck. She rose and waved. It was nice to see Colleen again. To her surprise, she was glad to see Shimmer too. They walked over to her. Colleen's face was grim, but Shimmer returned Sloan's smile.

"So, you are out of quarantine." He looked her up and down. "You have not gotten the virus?" He leaned back, still smiling, and crossed his arms over his chest. "You won't get it here. Clare is too careful."

Colleen looked around. "Where is she?"

"She's at the creek. Washing clothes with Rosemary." They had both been out of quarantine for two days.

Colleen and Shimmer looked at each other.

"What? What is it?"

"At some point we need to talk about what to do with the Whitbeck girl." Colleen looked at the ground then directly at Sloan's face. "But the pressing thing right now is… Annie and Marshall have gone missing."

Shimmer raised his eyebrows. "Is nothing really. Only two days. Has happened before. Often. And is only for two days. I told Colleen no need to come out here and bother everybody."

Colleen said, "I'll get Clare."

"Don't be so sad and serious. Is no big deal. Stop being so pale and scared." He flopped an arm around Sloan's neck. "You are worrying our friend here."

Colleen said nothing and started for the creek.

Shimmer shrugged. "She worries all the time. Come, tell me what you have been up to now that you are out of quarantine. And the Whitbeck girl is with Clare, so she is free too. Where do you sleep now?"

"I sleep in the stable if it's any of your business. Rosemary sleeps in the shed."

"And why are you still in the stable?"

"I like it there. It's not so stuffy."

"And the girl, she is with Clare most of the time?"

"What are you getting at?"

"Nothing, nothing. Just like to keep track of things, is all. Am a nosy bastard." He smiled and Sloan couldn't help smiling back.

When Clare, Colleen, and Rosemary returned, Clare's face was closed off, a look Sloan had seen before. She had been trying to talk Shimmer into helping her weed and laughing at how horrified he looked at the prospect. Seeing her mother's face silenced her. Colleen and Rosemary held a basket of wet laundry between them. They settled it on the ground and Rosemary asked Clare if she would like her to hang up the clothes. Clare thanked her then turned to Colleen. She spoke quietly. "You should stay here for a while."

Shimmer lifted his chin. "No need. Colleen has worried you unnecessarily. Annie and Marshall are often gone, taking care of business."

This wasn't entirely true, but Clare let it ride for now. "Stay the night anyway. We've plenty of food. We'll talk in the morning."

Shimmer shook his head. "No need to talk."

Sloan said, "Tomorrow, you can help me in the garden or all we'll have is weeds to chew on. Honestly, you'd think since this is the only source of vegetables, someone would have taken better care of it."

They all looked at her blankly until Shimmer said, "Looks fine to me."

John had caught three fish, which they ate sitting around the fire pit, along with tomatoes, sliced cucumber, and potatoes baked in the coals. Jack had shown up and ate with them. It seemed to Sloan he'd been there every day since she'd returned. He helped Clare and John fence in the upper pasture with the wire he brought them then hung out with Rosemary.

Dinner was mostly a silent affair. Jack and Rosemary were too busy not looking at each other to say anything and Colleen glared at the fire. Sloan studied the delicate way Shimmer ate. He picked the meat from the fish ribs with the ends of his fingers, licked them clean before taking a cucumber slice. In between eating, he made conversation. "This is delicious. Bountiful. I can truthfully say Valley Farm is best restaurant in New York."

Colleen turned toward him. "It won't last. You do realize that, I hope. We'll run out of food and tools and supplies just like everyone else."

"Why say such a thing? You must not be so glum. You depress me. And everyone else."

"Oh, shut up, Shimmer. I'm sick of your little Miss Sunshine act."

After that, the silence became complete. Once the food was gone, the group sat staring at the embers until Clare roused herself. "Tonight would be a good night for poker."

In the kitchen, she went to the pantry and brought out a worn pack of cards along with a cloth bag, round and heavy with coins. She divided the money evenly among the seven, then placed the cards in the middle of the table. The game was always five-card draw.

Sloan knew about her mother and poker. She couldn't wait to see how the others took it. She reached out and cut the pack then tapped it. Clare dealt and the game began. Sloan was most interested in how Shimmer played.

As the game progressed, Shimmer appeared at times bored, at other times keenly interested. He played his cards erratically, sometimes obviously bluffing, at other times playing an excellent hand too conservatively. His pile of winnings grew or shrank, and he didn't appear to care which way his luck was running. John played an elegant game, knowing when to hold and when to fold. His expression was always serene, and he laughed when his "winning" cards were beaten by better ones. Colleen cursed when she lost, throwing down her cards. Sloan wondered what had happened to the merry girl she'd grown up with. Jack played wildly, betting all his coins and having to borrow money. When he won big, he shouted and pumped his fist. Rosemary didn't have a clue, forgot to anti-up or ask for cards, and had to be prompted to bet or throw down. Jack would touch her hand or her cards to wake her up, and once he looked over her shoulder and told her how many cards to ask for. Colleen pushed back her chair and went to stand behind him. "Change places with me."

Jack twisted his neck and looked up at her. "Why?"

Colleen stared at him.

"All right. All right." He rose and switched places.

Sloan saw Clare hide a smile.

When the light in the kitchen grew too dark to see, Clare fetched candles from a drawer, lit them, and set them around the table.

About two hours into the game, Shimmer showed a full house, kings over jacks. Colleen shoved his cards across the table. "You're cheating. You always cheat."

Shimmer reached for his money. "Of course I cheat. Why wouldn't I? If you can't catch me is fair game, right?" He smiled an open, easy smile.

"You shouldn't be able to have that money."

"But why not? Can you say how I cheated? No. So, money is mine." He rubbed the top of Colleen's bald head. "Cheer up. Night is young. You have plenty of time to make it back."

"I'm watching you," Colleen said grimly.

John's pile grew slowly and steadily. Jack went from rags to riches then back to rags. Colleen, sullenly, held her own. Sloan was a good poker player having learned from her mother, and she built a growing pyramid of coins in front of her.

Towards midnight, Clare yawned and said, "One last hand."

"No, at least two," said Jack. "I need to get some of my money back."

Shimmer raised his eyebrows. "But why? All goes back into bag anyway, for next time."

Jack brightened. "I've got an idea. We should keep score of how much money each person wins and… oh… let's say by Christmas, the winner gets a prize."

"You think we'll still be here by Christmas?"

"Yes, Colleen, I do. We've got food, water, guns, bullets. No reason we can't be here forever."

"God forbid," said Sloan.

Everyone looked at her. She waved the words away. "Don't pay any attention to me."

"Two more hands and I'm going to bed," Clare said.

Sloan watched the play carefully. John won the first hand with three fives.

The rule for the last hand was you could fold or hold, but if you held, you had to bet your whole pot. Sloan watched their faces. Smiling, John drew three cards then folded. Colleen's eyebrows knit together, and she held. Rosemary put her cards face down. So did Sloan. Jack stared at his hand long enough to be just shy of unacceptable, and smiling broadly, he spread them on the table. A straight to eight high. His white cheeks flushed a pale pink. "Oh boy, oh boy," he said as he reached for the money. He stopped short as

Clare winked at him and showed a full house, aces over queens. Jack flung himself against the chair.

The look on Colleen's face was murderous. She shoved back from the table, and for a moment it looked like she might kick it over. Then she laughed a knowing, brittle laugh that held a current of admiration under it. "I swear, Clare, I love you. But sometimes." She turned to look at everyone else. "She always wins. Except when she chooses not to. You never know."

Sloan walked back to the stable in a wordless miasma of love, her mother at the center.

⸻✶⸻✶⸻

Before dawn, a horse nickered and a faint voice whispered, "Shhh." Sloan's first thought was Shimmer. She called out, "Hey."

Colleen answered back and walked over to her.

"What are you doing here so early?"

"I wanted to check on the horses."

"They're fine."

"They're too thin."

"Clare does her best."

"I know. That's what worries me." In the pre-dawn, Colleen's sharp edges faded.

She looks so sad, Sloan thought. "Have you been worrying all night?"

"John and Clare spent the night 'praying.' They woke me up and I couldn't go back to sleep."

Sloan rose and started to make her bed.

Colleen helped. "You really don't mind sleeping out here?"

"No, I like it."

"John and your mother are good for each other, I know that. He's my brother, so of course I'm into his business. I don't know why I feel so cross about… you know… how they behave."

Sloan frowned. "It makes me feel a little icky too, but it shouldn't. We should be glad they're happy."

"Clare won't show it, but she's terribly worried about Annie. Even when she's not missing, Clare worries."

"Does she need to?"

"Coleton may be a backwater no one cares about, but the Nationalists are growing all the time. Especially in sleepy towns like this. What else are the unemployed going to do with themselves? Now they can put on a uniform and bully people. Even get them killed."

Sloan stopped tucking in the top sheet and looked steadily at Colleen. "How dangerous is it?"

"Pretty damn dangerous. Two of the runners have been gone over a month."

"Jesus. When do you have to go back?"

"Soon. Shim wants to see what's going on."

"I want to go with you."

Colleen frowned. "I'm not sure. He wouldn't like it. It's dangerous. Especially for someone who doesn't know their way around."

"Take me with you. Help me finish weeding that damn garden and I can go."

"I'm going to pony the horses to the upper pasture for the day. Clare says if we get rain tonight, we can start using the pastures here."

They studied each other.

"I can't let them die. Or be shot." Colleen's eyes were dark hollows. "Sooner or later, we're going to be found out. You know that."

"Clare won't let that happen."

Colleen ducked her head, closed her eyes, and said in a husky voice, "God, I've missed you. I miss the way it was. The horses. You and me together all the time."

Sloan's chest tightened. "I missed you too," she said.

The words *but not enough to come back* hung unspoken between them.

## CHAPTER SEVEN

The next day Sloan began weeding at sunup. She'd been at it for half an hour when Rosemary joined her. The girl had never been in a vegetable garden before and stood next to where Sloan was kneeling and looked down at her. Sloan sat back on her haunches. "Do you need something?"

"I need to help you. I need something to do."

"Great. Just start on the row next to mine."

Rosemary dropped to her knees, watching Sloan, who had gone back to her work. When the girl didn't move, Sloan turned to her. "What's the matter?"

"I don't know what are weeds and what are vegetables."

Sloan felt the burst of anger she experienced in the restaurant when a chef didn't know how to do something he should have learned in cooking school 101. In the restaurant her normal reaction was to grab the whisk or knife or measuring cup, whatever utensil the novice was holding, and do it herself while yelling instructions at the cowering young cook. Now she looked at Rosemary for a long moment while regaining her temper. She really was a forlorn young thing. "Okay, I'm going to give you a quick tutorial." She lifted a vine laden with tomatoes. "Do you know what this is?"

"Tomato."

"Good." Sloan pointed to the pole beans. "What do you think those are?"

"Green beans."

"Good. Now over there, those plants with the big, dark, green leaves and delicate flowers. Those are squash." Sloan continued pointing out the various vegetables and then picked up a weed between her and Rosemary. "This is a weed." Rosemary nodded. "If you have any questions, ask me."

The girl bent to her task.

Sloan glanced at her from time to time, but she seemed to have gotten the hang of it. It was a statement to Sloan's preoccupation with the farm, and her desire to go to Coleton with Colleen and Shimmer to find out about Annie, that she didn't wonder about Rosemary's story.

The sun rose over them, causing their bodies to throw small, round shadows. A truck door slammed. Sloan didn't bother to turn around, not even when footsteps approached. Soon the feet making the sound were right in front of her. She looked up. Jack.

"You're back soon."

"Yeah, I brought a piece of clothesline so she can hand graze Wilson in the yard."

Rosemary had stopped weeding and looked at Jack.

"How about it? You want to try? Get him out of the stall?"

"I ride him every day."

"Well, there's grass in the yard."

Rosemary looked at Sloan.

"Go ahead," she said, rather crossly.

Jack helped Rosemary to her feet and the two walked across the yard to the stable. Sloan went back to her weeding and didn't give the other two a second thought until she wiped sweat from her forehead. Looking at the sky, she guessed it to be about eleven o'clock. She glanced over her shoulder. Jack and Rosemary were just now leading Wilson out of the stable. Apparently, it took almost two hours to tie the clothesline to Wilson's halter. Sloan watched them as they led the horse to the yard. Rosemary held the clothesline, leading the horse, and Jack walked next to her, their shoulders almost touching. Sloan didn't know much about Jack, but she knew he was too old for Rosemary.

She continued to watch as the girl let Wilson drop his head to the grass and begin the slow, steady job of cropping the sweet blades. Jack stayed right next to her.

Huh, thought Sloan. But mostly she was annoyed she'd lost her weeding partner.

As the sun started its descent, Sloan's clothes had become as wet as if she'd been in the eddy. And only half done. Sweat dripped from her head onto the ground. She felt sick to her stomach.

"You make good progress, eh."

Sloan nearly jumped out of her skin. Shimmer hunkered down at the edge of the garden. "You are industrious worker, I must say. Me. I prefer telling others what they should do." He smiled. "But they don't always listen. Fact is, they almost never listen. Is okay." He stopped smiling. "Colleen tells me you want to go to Coleton with me."

Sloan raised her arm and wiped sweat off her brow with the sleeve of her shirt. "Yeah, I would like that very much."

"Normally I would say no. But you are daughter of Clare. So, you can come. But I warn you, you must not say anything of what you see at this farm. Can you make this promise?"

"Absolutely."

Shimmer stood up. The sun hit him at an angle, making his spots glimmer. He looked more statue than man. "Come on. We need to go now."

"Now? Colleen's up the mountain. And I thought you like to travel at night."

"I need to get back. Colleen is staying here for few days. I told you… she worries about the horses. She wants to stay here and make sure they… hell, what do I know what she wants to do with them. I don't even try anymores to talk her out of it. Is one stubborn girl, your Colleen."

Sloan jumped to her feet. "I'll go change my clothes."

"Why?"

"They're soaked with sweat."

"Doesn't matter."

"I'm covered in dirt." She held out her hands. "Look at me."

"Doesn't matter."

"Shimmer."

"We are going to the Southside. No one will care how you look."

Once they were in the truck and on the Creek Road, he turned to smile at Sloan. "You might want to hold on to the handle over your head. Will be a little bumpy." He yanked the wheel right and the truck jumped over the roadside ditch onto an open, recently cut hay field. It was steep and Sloan felt herself pushed back against her seat. The newly cut hay was wet and slippery, and Shimmer had to work to keep from skidding. The incline near the top was so steep, Sloan yelled *Shimmer*, sure the truck would flip over backward. A second later they reached the summit and became airborne. She grabbed Shimmer's arm as the truck sailed to the next smaller hilltop, bounced off it onto the tallest of the three hills, and settled itself on all fours. Shimmer drove it over the crescent and began the long descent toward the woods at the bottom. "Next time might be a good idea not to grab my arm. Makes driving a little difficult." He laughed until he saw her terrified face. "No need for fear," he said and patted her shoulder.

"Why didn't you warn me?" Sloan gasped.

"No need to. I had control the whole time. Nothing to fear. Anyway, if I warn you, you get all tense, and this is not good."

The truck slid and shimmied down the long hill.

"Where are we going?"

"To Coleton, of course. But is best to avoid the roads in broad daylight when we can. Soon we will come to a dirt road that takes us to the Southside. The back way. Is a safe way to go for now."

Sloan stared out the front for a long moment before asking, "Just how dangerous is it here?"

"Not so dangerous as New York." Shimmer turned the wheel this way and that, trying to prevent the truck from going into a slide on the slick descent. "Why you not come home sooner? You must have noticed what was happening. The takeovers, peoples disappearing, the Nationalists everywhere."

Sloan put her hand on the dash to keep from sliding. "I guess I just put my head in the sand, or maybe I should say salt, and focused on work. Even though we had fewer and fewer customers, and it was harder and harder to get supplies, and we lost some staff. It was just easier not to think about anything but getting food on the tables."

The ground had started to level off. Sloan took her hand off the dash and leaned against the seat back. "How did you end up in Coleton?"

"Hopped a train."

"That's not what I meant."

"Just kidding. I bought a ticket."

"That's not my point. Where did you get on this train?"

"Pittsburg."

"So, tell me why you left Pittsburg to come here?"

"Maybe someday I tell you. Not important now. Best to know as little as possible about anyone. We don't even know who's in the resistance. Just the ones necessary to transport things. Get info around. And don't ask what things. Maybe you'll find out, maybe not. But like in New York, best to focus on the next step and not so much else."

Sloan didn't recognize the dirt road they took to Coleton. She tried to memorize it as they crept along. There weren't many landmarks to hang in her mind until suddenly the dirt turned to concrete, with houses, fences, sidewalks, trash cans, cars, and trucks on the sides of the street. She didn't see one person walking on the sidewalks or standing at a street corner.

The Southside was Coleton's version of a ghetto, though in any big city it would merely be a seedy neighborhood. A main thoroughfare, Evelyn Street, led out of downtown Coleton, through the business section into Southside and then on out the other end where it turned into a highway. Just before Southside, Evelyn Street was divided by a railroad track. None of the "decent" folk of Coleton crossed this track unless they had to. And if they had to, they didn't get out of their vehicles unless they were social workers, medics, or police.

Shimmer pulled onto a patch of dirt and grass behind a two-story clapboard building. A few of the downstairs windows were gone and boarded over. A rickety wooden staircase led to the second floor. The house was the same indeterminate pale yellowish color as most of the buildings near it, its aging paint peeling and neglected.

"Come on," he said to Sloan and led her to the back door. He knocked five times and waited. Sloan heard footsteps along with a rhythmic thump. The door opened, but it was too dark to make out anything except the person on the other side: a tall, Black man leaning on a cane. "Who's that?" he demanded.

"Sloan Raffienne. She's okay. Lives out there on Valley Farm. Is Clare's daughter. Sloan, this is Jamail."

The man opened the door enough so they could walk through. As Sloan's eyes adjusted to the dark, she made out three people in a room directly off the hall. They were sitting on the floor. She looked at them for signs of having had the virus. In the dim light it was hard to tell.

The only furniture in the room was a sunken couch.

"What's this?" said Shimmer. "Why so many altogether?"

"Something's happened." Jamail pointed his crutch. "Go on in. We need to talk."

Shimmer and Sloan stood in the middle of the room. Shimmer put his hands in his front pants pockets. "Why so many people gathered altogether? Is it about Annie and Marshall?"

"They're still missing," a woman said in a whiskey voice.

Sloan's hand flew to her mouth. The woman looked at her then back at Shimmer.

One of the men on the floor tapped a cigarette out of its pack. He lit up, took a deep draw, and spoke while exhaling smoke and squinting through the fog. "That ain't the only reason we're here. Several nights ago, the McMannises raided and moved into the Whitbeck farm. Someone must've warned them, cause the Whitbecks was long gone when the McMannises got there. The Nationalists are comin' into Coleton; word is, they're lookin' for a girl comes from the estate."

The McMannises, like the Holler people, were a country unto themselves. A family of forty or fifty, all inbred to cousins, uncles, aunts, grandparents, even siblings, in a complex web that not even they could sort out. They lived in groups of five to ten, mostly in condemned houses where they squatted until they were forced out. Generally, the places had to be torn down or burned once they were gone. Their dogs filled the places with fleas. They cut holes in the floor for latrines, left scraps of food everywhere drawing rats, and cooked crystal meth. Unlike the Holler people, they didn't hunt or fish. They ate fast food and whatever they could steal from grocery stores. They were nomadic, moving around Coleton and its environs, one step ahead of the law, which wasn't hard since the law considered them an inescapable evil and only pursued them when violence was involved, which was rare.

Like the Holler people, you could tell McMannises by looking at them: overweight, short, thin light-brown hair, acne-covered skin and bowed legs. Unlike the Holler people, they didn't keep to themselves but wandered around Coleton openly looking for something to steal.

Shimmer crossed his arms over his chest. "How do you know these things?"

"Rusty came by and told me. He went to give Marshall some news, something about more Nationalists coming into the area. And the house was empty."

"When?"

"Two, three days ago. He said he'd be back here with more info, but I haven't seen him since. You know how he is."

Rusty's parents and younger sisters had been killed by the virus. With ginger hair, flaxen eyelashes, and eyebrows the color of Arabian sand, like a roadrunner, the eighteen-year-old now lived in a place of perpetual motion.

Jamail leaned more heavily on his crutch. It was then Sloan noticed he was missing a foot.

Shimmer motioned to the people on the floor. "You. Out. Can't believe you gather like this when the Nationalists are making a swarm."

When the three were gone, Jamail eased himself into the broken-down couch and stood his crutch upright next to him. Shimmer sat cross-legged in front of him. "So, tell me everything. What were the McMannises thinking, going to that place?"

Jamail looked at Sloan, who stood in the middle of the room.

Shimmer nicked his head in her direction. "Is okay. Go sit, Sloan. He won't bite."

Sloan sat as far from Jamail and his crutch as she could. He had hooded eyes in an unfriendly, melancholy face.

"Not much to tell you, brother. The Whitbecks are gone, and the McMannises have taken over the place for now."

"Well, is not good news but not so terrible. What do we care about the Whitbecks? Good riddance." He glanced at Sloan, his expression clear, the heft of which she understood at once. No need to say anything about Rosemary.

She sat up straight. "Aren't you forgetting something?" She could hear the tears in her voice. "Why aren't you talking about Annie and Marshall? They're our people. Who cares about the Whitbecks and McMannises? It's Annie who matters."

"We haven't forgotten them," Jamail said. His eyes were like a blind man's, impenetrable.

Shimmer reached in a pocket and handed Jamail a set of keys. "Do you mind if I leave the truck here two or three days? I'm going to check around for them."

Once they were outside, Shimmer took Sloan's hand and led her through a series of crisscrossing lawns going deeper into the Southside. When they came to a barely there alley, he dropped her hand, placed his on the small of her back, and directed her from one shadowed alley to another until they were in front of a tiny blue cottage tucked between houses so disproportionally bigger that it could have been a shed belonging to one of them. Shimmer lived in this postage stamp of a house, though he only stayed there two or three days at a time. The front door opened onto the living room. A door in a side wall opened into a galley kitchen. On the other side, a door led to a bedroom with a bathroom so narrow it could hold only a claw-foot tub, small pedestal sink, and toilet.

The house had been owned by an old woman who died of the virus alone in her bed. When he moved in, Shimmer had dragged the bed and mattress into the tiny backyard and set it on fire, any Nationalists around be damned. He'd watched that fire all night, poking the flames with a stick and praying his kind of prayer for the woman whose house he had taken over.

The old woman had left behind a couch and two stuffed chairs in the living room, a refrigerator and gas stove in the kitchen. Shimmer tossed a bedroll on the floor in the bedroom, unplugged the fridge, and used the stove only to make coffee. "Sorry is so dark in here," he said. "But this will help." He lit a candle and put it on a plastic storage container in front of the couch. "Are you hungry? I'm starved." He dropped a plastic bag in the middle of the couch and plunked down beside it. "Let's eat. Oh. I forget." He jumped up, went into the kitchen, and returned with a plastic jug of water and two glasses. "Now come. Sit with me and drink and eat something. I am very tired, and you must also be. We will eat something, sleep a little. You can sleep on the mattress in the bedroom, and I will sleep on the couch, and then later tonight we will go looking."

Sloan slipped off her sneakers and sat gingerly at the other end of the couch, drawing up her knees. The near dark made her eyes huge smudges in her pale skin, but it was her bare feet that held Shimmer's attention. After four years as a chef in New York City, they were as white as the day she was born. In the flickering light he imagined he could make out the bones under the skin. He bit off a piece of jerky and chewed. "Eat," he said around the food. "You must be hungry."

"I'm not hungry and I can't sleep."

Shimmer considered her for a while. He placed his hand on one of her feet, his fingers tracing the bones so lightly she could pretend she didn't feel them. She closed her eyes. "Okay," he said, sitting back and removing his hand. "You need something to help you sleep. Maybe I do too." He disappeared into the bathroom, returned with a plastic water bottle, and settled himself back on the couch. He handed her the bottle. "Now, drink some of that. It will help." Sloan unscrewed the cap and sniffed. Vodka. She tilted her head back and swallowed a large gulp. It hit her empty stomach with gratifying fire. She took another nip then handed the bottle to Shimmer, who lifted it in the air. "To the resistance."

"What exactly is the resistance?"

"Good question." He drank and wiped his mouth with the back of his hand. "Is not a resistance really. Is just a bunch of people trying to stay alive and free till this blows over."

"Blows over?"

"Yes. You don't think this country will let Diamond stay in power forever?" He smiled indulgently and shook his head. "Course not."

Sloan reached for the bottle. "How will they get rid of him?"

"When… and I say it will be soon… enough generals get together and force him out. Believe me. At least half the generals hate him."

"And you know this how?"

Shimmer gave what looked to Sloan an Eastern European shrug. "I just do. How could they not?"

"How will they get him out?"

"With violence, of course. Like always."

"Are you talking nuclear weapons?"

"Of course not. There would be nothing left. They will use assault weapons. Maybe napalm. How do I know? I am not soldier or military of any kind. Innocent people will die but that is always true. In the meantime, people like us will collect guns, rifles, pistols, whatever, and kill off the Nationalists." He leaned toward Sloan and reached for the vodka. "Here, share that a little."

She handed it to him. "You are so naïve."

"Why do you say that? You think Diamond and his peoples will be in power forever?" He flung his hair out of his eyes. "Nonsense."

"So, if you think the generals will eventually take care of it, why all the sneaking around?"

Shimmer left the couch to retrieve another plastic water bottle of vodka. When he returned, he said, "What do you think happens to the peoples that disappear?" His tone was indignant. "They are put to work in factories or on farms. Or, if not fit, they are killed."

"You mean like slaves? Or the Jews in Nazi Germany?"

"No, not quite. They are paid. They can shop in government stores. The government wants them to spend money. Good for the economy. They live in government houses and apartments. They just cannot leave. So, to answer your question, *that* is why all the sneaking around. Unless you want to be a government drone. Then, by all means, walk around as you please. Except you don't see Clare or John or Colleen or Annie walking around like all is normal, do you." He lifted his hand, palm out. "Sorry, sorry. I should not talk of Annie. I know. Makes you sad. But shouldn't. We will find them. And even if they have been caught… and am not saying they have… government does not want them hurt. They are too valuable."

"What does that mean?"

"Important people are not hurt in this mess. They will try to recruit them. Ask lots of questions. Keep them around. Put them high in the organization. Tempt them with money. That's all that matters to these peoples. They think money can buy anything—even loyalty. That's the way it works. Some are turned into drones, others treated like kings so they will betray their friends. Marshall and Annie will not turn, though. They may pretend, become double agents maybe, but will not turn."

"You sound so sure of yourself."

"I know." He looked done in. "Where do you think I've been before coming to this place? What do you think I've been doing? Is important to spread resistance or whatever you call it across this country. The small towns, very important. And they are ready. It will be all right. Trust me. Here," he said amicably, "have some more vodka."

"Sounds like some sort of bad movie." Sloan took a deep drink.

"I know."

She stared at him.

"If you don't believe me, why you run from New York City?" He was cross again, waving his hand in the air. "Why be so careful when you did?"

Shimmer took the bottle and screwed on the cap. "Our job is to stay alive and free so we can help when the time comes."

"And what will happen after Diamond and his minions are gone?"

"It will go back the way it was."

"You mean free elections and everything?"

"Why not?" He unscrewed the cap and drank more vodka.

Sloan leaned back against the couch. "I don't know. That just seems so… naïve."

"There you go with the naïve again. I can't persuade you, so won't try." Shimmer got to his feet and smiled at Sloan. "We should not argue. Takes too much energy. We both need some sleep." He rubbed his eye with the tip of a finger and opened his mouth in a deep yawn. He shuddered on the exhalation and motioned to the tiny bedroom. "I will stay here. You go in bedroom, and I will wake you in an hour or two. Then we will look for your friends."

Sloan stood up. "You wouldn't happen to have any sheets, would you?"

"Sheets?"

"So I can make the bed."

"You cannot be serious. But I see by your face that you are." He looked around the living room. "No sheets here." A glance into the bathroom showed there wasn't even a closet or shelves. He strode to the kitchen where he opened all six cabinets. When he opened the last one, a set of sheets and two towels fell out.

In the bedroom he helped Sloan put the fitted sheet on the bedroll. "Is complete nonsense. You know that. We are in middle of war, and you have to have sheets on your bed." Shimmer took hold of one side of the sheet and helped Sloan snap it until it was tight. He leaned over and helped her fit in the bottom and sides. "You are insane, you know that. This makes no sense. We will only sleep for an hour before we go looking. But if you must have sheets, who am I to say no. There, are you satisfied? The corners meets your approval? Now I suppose you want a pillow."

"No, I'll be…"

Shimmer went into the living room and came back with a beige chintz couch cushion. "Will this do, your majesty?" He dropped it onto the bed. "Don't worry about me. I will be fine."

Sloan started to apologize, but he leaned close and kissed her forehead. "Do not apologize. You are good sport, and I don't mind. Well… maybe not always good sport but most of the time. You look terrible. Take a bath. Will make you feel much better. Just don't use too much water. We don't want the meter to suddenly jump and cause attention."

# CHAPTER EIGHT

**S**loan laid on the bottom of the tub, letting the water rise until it covered her hair. There was no hot water, but it was no colder than the eddy. She found a half bar of white soap in a metal soap dish and scrubbed her hair, her arms, legs, torso, the bottoms of her feet. She would have liked to empty and replace the tub with fresh water, but out of deference to Shimmer she didn't. He had given her a towel and she rubbed it from her head to her toes, wrapped it under her arms, then stepped through the tiny bedroom to the living room. Shimmer handed her a sleeveless nightgown made of yellow cotton decorated with colorful posies. She stared at him.

"There is no point putting on your damp and filthy clothes. Hang them somewhere to dry. We can wash our clothes when we get to the farm. You could sleep naked if you are uncomfortable with dead woman's nightie. However, I don't recommend it."

Sloan retrieved the nightgown and shook it. The cotton, washed to a tender cloth, hung at her feet. She smelled it. It smelled like laundry soap.

"Now is my turn. Hope you left some hot water." He winked at her.

Shimmer had been right. The nightgown felt delicious. She sat on the couch and listened while the tub filled with water. She wondered if he would drain and rinse, but he didn't. He walked out of the bedroom wearing a blue and white polka dot nightgown similar to hers. With his black curls, broad shoulders, brown skin, and slender build, he could have been a desert dweller on his way to a revelry.

He stood straight and still in the middle of the living room, his arms crossed over his chest. Sloan watched him, thinking he looked like a Maasai warrior. Eventually, he turned and said, "Are you hungry? I am starved again."

"Me too."

Shimmer produced more bear jerky, tomatoes, and squash on a plate, along with two glasses of water. "Do you want some vodka?"

"No, I'm exhausted. I'll be able to sleep. What do you think we'll find when we get to Annie's?

Shimmer held up his hand. "We will talk about that tomorrow."

They sat on the couch facing each other, sharing the plate of food. As usual, he delicately nibbled his from his fingers. Sloan suddenly considered kissing his mouth. But he stood and took the plate and glasses into the kitchen and washed them. When he returned, he smiled. "You are looking not so worse for the wear. The bath did you good. Now, please, go into the bedroom so I can lie down here and sleep."

A sliver of sunlight coming through the window traveled across the floorboards, onto the bed, and spread across Sloan's face, waking her. They had overslept. She laid still and listened. Nothing. The jerky had left her with a terrible thirst. She tiptoed into the living room. Shimmer was still asleep, curled in a fetal position, his knees held in the well left by the cushion he had given to Sloan, his fists tucked under his chin. With his curls and peaceful face and nightgown, Sloan thought he looked like an angel. He also looked cold. She should have given him one of her sheets.

She tiptoed past him into the kitchen, filled a glass with water from the sink, drank it and was about to fill it again when Shimmer called to her, "Bring me one of those, please."

He sat with his back against the arm rest, his knees pulled up to his chin under the gown. Sloan handed him the glass and he drank it dry. "What time is it?"

"I don't have a watch."

"You're half Indian. Go to the window so you can see by the sun."

"I'm not half Indian."

"I know. Just saying because you are Clare's daughter, and she is part Algonquin."

Sloan went to the window, but the tall buildings blocked the direction of the light. Apparently, it wasn't noon since there was no golden orb overhead. "I can't tell because of the houses. It must always stay dark in here."

"Come," said Shimmer. "Sit with me and we will talk about options." He pushed one of the cushions to the other end of the couch. Sloan sat facing him as she had the night before and drew her knees up and there they were, sitting in an old woman's house wearing her nighties in 2026, living off jerky and vegetables, with no hot water or refrigeration, wondering how they were going to stay alive and free.

"We have three options." Shimmer pulled his nightgown over his toes. "Number one, you go to Jamail's and stay there with the truck until I come get you. It will take all day because of the long walk to Adams Street but is safest for you. No one will notice you walking alone if you take alleys. If a Nationalist does see you, they won't think you are in the resistance. Course they might want to grab you for their purposes, but not likely. Well, maybe is a little likely, so be careful. Keep your eyes sharpened. If you see a man coming, duck out of sight."

"I'm supposed to walk to Jamail's from here?"

"That is correct. I will set out from here for Adams Street. Is a long walk but I don't mind. When I am finished, I will go to Jamail's and pick you and the truck up."

Sloan had no idea how to get back to Jamail's, but since she would never choose this option, she said nothing.

"Option two. You and I park several streets away from Marshall's and I go in the back way. You stay in the truck. Third option, you come with me as we sneak into house."

"No way am I staying in the truck. I'm going to sneak with you."

Sloan had been to Annie's home on Adams Street more times than she could count, yet as she and Shimmer approached the back door with its arbor of roses and narrow stairs, she could barely breathe. Her hands were shaking so badly she handed him the key. The back door opened into the kitchenette; a room once meant to be used only by the cook. Now Marshall and his paralegal used it for coffee and a small refrigerator. Annie had designed a moderately sized, updated and efficient kitchen upstairs where Sloan had spent many hours trying out recipes.

The kitchenette showed no signs of disturbance. Shimmer and Sloan walked into what had once been a dining room and now served as Marshall's office. Sloan stood in the doorway, her body turning to jelly. At first her eyes saw the whole room as a single image of rage. Slowly she shifted her gaze from corner to corner and took in all that was in-between—desk drawers pulled out and left on the floor, their contents strewn across the carpet. The books from the bookshelf were in heaps as though someone had swept them off their shelves with an extended arm. A file cabinet's drawers hung from its rails; the folders flung around the room.

Shimmer pushed Sloan past the rubble into the paralegal's office, which was in just as bad shape, then across the hall to where most of the documents were kept. Toppled file cabinets were covered in dent marks that looked like they came from a boot. Torn folders and papers covered every inch of the floor.

Upstairs, clothes were thrown everywhere, tables turned over, pictures torn from walls, the mattresses slit open. Sloan did not say a word. Shimmer picked up a cushion that had been thrown from an overstuffed chair, its white-fluff-filling leaving a trail. "Looks like someone was pretty mad, eh. This is good news. They didn't find for what they were looking."

Sloan gasped a deep breath. "You can't possibly be that stupid. Now they will torture them to find out what they want."

Shimmer stepped over the debris and wrapped his arms around her to stop her violent shaking. "I admit it will be very unpleasant for a while."

"Unpleasant?" Sloan hissed, trying to pull free and failing.

"Unpleasant, yes. But Annie and Marshall are smart. They will give just enough and make them believe they will become pawns. Work for the government. They will figure out a way." He put his hand on the back of her head and held it next to his. "The Nationalists around here are not so smart," he whispered. "Easily fooled. Annie and Marshall will get word to us somehow. Now hush. We must get back to the farm and tell Clare what we found."

Sloan wept bitterly and silently as Shimmer snaked the truck out of Coleton. Once they were on the dirt road they came in on, she stopped crying. Her breathing was deep and harsh. "Just for your information, I am crying for Annie, but mostly I'm crying for my mother. Throughout their teenage years and most of their adulthood, all they had was each other. This will kill her." Sloan dried her face with the bottom of her t-shirt. She sighed. They drove in silence while she settled herself down and could think more clearly. Finally, she said, "Shimmer?"

"Yes."

"I'm worried about Colleen. You didn't know her before when she was, as the saying goes, sunshine on a plate. And now—you see how she is."

"Yes." He rolled down the window and rested his elbow on the sill. "It is true she is not a happy soul right now."

"Was it the virus? Did she change after she got sick?"

"She almost dies. The fever so high she was delirious for days. Burned off her hair. She can't eat much now. Her liver is too damaged but is my understanding the liver heals itself very well." He looked over at Sloan. "You know she worries the horses will die a slow and horrible death."

"Clare won't let that happen. She'll euthanize them if it comes to it, but it won't. I just can't think the horses are all there is to the change in her." Sloan paused, gazing out her side window at the wild grass growing along the dirt road. "We were so close."

"Were you?"

Sloan frowned. "Yes, of course."

"In my mind, if you have such a close friend as you have in Colleen, you do not leave them except for a very good reason, which I suppose you must have had to leave your mother and best friend. Me, I never make close friends for that reason. Easier to leave. But…" He shrugged in a Russian-esque way. "You and Colleen love each other. At least Colleen does."

"What's that supposed to mean? You weren't even around."

"I come very soon after you left. She is sadder and sadder every time we meet. Your mother told me the story."

"She did not! She wouldn't say anything like that! She'd never talk about me." Sloan flicked a hand. "I assume you and Colleen are lovers, so she must have told you some story. We had started going separate ways before I left. My mother would never get into my business, much less talk to a stranger about it."

Shimmer raised an eyebrow and gave Sloan a sideways smile. "So, you think Colleen and I are lovers? Have it your way. But I tell you… Colleen mourns you. Even now."

Sloan studied Shimmer's face, the brown skin with its specks of gold picking up the light coming through the truck window, his high-bridged nose which had the look of an ancient warrior. "Where are you really from? Ethiopia?"

Shimmer tossed her a glance. "You've been reading too many novels."

They were approaching the three hills and their rollercoaster apexes. Sloan's body grew so tense all thoughts of Annie, Colleen, and her mother were pushed out of her. She closed her eyes. Shimmer floored the truck, not giving it a chance to shimmy into a slide, ricocheted over the pinnacles, landed with a jolt on the other side and laughed aloud. "We should charge money for this. Peoples would line up. What? Why are you looking so pale? You don't trust my driving. I am a regular bronc buster only in a truck, not a horse."

"You're lucky you have a truck left." Sloan laid her head against the back of her seat as she caught her breath. When they were on Creek Road, she said, "Do you mind if we drive to the Post Office? I'm looking for a letter from Luther."

"Luther?"

"He was my sous chef in New York. We promised to write to each other.

I sent him a letter as soon as I got to the farm and haven't heard anything back."

"Hasn't been that long."

"I know. But I'd feel better if I heard."

"Of course. What are a few more miles. Glad to make you feel better if I can. This Luther? You are close?"

"We're good friends."

# CHAPTER NINE

**A**s Luther walked the long driveway to his home, he surveyed the miles of young corn stalks growing bright green and hopeful surrounding the lawn to the white clapboard house. The air was still and quiet. He listened but did not hear the gurgling rumble of a tractor, the loud hum of the fertilizer, a hammer hitting a nail, or the lowing of cows in the pasture behind the barn. The closer he came to the house, the louder the silence became. He walked up the stairs, crossed the wide front porch, and opened the oak door, which as always, remained unlocked. From the hallway he could see most of the downstairs. The place was spotless. Too spotless. Nothing stood out of place. No magazines on the floor, no blankets tossed on the couch or open sewing baskets on tables, boots stepped out of and left by the door.

Only a group of farmer's wives coming to clean up after departed neighbors could create such tidiness.

Luther moved through the rooms. He didn't call out, unable to bear the sound his voice would make bouncing off the lifeless walls. He knew they were dead but kept going through the living room, dining room, kitchen, back porch, then up the stairs to the bedrooms. After he had looked in each place, he sat on what had once been his bed, clenched his hands together on his knees, and stared out the window at the miles and miles of flat land. The two silos were still in good repair. The entire farm was in good repair.

He sat staring for a few minutes or a few hours, he didn't know.

His journey here had been a hard one. Unlike Sloan, who had only needed to transfer once and that from car to car to arrive in the Allegheny Mountains, he'd walked, hitchhiked, taken buses, jumped or paid for trains, walked and hitchhiked some more until he reached his home in the Idaho cornfields.

At some point, Luther roused himself enough to become aware of the fact that he would need to find out what was going on. This well-kept house, generous land, the obsessively tended farm equipment would not remain unclaimed for long. The reptilian part of his brain kicked in and told him all of this was in danger, and so was he.

Tired and hungry, he forced himself to leave his room. The key to the truck was not on the hook in the kitchen where it normally hung. The key to the chevy was also missing. Luther walked to the barn and pushed the wide, heavy doors along their metal tracks. He stared and stared at the empty place where the vehicles should be parked, thinking that if he stared long enough, they would materialize and knowing, of course, they wouldn't. His mind didn't seem able to form words, much less coherent thoughts. A swallow swooped across his line of vision. The dust motes floating in the sunlight made him sneeze. At least he guessed it was the dust motes. Luther turned and, arms dangling at his sides, he started the five-mile walk to the Cook's farm.

Mr. and Mrs. Cook opened the door as though expecting him. They ushered him into the kitchen with hands inches from his back, knowing he wouldn't be able to endure being touched. Mrs. Cook's fluttering hand showed him to the table. She poured him a mug of tea so steaming hot it could have been waiting just for him. Without asking, she spooned in a large dollop of honey then sat across from Luther, and folded her hands the same way she would in church.

His parents, Mary and Joe, and his younger brothers Mark and John, were all dead. His brothers died first, his parents three days later.

The air around his head began to swirl, pulling away his thoughts. He broke out in a cold sweat, shivering from head to toe, his body able to take in the words his mind couldn't. To his horror, he gagged. He clapped his hand over his mouth and swallowed back stomach bile. He hadn't eaten that day. Finished, he slumped back into his chair. Mrs. Cook pushed his tea closer. "Drink it," she said with kind firmness. "You'll be going into shock. All the arrangements have been taken care of. They are buried next to your church as they wished."

Luther tried to focus on her words, her face.

Mr. Cook said, "I'll be going. I've got to get that truck fixed this afternoon. I'm sorry, Luther. Real sorry." He patted the young man's shoulder, brief and soft as a drop of rain.

After her husband had shut the door behind him, Mrs. Cook continued. "We didn't have a service. We were hoping you'd show up. You'd not want to miss it. I'll arrange something if you want."

Luther stared at her blankly.

"You don't need to decide now."

Silence filled the room while they observed each other. Luther spoke first. "What about Susan?" Susan was the Cook's daughter.

"She married a farmer from the next county, twenty miles from here. She's moving back. Her husband died."

"I'm so sorry. And Bryce?"

Mrs. Cook slid her eyes away and cleared her throat. When she spoke, the quiver in her voice took Luther by surprise.

"Son, there is something I need to tell you."

"Yes?"

"You must have noticed your truck and car are gone. Truth is, Bryce took the truck. He's on his way to Canada. Rumors have started. About how men in their twenties are being picked up all over the county. Lots of folks have left. Just abandoned their stock or sold it, though no one's really buying. We brought your cattle and the goat here. The dog too."

"Okay."

"Russell Sapaugh took the Chevy. He and Mary Beth got those two babies you know. He wasn't sure where they were heading. The Sapaugh's got relatives somewhere. Rockies, I think he said. Some place like Wyoming. Real remote. He thought he might go there. You can get lost in those mountains."

"I believe you can."

"You can have our truck. It's only right."

"No, that's okay. You need it."

"I feel real bad about this."

"It's okay. I understand."

"How'd you get here?"

"It wasn't hard."

"Do you need money? We could give you some."

"No, I've got plenty."

Mrs. Cook sat clenching and unclenching her hands. "Cletus and I haven't been sick. Susan hasn't either, but she stayed with her husband till he died. Couldn't let him die alone in the hospital. Besides, hospitals are too dangerous now. You know what I'm saying. We've all been exposed."

"So have I. I think. I met lots of people on my way home. Who knows? They might have been contagious."

"You're welcome to stay here. No sickness is going to take away our humanity. And I can't imagine you'd want to stay in that empty house."

"I would, I think. I…"

Mrs. Cook continued folding and unfolding her hands. "Honestly, I'm not sure what we're going to do. Susan's pregnant. But if the Nationalists are here, maybe we'll leave. I don't know. Our families have always lived here."

"I think I'll head on home. For a day or two, anyway. See to things."

"We've done everything we could over there. Left the fridge on. That's about all. Stove's off. There's some bread I made in the fridge. Case you came back hungry. And the well still works if you need it."

"Thanks."

Mrs. Cook rose and rinsed out Luther's mug. "No one's been around so far. Not directly here. But prime land like yours. It won't be long before the Nationalists find it. Find all of us. Surprises me they haven't already. You should probably leave as soon as you can. What do you think you'll do?"

"I don't know."

Luther watched her back, her strong shoulders as she poured dish soap on a rag and ran it around the sink and his mug, scrubbing vigorously. He'd known her all his life. Her son had taken his truck, his friend the car. His whole family was dead. He wanted to get up and walk out of this house and keep on walking until he fell off the earth. He felt weightless, tied to no one, all connections to this world severed. Except maybe to Sloan, who seemed light years away and he too gut wrenched to put one foot in front of the other.

"Strong boy like you and blond. Just the right type," Mrs. Cook said, still scrubbing. "Don't know where you'd go, but if you have a place safer than here, I'd leave soon."

Luther made it home by staring at his feet as he walked along the macadam road. Left then right, left then right, while the sun zeroed in on the back of his neck. Once in the house, he crawled into bed and dropped into a sleep so profound he might as well have been dead. Not until the sun poked over the horizon did he emerge from this merciful state to confusion, curiosity, and then an explosion of despair. After scrubbing his face with cold water, Luther looked around and wandered into his closet. Having lived in New York City for several years, he only owned one change of clothes. His backpack, as he made his way to Idaho, hung loosely from his shoulders. Here in the middle of the vast Midwest, closets overflowed with shirts, khakis, jeans, perhaps a sports coat or suit. Boots of every kind, sneakers, whatever wasn't needed and long forgotten covered the floor. Dressers in New York, if you had one, were shared with one or two other people. T-shirts, underwear, socks, and outgrown items were not crammed haphazardly into every corner.

Luther's clothes had been left alone, untouched or moved in any way. A bubble in his chest pushed against his ribs as he pictured his parents standing on the porch waving him goodbye. He knew if he didn't get moving, he would end up in bed curled in a ball.

It took over an hour to sort through what seemed now an unforgivable excess of belongings and choose the right ones to put in his backpack.

Downstairs, he peered into the refrigerator. Two loaves of golden-brown bread stood as though framed, on the top shelf. And, yes, next to them a block of butter glistened through the wax paper wrapping.

He drew a glass of water from the tap, sliced a thick section of the homemade oatmeal bread. Even cold, its aroma escaped, rose to his tired, slack face. Tears stung his eyes, but inhaling and exhaling sharply, he pushed back the storm of emotion threatening to capsize him. He sliced the brick hard butter with a butcher knife, laid greedy pieces on the bread and took a bite. His eyes closed. The smooth, solid butter began to melt on his tongue. The bread offered just the right amount of resistance. He barely had finished his first bite when he opened his mouth and stuffed in another as he leaned against the counter. He was about to begin on a third when his stomach rolled. Excess saliva spilled from the back of his cheeks. When Luther looked at the bread, his gorge rose. Tears ran down his cheeks. I'll just lie down for a while, he told himself.

He fell into a haunted sleep, roamed through twilight, shadows following him, all of them familiar. He shied from some, hunch shouldered and ashamed. Others he reached out to, desperate to hold on, but they eluded him, slipped through his fingers, grinned, and mocked him. At some point on this ghostly journey, a brace slid around his head and an unknown force squeezed tighter and tighter. Thirst closed his throat. He woke up enough to lick his lips and consider getting a drink of water. The moment the thought landed, he catapulted out of bed, ran to the bathroom across the hall and threw up the two bites of bread and more. He wiped his mouth on his sleeve and turned to go back to his room. Nature had other plans. He sat on the wooden seat, held his head in his hands, and moaned. At last, he staggered to his bed only to leap up as soon as he laid down. This happened six times until he dragged his blankets and a pillow into the bathroom and curled around the commode, his forehead resting against the cool porcelain. Relieved, he shuddered and slipped into a real sleep where he was carried away by fever dreams. Fire burned around the room but did not touch him, a horse he'd owned as a boy approached, stopped, and offered him a ride, finally lost patience and galloped away. His brothers cried, stretched their arms to him, and cursed him as they drowned in the lake they had all swum in as children. His head bulged around the metal ring till his eyes rolled onto the floor and laughed because he could still see without them. Sloan walked around the kitchen in the restaurant on her hands, toes pointing toward the ceiling while the pots and pans banged together, drowning out her voice as she issued orders. He pulled himself up, touching his lips to the faucet, wet them, then fell like a rag doll onto the foul blankets, and shivered so hard his teeth rattled. He had no idea how long he stayed in this unknown place, where three times he left his body to float against the too bright ceiling before returning to the carnal world of pain and unbearable sick, light and utter dark. He found himself lying naked in the desert, nothing but sand and sun-drenched pale blue sky overhead, slowly turning his skin to parchment and him not able to move. His joints grew to the size of baseballs and throbbed against his brittle skin. Dark angels with beaks for heads and wings ending in claws swooped, threatened to drag him to a place where the earth disappeared and, "even if you checked out, you could never leave."

His parents traveled with him, and though reduced to skeletons they smiled encouragement, assured him they did not blame him for leaving. His father put his arm of bones around his shoulder and told him he would help him walk through the valley. His mother clattered to her knees and held a glass of cold delicious nectar to his mouth, tipped it down his throat. Luther opened his eyes and wanted to die all over again when he recognized Mrs. Cook.

"Looks like you're through the worst of it. You must have had the wit and strength to drink from the faucet, otherwise you'd be dead by now. Been about two weeks. We would have come sooner but weren't sure you wanted company. Drink some more." She handed him a glass and said, "You've got tan patches on your skin. They'll darken, no doubt. I see you've lost some hair, and you're white as a sheet, but I think you've come through."

Luther swallowed the cold sweet tea, and this time it traveled through his stomach to his limbs where it could do some good. He closed his eyes and cursed the ministering angel.

Mrs. Cook tended Luther for three days, and because he had grown to manhood breathing fresh air, eating wholesome food, and putting his bones and muscles to good use, he recovered quickly, though he didn't regain his appetite. He lived on sweetened tea and last year's pears.

He had always been a saver and had brought a significant amount of money with him to New York. But the city was expensive and his bundle of cash, which he carried in a leather pouch tied around his waist, was not as large as he had hoped when he made his escape toward home. Even so, Sloan or not, he knew he would never make it on foot. He knew her address and squandered most of his stash on an Amtrak ticket that dropped him smack dab in the middle of Coleton.

# CHAPTER TEN

Clare's hay-loaded pickup sat in front of the stable. "I'll tell her after I help unload the truck," Sloan said as she and Shimmer drove up the driveway.

Shimmer waved to Clare, who came over and leaned against the driver's window. "Colleen around?" he asked.

"She's up the mountain grazing horses."

"I'll go look for her. Which pastures?"

"The highest. The one that's not fenced."

Sloan jumped down from Shimmer's truck. "I'll help with the hay."

Clare nodded, reaching for a bale.

Sloan watched her mother as she lifted the bale off the truck's bed, hoisted it against her chest and carried it into the barn. Even gaunt, she moved with the same ease she'd had as a young woman. Sloan grabbed a bale and followed her. "This is good looking hay," she managed to say, though the sudden dead weight took most of her breath.

"Green… sweet… smelling," she panted.

"My buddies in Somerset are still growing it, just as good as before. No one bothers with Somerset. Not yet anyway." Clare's voice came out evenly, unstrained by the bale she carried.

When they finished, Sloan asked her mother to sit with her on the tailgate.

She waited until she got her breath back then said, "You know we went into Coleton?"

"Yeah."

"Long story short, Annie and Marshall are definitely missing. We went to their house. It was ransacked." She struggled to keep her voice steady.

Clare didn't look at her daughter but at the mountain behind the farm. She swung her legs back and forth, her expression impenetrable.

Sloan waited. She'd sit here all day if she had to. Annie being gone was too important to let her mother put up a barrier the way she did when confronted with trouble. Clare Raffienne suffered from the sin of pride, fed by the fact people feared her. She'd been sixteen when she crippled a boy in the act of assaulting a girl, that girl being Annie. Four years later, a man drank himself to death when she refused him. She burned another man's house to the ground because he'd dared to hit her. Even when the US government took Sloan away, her mother got her daughter back in record time. The bureaucrats had thought of her as poor and alone, which meant weak. They underestimated her power.

Sloan's memory of that time was caught in fog, a haze so thick she could only retrieve shadows: a ghost of a man, hands touching her underwater, crooning, treacherous voices, and a tall, dark boy, the most deceitful of all.

But things were different now. Possibly even Clare's place in the world. A sudden sense of loss caught Sloan unaware, made her draw a deep breath with the need to penetrate her mother's shuttered arrogance. She turned to face her. "It's all changed. No regular people are safe. Annie and Marshall were head of the resistance. Do you understand that? The Nationalists are bad people, Mom. Good people disappear. Forever! You need to understand that."

Clare turned to her daughter. "I do understand. What do you mean ransacked?"

Sloan stiffened and described in slow, clipped words what she had seen. Her mother watched her carefully, letting the information fill her. "You find any sign what they were looking for?"

"Not really. We didn't go through stuff piece by piece."

"Does Jamie have any idea where Annie and Marshall are?"

"You mean Shimmer? Me and Colleen, we call him Shimmer. And no, he doesn't."

Clare nodded. "Got it."

"You're going to go to Annie's, aren't you?"

"Course I am."

"I want to go with you."

Clare turned to her daughter. "I'd like that."

Sloan looked away, not willing to let her mother see her surprised and pleased expression. She undid her sloppy ponytail, pulled it tight into the rubber band. "I have something else to tell you. About the Whitbecks. The McMannises raided their place, either chased them off or maybe they were already gone. And more Nationalists are coming into Coleton every day. Even to the Southside."

"Huh." Clare ran her fingers through her hair. "Are they coming because the Whitbecks got run off?"

"No one knows for sure." Sloan looked around. "Where is Rosemary, anyhow?"

"With Jack some place."

"Why do you let him hang around here? He's way too old for her. It's kinda creepy. Didn't he do something awful to one of your staff?"

"Staff? Is that what you call it?" Clare laughed.

Sloan shook her head. "It's not like you to put up with riffraff."

"Riffraff? Listen to me. The Holler was its own country long before you were born. No one bothers them. No one enters their world. God knows how they do it, but they always manage to get what they need. They're important to us now. Jack's gone over there to get some fishing line. Rosemary probably went with him."

"What does she see in him?"

"He's the only one who pays attention to her."

Sloan put her palms behind her on the truck bed and leaned on them.

"Why is that? Why don't you take the time to get to know her? She's going to cause us a lot of trouble. I can feel it."

"You're right. I should of taken more time to find out what happened over there."

"She doesn't seem to have a clue herself. Imagine her family just running off and leaving her."

"Important thing is to find Annie… and Marshall. I should have persuaded her to stay here."

"You couldn't have. You know how it is with a woman in love."

Her mother jumped down from the tailgate. "Daughter, I *do* know what's goin' on and how dangerous things is, but bad as it is for us, it's a whole lot worse in town."

Sloan's mother peered across the road. Rosemary and Jack were crossing, their shoulders touching.

"Believe me, Sloan, I hear what you tell me. What I can't figure out is how parents could just leave a child behind. No wonder that girl acts so strange."

The main thing that escaped Rosemary's understanding of the world around her was the depth of her father's love. She didn't know he thought of her as pure, clean, innocent of subterfuge. While most girls her age demanded the latest devices, the newest haircuts, clothing, trips to Hawaii, cars, Rosemary coveted nothing but a single horse. Mr. Whitbeck had never known her to lie or tattle on her brothers. He never heard her speak rudely to a servant. He couldn't imagine her bullying or stealing or betraying anyone.

In other words, she was free of all the behaviors he had taken on as greed propelled him further and further down a trail to hell where he joined the cursed group of humans for whom, no matter how much money or power they had, it would never be enough. His distance from his daughter wasn't because he didn't care for her. He cared for her so much he refused to bring her into his world.

The night they'd had to flee in a frenzy of terror, he'd made up his mind to let her go from his life, possibly forever. The less he knew of her whereabouts, the safer she would be.

Mr. Whitbeck had known his stable manager for twenty years. Pedro had his own resources; an underground Mr. Whitbeck denied knowledge of. He also knew him to be a man of integrity. If he told Pedro to do something, he did it. Like putting Rosemary on a horse and sending her into the mountains. Rosemary's father thought the mountains and the self-contained people living there would be isolated from what was going on in DC, New York, LA, or any populated area in the country. Anyone could hide in those hills, and this made them the safest place to send her. He thought of the mountain folks as independent but not cruel. Someone would take her in.

He didn't care what happened to the estate.

Let the locals take everything, move in if they wanted to, just so long as they didn't bring Rosemary back here. He'd told Pedro not to let that happen, and he trusted the Mexican.

What made his hands shake and his mind skid around instead of settling on a sensible plan was the phone call from President Diamond. President Diamond had summoned him to Washington. He also told him to bring his family, and Stirling Whitbeck knew the reason why.

# CHAPTER ELEVEN

In the hope he could get some sleep, Luther chose a seat in the back of the train. The ride to the station with the Cooks had exhausted him. They tried to hide it, but their fear of being on the open road in daylight leaked out of every pore and tumbled from their mouths even though they said very little. They had insisted on driving him since Russell had taken his truck.

Now he walked down the aisle to the back, threw his backpack overhead, and sank into his seat. The cushions were wide and soft. He lowered the back and laid his head against the window. There were only three other passengers: two middle-aged, chunky women and a younger one dressed as though she might be going to the city.

Luther closed his eyes when the train started rolling and fell into the sweet sleep that only comes when recovering from a life-threatening illness. If he dreamed, he didn't remember it. Once or twice, he surfaced enough to feel the swaying train then, suffused with peace and well-being, drifted into nothingness.

He slept through the stops in small towns, but when the train shuddered to a halt in Akron, Ohio, he woke. Slowly he became aware of where he was and why, but the feeling of well-being remained. He had left Idaho and his dead family in a dark, unknowing part of his brain. Now he concentrated only on Sloan. He'd put a letter to her in his mailbox at the farm saying he was coming, even though he didn't know if the mailman still came by. He'd spent most of his money on the train ticket to Coleton. When he thought of what he would do after he arrived, his mind went blank. He'd figure that out when he got there. Now he watched with curiosity as about fifteen young men, some in uniform, boarded. They emanated an aura of goodwill, good humor, joy in the freeing knowledge that their futures were golden. They laughed, punched, and shoved each other as they stowed their luggage, all the while smiling and chatting, taking two seats apiece, settling into them still laughing and talking back and forth. As Luther watched, he was infected with their good humor and fell back asleep with a half-smile on his face. He slept until he felt the train push back as it came to a stop in Coleton, Pennsylvania. Sloan had told him the station was in the middle of downtown. Once a booming railroad city, tracks still crisscrossed it, as much a part of the town as the highways that replaced them.

Sloan's address rested in his breast pocket: Clare Raffienne, Valley Farm, Pleasant Union, Pennsylvania. He also had directions on how to get there. Unfortunately, no way did he have the strength to walk the fifteen miles. Sloan had told him if he needed help to go to the Southside where most of the resistance hung out.

Grabbing his backpack from above, he followed the band of merry men out onto the sidewalk. The buildings were stone or brick with decorative wooden window casings. Grass lined the sidewalks. Once flowers had grown there and the sidewalks had been clean. Now, wrappers from fast-food joints and other debris clung to the crease where the sidewalk met the buildings. Luther felt hollowed out, all the good feelings gone. The thought passed through his mind that the people who had tended these streets were hiding, captured, or killed. And now he was mixed in with the group doing the capturing, perhaps even the killing. He was glad Sloan wasn't here, hadn't by some miracle gotten his letter and found a way to meet his train. He stood, backpack straps on his shoulders. His best chance was to walk quietly away. Other than his fellow passengers, the streets were empty. He was turning away, wondering how he would get to Southside, when one of the men in uniform came up to him and laid a hand on his shoulder.

"Hey, fella. You were out cold back there. We thought about waking you but decided you needed your sleep." The uniformed man dropped his hand from Luther's shoulder and held it out to shake. "Henry Reilly, from Ruckstan, Ohio. Nice to have you with us."

Luther stared at him. Another young man, this one without a uniform, joined them. "You look like you've had the virus. Those patches aren't too bad. I've seen many stranger things. What happened? You get a bad vaccine? Happened to a buddy of mine. They're in such a rush to get us all vaccinated sometimes they put out a bad batch. How you feelin'?"

"Okay."

"You're a rack of bones," Henry said. "But don't worry. They'll have you fattened up in no time. The food is great, I hear."

Luther looked around at the others. Most of them were blond and blue-eyed. He realized they thought he was one of them. The rest of the men gathered round. One of them asked where he was from.

"Western Ohio," he said vaguely.

"Most of us are from Ohio. A couple from Michigan. This is going to be a great gig, so I'm told."

Another said, "You don't have a uniform yet. They'll probably have one that fits at the hotel. They've taken over the Holiday Inn as headquarters."

A third young man looked around. "I thought they were sending cars to pick us up." As he said this, four SUVs pulled to the curb, and the men began shoving in their duffle bags and climbing in behind them. Henry Reilly put his hand on Luther's back and gently pushed him into the fourth SUV.

He sat in the back and shifted his backpack to his lap. Well, now I'm cooked, he told himself. His chest tightened when he thought of Sloan. He was too weak to put up a fight or any kind of resistance, so he went where he was pushed.

The small entourage crossed the tracks, drove to the middle of town, turned left, and made a steady climb up the four blocks to Madison Street where the

Holiday Inn, with its curved driveway in front, and wide-open parking lots providing no place to hide, overlooked the city. Luther noted several canvas-covered army trucks in the Nationalists' colors: white, gray, and tan, parked in the asphalt lots carved into the mountain. Frantic, disjointed sentences formed in his mind, trying to put together a sensible plan of escape as the momentum of the group carried him out of the truck and forward up the steps to the hotel.

Inside, the lobby had been renovated. The welcoming counter and staff were gone, replaced by a rectangular desk in the middle, where a young man, boy really, sat taking names. A line of men stood in front of it. Somehow, in his haze, Luther found himself only five men back. Henry stood in front of him. Each man in turn told their name and the boy checked it off on a sheet of paper. Luther hastily went through his options. Give his real name and see what happened, make up a fake one claiming he lost his I.D. or slip out of line and out the door, into the streets of Coleton and disappear. He decided the latter was his best choice but then realized he'd dithered too long, and he was just two men back and couldn't slide out of line unnoticed and anyway there was Henry. When it was his turn, he grasped the name Peter Jones out of the air. The boy ran his finger down the three pages, scowled and did it again, squinting earnestly. "How do you spell that?"

"P E T E R J O N E S."

The boy once again ran his finger over the names then for the first time looked up at Luther. His expression turned from worried to keen interest. "You've had the disease."

"Yes, but I'm fine now."

"Didn't you get the vaccine when you signed up?"

"Apparently I got a defective shot."

"I've heard of that." The boy looked at his papers again. "You're not listed here. Did you go to the hospital?"

"Um, yes."

"That explains it. The hospitals are a mess. They can't keep anything straight. It's a wonder they haven't killed half the patients with the wrong medicine. I'm not sure why they keep treating people anyway. I heard soon the government will have their own hospitals where they'll treat only Nationalists. Things will be run well there; you can be sure." He reached for a yellow legal pad. "What was your name again?"

"Peter Jones."

The boy wrote it on the legal pad. "Where did you come from?"

Luther gave the name of the western most city in Ohio he could think of, and the boy wrote it down. "Your name will turn up. I'll start checking on it tomorrow or tonight after I get this load processed." He reached for a key card from the stack. Before he could hand it to Luther, Henry was by his side. "He'll bunk with me. Room 312." He put his hand on Luther's shoulder.

"Go through the middle door on your right, down the hall, and you'll come to the elevators. Third floor." The boy watched them for a moment then resumed taking names.

"Might as well bunk together and not with a total stranger," Henry said.

And we're not strangers, Luther wondered.

The ugly, narrow hall was newly constructed with three doors on each wall. One gaped open, revealing a conference table and chairs with several men, all in uniform, inside.

Their room looked like any Holiday Inn bedroom: two queen beds, two chests of drawers, a small round table with two chairs, a small stuffed chair, and the ubiquitous large window framed in steel.

"Which bed, Patch? The air conditioning/ heating unit bothers me, so I'll take the one near the door if that's okay."

"Patch?"

Henry put a finger next to his own eye.

So now he was no longer Luther on his way to hook up with Sloan, but a fool named Patch. One of Luther's mustard-colored patches covered his left eye. "Take whatever bed you want," he said and threw his backpack on the one near the window.

Henry plopped onto the side of his bed, his feet on the floor. He slapped his thighs. "Here we are. In good old Coleton. What do you think of all these mountains? Kind a creepy, I think."

Luther sat on his bed facing him. "I don't know. I think they're kind of pretty. Hey, did all you guys come from the same place?"

"No, most of us came to Akron from all over the state. My folks brought me. You been to Akron before?"

"Once or twice."

Henry stood up. "If you don't mind, I'm headed for the shower. Get the road stink off me."

When he heard the water running, Luther let his upper body fall back on the bed with his arms stretched out. What the hell, he thought. You've gotten yourself in a fine mess. They'll probably kill you when they find out you're a fake. He tried to formulate a plan of escape, but nothing connected and then Henry came out of the shower wrapped in a towel. "Your turn. Plenty of hot water."

Luther took his backpack into the bathroom with him. He undressed in front of the mirror. His normally fair skin was whiter than a sheet, as his mother used to say, and it was covered all over with unevenly shaped tan patches the size of a small fist. His ribs stood out, as did his shoulder joints and hip bones. He touched his dry, flaxen hair. Some came away on his fingers. Even in these circumstances, he was vain enough to hope he didn't go bald. He leaned forward, peered at his face. Nope, not a single hair showed itself through the pores in his skin. Great. First a dog, now a woman. He turned the water as hot as he could stand it and stood not moving under the shower's delicious spray. Eventually, he scrubbed himself all over with a bar of soap and then used complimentary shampoo on his hair. When he looked at his fingers this time, no strands clung to them, and he felt grateful and embarrassed by his gratitude. He thought of Sloan. Tan patches were bad enough but bald was worse.

After drying himself, he put on clean clothes, wondering if this new version of a Holiday Inn had laundry service.

Henry curled on his side under the covers, snoring lightly. Luther laid down on his bed and stared at the ceiling, knowing he would never be able to go back to sleep. He sat up and picked up the phone receiver on the nightstand. A laminated card told him to dial nine for reception and zero for an outside number. He dialed zero and was taken aback when he heard a dial tone. He hung up quickly and looked at his roommate, who continued to snore.

Luther sighed and rolled onto his side, his back to Henry. It felt wonderful to be clean. He tried again to formulate an escape and was climbing over an iron fence when Henry woke him.

"Hey, Patch, it's time for chow according to this list of instructions here. I don't know about you, but I'm starved."

The dining room had not been changed structurally, but the normal small tables had been replaced by cafeteria style rectangles. Most of them were full. Henry sat at the end of one in the middle, Luther opposite. A group of three men sat at the other end. They all looked at each other and smiled. "Where you from?" one of them asked. Before either Henry or Luther could answer, the waiters brought in the food and began placing it in front of the seated men.

The first course was a mixed green salad with black olives, sliced red onions, tomatoes and cucumbers. The dressing was in plastic cups. Italian as far as Luther could tell. He noticed the oil floating on the top and put the dressing aside. The next plates, heaped with medium-rare prime rib, baked potatoes, and roasted squash, arrived. It all looked delicious. There were baskets of rolls, Italian bread sticks, and cornbread on each table. Luther felt like weeping. He could tell by the saliva in his mouth if he ate anything but plain baked potato and bread sticks, he would be sick. "My body isn't ready for this food. You want my steak?"

"Hell, yes," Henry said around a large piece of meat. "Sorry, Patch. It really sucks to be you right now. You won't get far on just carbs."

The room settled into the sound of cutlery hitting plates and murmuring voices as the men concentrated on their food. Luther glanced around the room. Most of the men looked Aryan like Henry and him, but there was a faction of darker, less well-proportioned men sitting in a far corner. They didn't share the aura of happiness and goodwill like the others. Their expressions were guarded, perhaps hostile. Also, unlike the crowd Luther now seemed to belong to, most of these men had longish hair and often beards. They must be locals, Luther thought. Volunteers or recruits or those that had been persuaded by means he didn't like to think about. They tended to be heavy shouldered, some overweight, and they kept their eyes to themselves.

After dinner everyone was herded into a large conference room where a huge TV screen dominated front and center. The men found seats and began to wait. In five minutes, a potbellied man wearing both a belt and suspenders over his uniform bustled to the head of the room and welcomed them. "Some of you obviously don't have uniforms. They arrive tonight. Report to room 103 tomorrow, nine sharp, and you will receive three sets of shirts and slacks." He then turned to the far wall and switched off the lights.

President Diamond filled the TV screen. He was a big, orange man with tiny eyes, puffy lids and what was obviously a black wig looking like it had been chewed by rats. His silicone upper lip protruded over the bottom one, making his mouth look like it belonged on a turtle. When he wasn't gripping the podium, he pounded it for emphasis. Sometimes he opened his mouth and sucked air between his teeth. Despite the ten-thousand-dollar suit and five-hundred-dollar tie, there was an aura of Halloween about him.

This was a teleprompter speech, used over and over for new recruits.

How, Luther wondered, do his people allow him to go out in public looking like that? A new five-figure designer wig would be an improvement. His mouth could have been allowed to fall into its natural shape and, dear lord, someone could tell him to stop spraying on that awful color. Was everyone really so afraid of him?

Tables covered with uniforms filled room 103 and several men, crisp and official looking, handed them out to a surprising number of men in street clothes. Waiting in line, Luther heard two men, bearded and unkempt with the same heavy shoulders he had seen last night, talking in whispers to each other. He inched two steps closer.

"Heard they're bringing a bunch of new men arriving tonight from all over. It's too expensive to truck food to every small town, so the boys is movin' here."

"Be crowded as hell then."

"Yeah. Heard some men might have to sleep three to a room."

"Not me. No way. I ain't sleeping next to no stranger."

"You know the Whitbecks, right? They was called to Washington by Diamond. Funny thing though. One's gone missing. The daughter, I heard."

"Gone missing?"

"Yeah, wasn't with the family when they got there. Big to do about it."

"Why would anyone care about some girl?"

"Stirling Whitbeck is richer than God. You know Diamond. Likes to keep his billionaires close. Their families too. For leverage. Some say that girl might be right here in these mountains." He stared at the other man, who stared back. After they had stared long enough the first one said, "I'm the only one in my family who signed up."

"The others?"

"Hidin'."

"Yeah, I hear ya."

# CHAPTER TWELVE

After their exchange on the tailgate of Clare's truck, Sloan's mother left without saying where she was going and Sloan went into the stable to throw hay to the horses. Made restless by its sweet smell, they chortled and banged their hooves against the stall walls. She tossed a slim flake over the half doors then watched as they dipped their heads to snatch the pale green stalks and grind them to a pulp with a side-to-side motion of their jaws. In her late teens, Sloan had come to resent cleaning stalls and other barn chores. She even grew sloppy with the grooming her mother demanded before and after each ride. But she always found pleasure in feeding time, feeling to its fullest the special something that happens between the feeder and the fed. Now she crossed her arms and rested her chin on them at each stall door and happily imagined each horse's satisfaction. It was so silent in the barn she could hear teeth coming together and stalks breaking up.

Sloan could remember a time when the barn was full of horses and people coming and going. Sometimes all the cross ties were full, and she and Colleen had to tack-up in a stall. Being in 4-H, they rode every day to prepare for the required shows. Sometimes they rode in the riding ring; other times they took the Pensy, a path following the railroad tracks into the tiny village two miles away and beyond. They rode next to trains and over bridges, the horses' hooves ringing on the steel while water rushed below. They rode down the middle of streets, still allowed in the Commonwealth of Pennsylvania. Sometimes they trailered the horses to cities like Coleton to ride in parades with marching bands and cymbals, people shouting and applauding, and firetrucks, with their whistles blowing. All this gave them an edge in horse shows where most of the participants never took their horses out of the practice ring. As a result, those horses spooked when a trailer door banged shut, or a child screamed, or any other loud and unexpected noise happened. Sloan and Colleen always won Regionals, most of the time the State Championship, and could probably have won Nationals, but Clare wouldn't go that far from home.

Now, not wanting to see the horses finish their flakes and fruitlessly look for more, Sloan walked out of the quiet dimness into a blaze of sun. Out of the corner of her eye she spotted Shimmer and Colleen. Each led a horse and a third followed behind them. She stood still and watched. The horses caught the keen, familiar smell coming from the barn and began to toss their heads and prance. The free one bolted toward her, and she flung up a hand to stop him then grabbed his mane and took hold of an ear. Turning him in circles, she said over a shoulder, "How was the upper pasture?"

"It sucked," said Colleen.

Shimmer's mare began crow hopping beside him, and he put his free hand on her neck. "Do not listen to her, Sloan," he called to her while stroking the horse. "Colleen is crabby just now. The pasture is not great, all thick and moist like we would wish, but is okay. Will last for a while. You have unloaded the hay, I see. Good. Not a job I like. Now, let's put these beasts away before my arm is ripped from its socket."

In a flurry of prancing, head jerking, snorting, and pulling, they got the horses in their stalls and Sloan settled them with small flakes of the sweet-smelling grass. Colleen leaned against an empty stall, her arms crossed over her chest, and watched. Sloan, after giving herself a moment to watch the horses' pleasure, turned to Colleen, took her hand, and led her toward the corner of the barn where the hay was stacked on pallets. "Look," she said, pulling a bunch from under the baling twine and handing it to her. "Nice, isn't it? Admit it."

Colleen rolled the hay in her palm then in the time-honored tradition of horsemen everywhere, leaned forward and sniffed a bale. "It's nice," she said.

Sloan grinned.

"It'll be gone in a month."

"Jesus, Colleen." Sloan nudged a bale and shook her head.

"Well, it will be."

Colleen turned away, but Sloan grabbed her shoulder. "It doesn't help, you know. Being so bitchy about everything. If we all just suck it up and do our best, it will be okay."

Colleen turned so she faced her straight on. She cocked her head to one side, her eyes wide and menacing. "Will it? Dragging things out like this? Just prolonging the suffering."

"What the hell does that mean? What are you saying?"

"You had to run out of New York City, remember? With your tail between your legs."

Shimmer flung his arm over Colleen's shoulders. "Don't fight. You are giving me a headache. Am already hot and sticky. Let's all go to the eddy and swim. Take off the rest of the day." He smiled and placed his other arm around Sloan. "We are all friends, remember." He squeezed the two women against his sides. "Now let's go swimming. Forget everything for a while."

That evening, Clare made an extra effort with dinner. She fried thick well-marbled bear steaks, roasted new potatoes in the coals, turning them over every once in a while, and sautéed zucchini in the bear grease, never taking her eye off it so as not to let it get limp. She was vain about her cooking. Her repertoire was small, but she strove for perfection within her limited scope. Sloan wanted her mother to talk to Rosemary and winnow more information but knew it wouldn't happen while Clare concentrated on a task. Anyway, she'd probably have better luck if she talked to the girl alone.

Sloan, Shimmer, and Colleen were sitting on the three stumps John had brought to the pit months ago. He and Clare shared a log. Jack had gone home. The evening was fine, not too hot, and the light coming through the trees had a gentle wavering quality from the slightly swaying leaves. Clare filled plates and passed them around. Knives and forks had been abandoned weeks ago. Balancing plates on laps to cut anything or spear food with a fork proved far less comfortable or efficient than using one's hands. Shimmer ate with his usual delicacy, licking the tips of his fingers before running them over grass made moist by the evening air. Clare and John's style of eating was frank and efficient. When the meat was cool enough, they picked up their steaks and bit off chunks. They popped the small potatoes into their mouths and nibbled the zucchini like rabbits. Colleen slowly and absently put potatoes in her mouth one after the other until her plate was empty. She ate nothing else. Shimmer watched her put her plate on the ground then turned to the group in general. "Here we are again in this beautiful place, eating this bountiful food. I think we should give thanks."

"For God's sake," said Colleen.

Shimmer raised a Super-Sized Big Gulp container in the air. It had been batting around the farm, scratched and faded, for as long as anyone could remember. "Thank you, Universe, for these blessings," he said. "May we all live to be together same time next year."

Everyone except Clare—who looked half asleep—stared at him, too surprised to respond. He lowered his Big Gulp, took a sip of water, and handed it to Colleen, who passed it off to Sloan. Sloan drank long and hard then started to lean over to give the plastic red and white growler to John when she remembered Rosemary sitting on the ground next to her. That was the thing about Rosemary. She was so easy to forget. Quiet and compliant, people barely noticed her despite her potential to cause disaster. Remembering this, Sloan looked at her mother, who was leaning with her head on John's shoulder, her expression blank.

Sloan handed Rosemary the Big Gulp, thinking she'd have to be the one to find out what happened that day at the Whitbeck's and the days leading to it. Getting people to open up wasn't her forte. After shouting commands for hours over the sound of clattering pots and pans in the restaurant, all she wanted was to be left alone in the silence of her bedroom. When she went out with chums, no one had any interest in a heart-to-heart. However, this girl was so ready to do as she was told, Sloan might be able to coax out some information.

Clare began gathering plates from around the fire pit.

"No, no." Shimmer jumped to his feet and plucked a dish from her hand. "Sloan, Colleen, and I will clean up. Is the way it works. You prepare the food. Someone else does the washing." He picked up the tin bucket they kept close for such purposes and carried it to the spring house. John stood up, raised his arms over his head and, groaning with satisfaction, stretched onto his tip toes. "Come on Clare, let's go fishing. It's getting too warm for fish to bite during the day. Now's the perfect time. We'll go to the nearest clearing."

Everyone's eyes followed them as they went into the house to fetch their gear then as they disappeared into the woods next to the path leading up the mountain.

Colleen tossed a stick into the fire. "Do you actually think they are going to do any fishing up there?"

Sloan pushed three stray coals back into the fire with her foot. "Sure."

"Huh."

Shimmer appeared with the tin bucket full of water. He set it on the ground and started to put in the plates. Sloan drained the grease from the two cast iron fry pans and put them on the grate to burn off any excess fat. Colleen sat with her elbows on her knees, her chin in her hands. "I bet they're up there fucking their brains out."

Sloan tried to decipher the look on Collen's face. Was it disgust, disdain, bitterness? Bitterness, she decided, mostly bitterness.

Shimmer looked Colleen up and down. "You have no muscles at all. How do you even walk around?" He touched her thin wrist. "I think you might have a fever."

Sloan pictured them swimming at the eddy earlier that day, the way

Colleen's bikini bottom hung from her hips. In the water, the top almost washed off her shoulders. She'd tried to float on her back, but with no body fat, sank to the bottom. She pulled herself onto the "sitting rock"—a large, flat boulder in the middle of the eddy with its surface just above the water line—and huddled with her bald head on her knees, her fingers grasping her toes.

"Go inside," Sloan said. "Take the north bedroom. It'll be dark in there by now. I'll bring you some toast and tea if you like. Clare made bread this morning." She stirred the coals.

Rosemary eased to her feet and turned to leave.

"Hey," Sloan said, "Wait a minute. I'd like to talk."

Shimmer took Colleen's hand. "Come. We are leaving exceedingly early tomorrow. Go to bed." He pulled her to her feet, placed his arm around her waist and walked her across the yard. Surprisingly, she didn't resist. He kept his arm around her, and it looked like maybe she even leaned against him a little. Sloan felt a thump under her ribs near her breastbone, followed by a sinking feeling she didn't understand. When the two disappeared into the house, she turned to Rosemary, who was perched on the log.

"Rosemary," she said. "We really need to know what happened the day Clare found you in the woods. And the days leading up to it."

Rosemary blinked. "What do you mean?"

"I mean tell me what happened that morning. From the start."

"When I went to the barn, Pedro put me on Wilson and sent me up the mountain."

Sloan waited.

"My family was gone. Nobody told me they were leaving."

Sloan continued to wait, wondering if the girl was simple or hiding something. She was trying to think of words that would encourage her to say more when Shimmer came up from behind and sat on a stump. "Rosemary, I think you must be very sad," he said. "Sad and scared and lonely. Here you are among all these people you don't know. I understand. *Believe me.* Tell us what Pedro said when he sends you off. And what happened the night before."

"Nothing. I went to bed."

"And what did Pedro say?"

"To go away and never come back."

Shimmer scootched forward, forearms on his thighs, leaning toward Rosemary. "Is hard to talk about. I understand. But it is necessary. We heard about your family when we were in Coleton. We know where they have gone."

Sloan turned to stare at him. Rosemary sat up straight, her mouth open.

"They are in DC."

Rosemary's eyes widened and became even darker. Tears formed in their corners. She put her hand to her mouth.

"They are safe. So, no need being scared. Do you know why they might have gone to DC?"

Rosemary shook her head.

"The President. Has he been to your house?"

Rosemary nodded.

"Tell us. It will help us find them. Tell us what happened when President Diamond came to your house."

"Nothing. They all had dinner. He brought a lot of extra servants." Tears started rolling down her cheeks.

"Who is 'all'?"

"The men who came with him. And our family. And the president, of course."

"So, all is friendly. Good times. Do you remember what they talk about?"

"No."

Shimmer got up and sat next to the girl. He patted her knee. "Is good all was friendly. Being friends with the president is helpful. We will find out about your family. Just takes time. Do you need anything?" Smiling, he held up the Big Gulp.

Rosemary shook her head.

"Do you want to go to bed now?"

Rosemary wiped the tears from her cheeks with the backs of her hands.

"How do you know they are in DC?"

"I talk to people."

No one spoke for several seconds until Rosemary stood up. "I guess I'll go lie down."

Sloan watched her drift to the shed—she preferred sleeping there to the house. When the door closed behind her, Sloan said, "And just who did you talk to?"

"People." Shimmer glanced away.

"You don't know they're in DC."

"They could be. Anyway, it was good way to start a conversation."

# CHAPTER THIRTEEN

According to the instructions in Luther's room, all the residents on the third floor were to be in Conference Room B by ten o'clock that morning. He'd never been in a Holiday Inn, though he used to drive by one on the way to town—a large rectangle building looking as though the architect had gone out of his way to make it as uninspiring as possible. Luther remembered all the windows on the flat surfaces, presumably one to each room. In his confused state the day before, he hadn't noticed much about this particular building except the parking lots and the stairs leading up to the reconstructed lobby. How many rooms, he wondered, did this Holiday Inn have? He gathered it was full, or nearly so, from the conversation he'd eavesdropped on earlier in the morning.

Conference room B was the size of a turn-of-the century ballroom with none of its charm. The place was full of milling men, all in the same military dress he had been issued earlier. A shiver of fear ran through him. If this group were only the men on the third floor, how many were in the entire hotel? Say there were ten double rooms on each floor. Twenty men times ten floors. Two hundred. What were they doing here? Whatever it was, it didn't bode well for the locals who were not part of this growing army. Sloan had described Coleton as a city of not much more than thirty thousand. That thirty thousand would include children. Then there were the outskirts, the tiny towns with little more than four or five businesses, sometimes just a post office and a cluster of residents. Beyond that would be the lone homesteads, the farmers, and the recluses. Thinking of this, Luther was able to relax a little. Most of the Nationalists didn't come from around here, wouldn't know anything about the people or the terrain. He thought of the Revolutionary War and the maddening frustration the British experienced trying to fight the rebels who kept popping out of nowhere, ambushing them. Then there was Viet Nam, impossible to define who was the enemy, an unwinnable war. He'd bide his time, wait for the right moment, and slip away in the confusion that was bound to ensue.

From a stage in the back left of the room a man in a fancier uniform, complete with epaulettes and even a medal, tapped on a microphone. Faces turned to him as the sound reverberated around the room. "Attention," he said, "attention everyone. I want you to divide yourselves into groups of seven, go outside, and wait in the parking lot. Today we will be showing you Coleton and its environs. If you don't have a good memory, take notes. There are notebooks and pencils near the exit. No cell phones allowed. You are to turn them in to the man standing by the exit door."

Luther hadn't owned a phone in months.

Outside, the sun-warmed asphalt sent up waves of heat and brought sweat to the back of his neck. As usual, Henry was by his side. "Nice day for sightseeing," Henry said. "As long as they have air conditioning in the cars. I thought it would be cooler in the mountains." He tugged on his collar.

Luther looked at him closely, wondering if this man had been assigned to keep an eye on him. A long, black SUV pulled in front of their group, the kind with two rows of bench seats behind the front bucket seats and two bucket seats in the back facing each other. It held nine people. Henry put his hand on Luther's shoulder and guided him into the middle of the first bench seat.

The driver, a little over six feet, walked toward them—ramrod straight posture, epaulettes, creases like razors on his long-sleeved shirt and trousers.

The corners of his collar sharp as knives. "I'm Captain Slater," he said as he flung himself in the car and aggressively clicked his seat belt closed. The man who climbed in next to him wore the same class uniform and his hair was also cut high and tight. Yet there was a difference, an almost infinitesimal slouch to his shoulders, a sullen, barely perceptible slowness as he settled in. He didn't turn around when he said, "Captain James Riddick here."

Captain Slater adjusted his rearview mirror. "Our goal today is to acquaint you with Coleton. If we have time, we will drive into the countryside around it. You will be expected to come away with a working knowledge of where things are located." He moved the mirror so he could look at the passengers' faces. "If we say to you, for example, 'go to 804 Center Street,' we expect you will be able to find it. Coleton is a small city but follows no patterns like DC. Or New York City. So, pay attention. Make note of markers if you need them. We have maps for you, but they contain no topography or lat/long, hence the tour. Hand them the maps, Jim."

Jim opened the glove box and brought out typical three folded maps and handed them to Luther, who passed them around. They looked like the kind found in a gas station.

"Eventually we will have better ones, but for now you'll have to make do. You can write on them but as you can see the paper is glossy and doesn't take well to pencil or pen. And don't think you can rely on GPS. Reception is lousy in these mountains. Even so, we'll be giving you your new cell phones soon. Just don't rely on them."

*For now*, thought Luther. How long would they be here? It occurred to him with a flush of anticipation his time with this unit could be an opportunity to find out their plans, their methods, their equipment, and anything else that would be of use to Sloan and her family. He tried to immerse himself in these thoughts, mixing them in with his nearly hysterical ideas about how to escape.

Captain Slater kept up a running description of where they were and where they were going but Luther only found him distracting as he tried to scribble notes and look up every few seconds to find markers to guide him later. Slater drove over the twenty-five mile-per-hour speed limit, the streets being mostly empty.

In different circumstances, the trip through Coleton might have been a tour of a city in a foreign country, so different was it from anything Luther had seen before: narrow streets, lovely solid brick buildings, and old, large trees. He got the impression of a great deal of black wrought iron. The streets—some made of brick and others of cobblestone—were so steep and twisting, Luther grabbed the bottom of his seat during a few turns. They were spookily empty. The man on his right suddenly thrust out his hand at him. "Spencer Corcoran, from Ohio. And you are…?"

"Lu…" Luther stopped himself and coughed to cover his mistake. "Peter Jones, also from Ohio." They could have been brothers: same coloring, same build, but Spencer's facial bone structure was much sharper. His cheekbones almost came to points. You could have dotted an i with his nose and his eyes weren't round but long and narrow. "Well, pleased to meet you, Peter. These red necks won't know what hit 'em."

Henry leaned around Luther. "I don't think you can call them red necks. Not much sun here. I googled it. Lots of rain. Clouds."

"What then? Mountain Men? Hill People?"

Henry thought for a moment. "Bushwhackers, I guess."

"That makes sense. Plenty of bushes around here to whack." Spencer leaned back, smiling at his joke.

A lone girl, hands in her jean pockets, head bent, her red gold ponytail swinging, strode up a street steep enough to qualify for mountain climbing. Luther's stomach flipped, thinking it might be Sloan, but when they passed her, she turned out to be younger and plainer. Spencer looked at him and wiggled his eyebrows. "Wouldn't mind whacking that bush. Why don't you tell the captain to stop and pick her up?"

"And just where would we put her?" Henry said crossly.

Spencer turned so he could continue gawking at the girl. "Always did like redheads."

Around one o'clock, Captain Slater pulled into the parking lot of a Burger King. Luther's head had been splitting for over an hour and he felt dizzy from hunger. He knew there would be nothing on the menu he could eat. The Holiday Inn had prepared its typical buffet along with extra eggs and sausage for breakfast that morning. Luther ate one banana, two pieces of dry toast, two large glasses of orange juice, and three cups of sweetened tea. By now his blood sugar had dropped miserably low and though his stomach was empty, he felt sick.

Inside, he shared a booth with Henry, Spencer, and Captain Riddick. Going through the line, he hadn't needed to look at the overhead menu. The smell of grease and frying beef patties gave him a curious mixture of hunger and nausea. He ordered two super-sized iced teas. When the four men settled into their booth, Captain Riddick stared at Luther's tray then up at Luther, who was doing his best to control his shaking while he poured packets of sugar into his tea.

"We've got at least four more hours to go this afternoon," Riddick said.

Luther met the captain's eye but made no answer. As they looked at each other, Luther could not help wondering if he didn't see something in the other man's expression—recognition? encouragement? possibly a threat? He'd thought these mountain men were supposed to be inscrutable then realized with surprise he'd assumed, for some reason, the captain was local.

"Our Peter here is feeling a little squeamish. It must be the altitude." Henry laughed. "He'll be right as rain in a day or two."

"You look white as a ghost," Spencer said, scooting out of the booth to put his tray on the nearest stack. When he slid back into his seat, he continued, "Makes that tan patch over your eye stand out like a sore thumb. What is it, a birth mark?"

"Christ," said Henry.

Captain Riddick took a large bite of his Whopper and continued watching

Luther. "I expect you got a bad dose of the vaccine," he said around the food.

"That's right." Luther felt wet circles forming under his arm pits.

When they returned to the SUV, everyone took the same seats. As Luther climbed in, Henry caught his elbow and leaned close so he could whisper in his ear, "Careful. You don't want the brass thinking you're not up to par. I'll see if I can get the kitchen to poach a chicken breast for you when we get back."

Luther would no more have approached the staff, kitchen or otherwise, let alone request a special favor than he would have jumped out of the vehicle and run away. Why did Henry think he could get away with such audacity? Who was this man?

When they arrived back at the hotel, Luther's clothes felt damp. He could feel droplets of sweat in his eyebrows. He stepped away carefully from the SUV, leaned on the door when he shut it. He turned to follow Henry. Captain Riddick put a heavy hand on his shoulder. "How you doin'?"

"Fine. Just fine." Luther forced himself to stand up straight and keep his legs squarely underneath him. "It's a lot to take in, in one day." He tried a cheery smile. "I'll be studying my notes tonight. Just like back in school."

"Fortunately for me I know these parts. If you have any questions, just ask me."

Riddick definitely didn't look the same as the new recruits or Captain Slater. They were strong, fit men, but Luther had the feeling if he turned and rammed this guy as hard as he could with a shoulder, he wouldn't budge. He seemed bound to the earth, a part of it. "You been in this unit long?"

"No one's been in this unit long." There it was again. That look, reading him.

"I guess I'll go and get cleaned up for dinner. Maybe I'll see you there." Luther wiped his wet eyebrow with his index finger.

"We've been waiting for this for a long time."

"What?"

"I expect you have too." Riddick's face gave nothing away.

"Well, sure."

"Let me know if you need help."

Luther waited for the other man to elaborate, but he said nothing, just watched as though expecting a sign. The air grew even heavier, lowered over them. Finally, aided by a burst of fear-induced adrenaline, Luther said, "I'll see you later," turned away, and hopped up the stairs two at a time. In the lobby, men were walking toward the hall. No one sat at the reception desk. Luther hurried to the elevator.

Henry left almost at once after he and Luther arrived in their room. Forty-five minutes later, he was back with a cloche. He bowed with one hand behind his back and presented a silver-plate tray to Luther. "At your service, sir." Under the lid were two pale, still hot and moist chicken breasts. "They're actually serving chicken for dinner tonight. In some sort of sauce. You might want to scrape the sauce away. In the meantime, you have these babies as pristine as the day they were slaughtered. I think they might be serving plain rice too."

Who is this guy, Luther wondered again.

# CHAPTER FOURTEEN

In the dark hours before dawn, Sloan woke to the sound of a pickup moving slowly down the driveway. She had been here long enough to recognize her mother's truck, and this wasn't it. It must be Shimmer and Colleen. Colleen and Shimmer. Sloan felt a liquid cold start in her chest and travel through her belly and limbs. There had been a time when Colleen was the most important person in her life. She loved her mother, but it was Colleen she wanted to spend all her time with. She'd felt that bond when she first returned, but since then it seemed to slip further away every time she saw her. Sloan laid on her back, listening to the drops of light rain on the tin roof. Another pickup engine started and then its tires crunched over gravel and stopped outside the stable. It was too dark to see a thing, but her mother walked quietly into the barn and unwrapped the hose from its holder. Starting at the far end, water splashed into buckets as Clare topped them off. When she reached the stall next to hers, Sloan said, "Good morning, Mom."

Clare stepped back. "Well, hell Sloan, you could of give me a little warning. What are you doin' awake?"

"You banging around in the barn might have something to do with it. Why are you here so early?"

"I'm going into Coleton before it gets light."

"I'm going with you."

They drove a circuitous route only a native could find in the dark. Sloan turned herself over to her mother's lead the way she had as a girl. They rode in comfortable silence, enclosed in darkness except for the dim headlights. Clare parked two alleys away from Annie's house. No lights shone from the surrounding homes; the only sound was the quiet tread of their sneakers. The light outside was just turning from navy to gray when they climbed the stairs to the back door.

Sloan had wondered what her mother's reaction would be when she saw the wreckage in the house. Clare flicked on a light switch.

Sloan drew a breath, taken aback all over again by the destruction.

Clare put her fists on her hips and looked around. "My," she said, hooking her hands in her back pockets. She then walked through the entire house, touching this and that and saying nothing. Sloan followed her. When they returned to the downstairs kitchenette, Clare began at the back door where they had come in. She proceeded to touch every surface, overturn every object, pull out anything remaining in a cupboard or drawer, picked up and read every scrap of paper. She looked behind what drapes were left hanging and under those on the floor. She looked under rugs, moved furniture for a better look, used chairs so she could see on top of dressers. Sloan helped her. It was tedious, exhausting work, and the sun was high when Clare finally folded her legs underneath her and sat in the middle of the living room. Sloan settled opposite her, looked closely at the familiar, lovely face and felt her world shift, move into the future, change forever. For the first time in her life, she saw doubt on her mother's face. And weariness. Clare looked tired in a way that rest or a satisfying meal couldn't cure. Her arrogance had deserted her. Watching her mother, Sloan learned something she didn't want to learn. Power comes and power goes. Her mother didn't know that, had come to rely on hers, and now she sat alone in her failure.

Clare picked up a piece of paper she had crumpled then dropped it on the floor. "You know, Annie once looked for clues just like we done now. Only she was successful. She found out right away where them foster parents who stole Colleen took her. It was because of her that John got her back before she was hurt. Even so, he left us after that. Took Colleen away. Said it was too dangerous at the farm."

Sloan remembered the frantic pain of those days. She'd screamed at her mother, refused to be comforted, raged for days until she decided to take matters into her own hands. She was eight.

As though reading her mind, Clare said, "And it was you who brung her back. Galloping Molly down 64, hell bent for leather, to get her. You didn't even know where she was stayin', but that didn't stop you." Clare laughed a mirthless laugh. "The police did. Corralled you and threw you in a cruiser. John got the message though, let Colleen come back for good."

As her mother talked, Sloan saw the obstinate pride grow in her face. She saw the bewilderment in her eyes, the need to put on a mask of confidence. To have touched her in sympathy then would have been a betrayal. Instead, Sloan said, "We'll find Annie," though she didn't believe it.

Even though it was broad daylight, Clare decided to drive home. Sloan persuaded her to take her to Shimmer's place first and, after getting lost three times, they finally found it. Her mother refused to come inside with her, said she'd wait in the truck to make sure she got in all right.

The door was unlocked and no one was in the living room or kitchen when Sloan let herself in. Before she called out, Colleen walked out of the bedroom wearing nothing but what looked like one of Shimmer's t-shirts. "Shimmer's not here," she said. "How did you get here?"

"Mom brought me."

"Is she still here?"

"Yes, I guess. She stayed in the truck till I got in."

Colleen ran to the front door and outside. She came back panting. "I'm going home with Clare." She dashed into the bedroom and began yanking on her clothes.

Sloan stood in the doorway watching her. "So, where's Shimmer anyway?"

"He knows a guy." Colleen pulled her own t-shirt over her head. "He and Rusty went to talk to him. Well, Rusty will do the talking." She snapped her jeans closed. "The locals would freak out if they saw Shimmer. Even in the resistance, brown and gold don't work for most people." She sat down on the bed roll and pulled on her sneakers. She tied the laces so quickly she tangled them and had to start over. "Shimmer drives then stays out of sight while Rusty does the talking." Colleen stood up and grabbed her backpack.

"When did they leave?"

"Hours ago." Colleen hung her backpack over her shoulder, walked out of the room, bent over on her way to the door to sweep a pack of cigarettes off the table.

Sloan hadn't noticed them before. When had her friend taken up smoking? "Hey…where did they meet this guy?"

"That's on a need-to-know basis. And trust me, I don't need to know."

"Is it dangerous?"

Colleen paused on her way out and stared at Sloan. "Hell, yeah, it's dangerous."

"What's he talking to this guy about?"

"Ask him when he gets back," said Colleen and then she was outside, slamming the door behind her.

When he gets back, Sloan repeated silently. She went into the kitchen. There were no dirty dishes lying around, just a jar of peanut butter on the counter. The refrigerator was empty. After five hours of sleuthing at Annie's, Sloan, still in that mind-set, poked around the bedroom, which produced nothing but Shimmer's backpack next to the bed roll. In the bathroom she lifted off the lid to the toilet tank. His bottle of vodka rested among the plumbing. Sloan gently removed it, unscrewed the cap, held the plastic bottle to her lips, and took a hard swallow, followed by a second. She replaced the bottle in the tank, returned to the living room, and sat on the couch. She noticed for the first time a saucer filled with cigarette butts. She felt sick. Nothing announced more clearly the changes in Colleen than this nasty residue. She was staring at it blankly when the door flew open, Shimmer following along with it. He spun around to close and lock it, calling out, "I told you to be sure to lock this." When he turned back to the living room and saw Sloan, he drew back for an instant then, to her surprise, he smiled. "Sloan, how did you get here?" He loped over to her, bent, and hugged her. "Good to see you. What a morning we had. How did you get here?" He sat next to her.

"My mother brought me. Colleen went back to the farm with her. We came to look at Annie and Marshall's place."

"And?"

"Nothing. We came up with nothing."

"I have much news. Diamond, for example, is hurting for monies. Some of the board of the federal reserve are becoming not so loyal. Diamond wants them to make more money, but they won't. They say it would only make it useless because of the run-away inflation. Like after the civil war. Some dudes on the Supreme Court are getting restless too, but it's just a bunch of puppets anyway." He noticed the cigarette butts and pushed them away, his face sour. "This brings out the matter of Rosemary. Whitbeck is one of the richest men in the world. And he dotes on his daughter. In the beginning, he was all for the president, but apparently, he's seen things. Whitbeck is greedy, crooked, ruthless, but not a pedophile."

"You saying Diamond is?"

"Would it surprise you?"

"No. So, what you're saying is Whitbeck got called back to DC for what— so Diamond can get hold of his money somehow?"

"Diamond has a sixth sense about loyalty. If one of his billionaires becomes less than enthusiastic, he finds leverage. That girl is his leverage. That's why Whitbeck sent her off to get lost in the mountains. I say is pretty damn radical to just send your daughter off to fend for herself. Must have been desperate." Shimmer sat back and flung his arm across the back of the couch.

"What about the rest of his family? Wouldn't they be leverage too?"

"Yes, of course, but not so much as this girl. The manhunt is on. You must tell Clare. She is in danger and so is everyone else at Valley Farm. Some think the reason extra troops are brought to Coleton is to find the girl. Is also true, Diamond is desperate to increase the size of the Nationalist army in small towns. Small-minded people make good resource. So do unemployed ones."

Sloan frowned. "What would Diamond do with Rosemary?"

"I hear Whitbeck would never let Diamond hurt her. You can imagine the rest. Clare needs to know what is going on." He smiled. "Lucky you are here, no? So, I can tell you right away."

Sloan looked around. "Where's Rusty? I thought he went with you."

"Oh, you know Rusty. Off on some other mission. I had to take him with me. My contact is not so ready to talk to a man who looks like me. Rusty's got the red hair, white skin and when he can hold still long enough, he is very smart. You have to keep an eye on him though. His mind jumps all around. Gets distracted and he is off on another job before he's done with this one. How you going to get back to the farm?"

Sloan shook her head.

"You stay here as long as you need, but someone needs to warn Clare. I can take you back tonight." Shimmer smiled again.

"Will you stay?"

Shimmer sat up straight. "No, I know some people in DC. I think I should talk to them."

"You're going to DC?" Sloan said, her voice nearly a shout.

Shimmer nodded.

"When? For how long?" She clenched her fists.

"Probably leave after midnight."

"How long will you be gone?"

He shrugged.

Sloan drew back and socked him in the face. They both yelped and Sloan's hand flew to her mouth. Shimmer cupped his hand over his mouth and nose, brought it away dripping with blood. He stood up and walked into the kitchen and spit into the sink. Sloan heard water running then stop. He returned to the living room, the back of his forearm under his nose. Blood flowed around it and dropped slowly on the floor. Sloan leapt to her feet and pushed him down on the couch. "Oh God," she said. "I don't know why I did that. I'm so sorry. Do you have a cloth or ice? Lie down with your head back. No don't. You might drown. Oh, Jesus."

"No ice."

Sloan ran into the bedroom and grabbed one of Shimmer's t-shirts. He held it tightly against his nose and mouth while she watched crimson spread in a Rorschach shape on the white cloth. Shimmer looked up at her. "You can sit down." His voice was muffled and sounded like he was talking through water.

She sat next to him. "Don't die. Just don't die."

Eventually the red stopped spreading, and he removed the cloth from his face. His upper lip was split down the center. Sloan covered her mouth and waited for him to hit her back. When he didn't, she went into the bathroom to retrieve the vodka. She dipped the clean part of the t-shirt into it and patted Shimmer's lip as gently as she could. The bleeding had stopped. They sat looking at each other. "I don't…" Sloan couldn't continue.

"I know." Shimmer leaned forward and kissed a place on her neck beneath her chin.

Less surprised than she might have been, she briefly leaned her head against his. "I'm going with you."

Shimmer pulled away. "You can't."

"Doesn't matter. I still am."

"It will be a long, nasty drive and who knows if we will find any sleep at the end of it. We should get some rest."

They slept on the bed roll until past nightfall. Shimmer held Sloan curled against him. She asked him if he'd heard anything about Annie and Marshall.

"I won't lie," he said. "It does not look good. The Nationals want them and want them bad. No one has a clue if they have been captured, and if they have, where they are."

# CHAPTER FIFTEEN

**A** breeze coming through the window caused the four candle flames to flicker, throwing uneasy shadows across everyone's face. Clare, John, Colleen, Rosemary, and Jack sat around the kitchen table; a Monopoly board splayed out in front of them. From the size of the piles of money and number of houses and hotels, it looked to Sloan as though they had been playing for a while. She and Shimmer stood in the doorway; everyone turned to them. A surprised, questioning silence hung in the air. No one mentioned Shimmer's damaged lip. Sloan figured the flickering light made it difficult to decipher. Clare pushed the empty chair next to her away from the table. Sloan sat and pulled it back in place. John stood. "I'll get another from the living room."

Shimmer placed his chair next to Colleen. "You are playing Monopoly. Wonderful." He rubbed his hands together. "We used to play for hours when there was no work."

Sloan stared at him. He actually looked gleeful.

Colleen handed him a stack of money and gave him her little car. "Here, you play for me. I'm bored." She rested her head on his shoulder.

"You sure?" Shimmer put the money under the edge of the board in front of him.

Clare shook the dice. The moving light made it difficult to see how they landed, but Clare managed and moved her character, a tiny horse, to Park Place, where she bought and placed a hotel.

When Rosemary picked up the dice and handed them to Shimmer, he blew on his fist and let them loose on the table, made a fist pump, and yelled, "Yes!" He'd landed on an empty spot. With Colleen's money, he put down a house.

Why was Colleen leaning on Shimmer, draped like a rag doll? How could he sit there, absorbed in a game, while Rosemary sat next to him, clueless, a magnet for the Nationalists? The whole scene was surreal, something nightmares were made of. He'd said he had to go to DC and now he lollygagged around playing a game, for God's sake. She turned to her mother. "May I have a word?"

John rose from his chair. "Excuse me folks, I have to go see a man about a dog."

Clare stood as well, touched Sloan's shoulder, and the three of them walked outside, John heading off into the trees. Though not a full moon, it was still light enough to follow silhouettes. John disappeared into the woods and Sloan faced her mother, told her about the Whitbecks and Rosemary and about Diamond's use of leverage. Clare listened, staring at her boot as she dug its heel into the ground. When Sloan was finished, she lifted her head. "Thank you for telling me this."

"What'll you do?"

"We'll keep watch, be real careful when we take the horses to the upper pastures."

"Keep watch? You can't keep watch 24/7. The Whitbeck Estate isn't that far from here. If Rosemary made it to the farm in a day, the Nationalists could be here anytime."

"I expect you're right."

Sloan shoved her hands in her pockets. "It was one thing when there was no particular reason to comb these mountains. Now they are bound to search here."

"Maybe we'll move to Pap's place for a while."

"That's not much safer."

"What are you suggesting?"

"Um… if they find her here, it won't go well for any of you—or any of us."

"Are you saying we should put her in a truck and take her… where? Who do you think would give her shelter? I guess we could just dump her on the side of the road. Or you and Shimmer could take her wherever you're going."

"Going? What makes you think we are going anywhere?"

Clare said nothing.

"Okay, so Shimmer and I are going to DC." Sloan expected her mother to be surprised, taken aback, at least to object. Instead, she pushed the hair away from her face. "Answer me, daughter. What ideas do you have about the problem of Rosemary?"

Clare's refusal to show concern made Sloan want to slap her. "Do what you think is best," she snapped, then because it would hurt her mother, she added, "No one knows where Annie and Marshal are."

"I think we are aware of that."

"Aren't you wondering why Shimmer and I are going to DC?"

"To find out what the plans for Coleton are, I guess."

Sloan shook her head. "Where did this man come from? What's his agenda? He could be the enemy. I mean, who is he?"

Clare laughed. "God knows."

"And you would just let me go off with him?"

"I'm not letting you do anything. You've already made up your mind."

"Do you trust him?"

"He's been around for over a year, maybe more. Been extremely useful. If he wanted to turn us in, he would of already."

Sloan looked away and then back at her mother. "What's his deal with Colleen, anyway? Are they attached?"

"How do you mean?"

"Like romantically."

Sloan could make out Clare's serious face, even in the dark.

"She needs him. The virus and Diamond's takeover hit her hard. I think she feels safe around him."

John came out of the woods, walked up to them, and leaned against Clare. "What's going on?"

Clare put her arm around his waist. "The Nationalists are on a manhunt for Rosemary. Seems they need her to keep Whitbeck in line. Keep his billions in line."

Sloan waited, hoping he would say the girl had to go. The idea of sending her back to the estate occurred to her. She'd probably be okay. If the McMannises were there, they probably wouldn't hurt her. She thought these things then let them go.

John put his arm around Clare's shoulder. "No one knows these mountains the way you do. You want to get lost in them and the girl with you; I've no doubt you could."

Shimmer stood as the three of them came into the kitchen. "We will be going now," he said.

Colleen looked up at him sharply, but he was watching Sloan, his face a question. She nodded. Clare blew out the candles. The sudden darkness was absolute.

Surprisingly, it was Rosemary who asked, "Where?"

Shimmer's voice floated in a ghostly vacuum. "Do you need to get anything: clothes, toothbrush, water?"

Clare fumbled in her pocket, found the matches, and, searching in the dark, found and relit one of the candles. She handed it to Sloan, who said, "I'll just get a change of clothes, hang on a sec," and made her way carefully up the stairs, the shadows jumping as she moved. Clare's voice followed her. "We need to be careful with the candles. They have to last."

Sloan was thankful for the dark when she returned with her backpack. She didn't want to see the expression on Colleen's face. Shimmer stood by the door, his hand on the knob.

They drove the back roads as much as they could. There was almost no traffic this time of night. They talked little as Shimmer navigated the curves and small hills. Sloan tried but failed to engage him in conversation. Finally, she asked, "Are you mad at me? I sure wouldn't blame you. I don't know what happened to me. I'm really sorry." She was flabbergasted when he laughed.

"Women have done much worse, believe me. I shouldn't have said I was leaving so fast, should have led up to it. Now. You can put your head in my lap if you want to sleep."

Sloan declined.

The only stop they made was at an abandoned gas station with a phone booth on the side. Shimmer made a call and was back in the truck in less than a minute. Half an hour later, he pulled into a driveway leading to a small, isolated house. A dim light from inside illuminated the yard. He turned off the headlights at the same time the front door opened. A man came out and trotted down the stairs, across the grass to a garage whose door had to be lifted manually. Inside, Shimmer pulled into a tight space next to a dark, nondescript sedan. The man sidled between the vehicles. Shimmer jumped out and exchanged keys with him. Sloan had to slide across to the driver's side to leave the car. The two men hugged, kissed each other on both cheeks, managed to open the car doors so Sloan and the backpacks could be squeezed in the dark sedan, and she and Shimmer were back on the road without a word having been spoken.

It was still dark when they arrived in a residential part of DC. Sloan had never been to this city, had no idea where they were. The streetlights shone on narrow, tall brick buildings. Shimmer parked in front of one of them. A light turned on inside the house. Once again, a man ran out at once. Shimmer handed him the keys, opened Sloan's door, and led her inside while the man started the sedan and drove away.

A woman, looking like she had been re-incarnated from the sixties—long, unstyled, thick, brown hair, loose fitting dress, barefoot, no make-up—greeted them. She introduced herself as Lena.

Sloan noticed her register Shimmer's spilt lip and her decision not to say anything about it.

Lena led them out of a narrow, high-ceilinged hall into a living room, also narrow. "Sonny will be back soon. He is just parking the car underground.

The garage isn't far away. Do you want something to drink? Tea, coffee, soda, water?"

"Do you have anything stronger?" Shimmer paced around the room, picking up objects, stopping to look at books.

Sloan had never seen him so jittery.

Lena went to the drinks table. "Scotch, vodka, gin?"

"Vodka is good. On the rocks if you have any. If not is okay too."

Lena filled a cocktail glass with ice from an ice bucket, added three fingers of vodka. Shimmer carefully held the glass to his wounded mouth and drank a long drink then sank gratefully onto a couch and leaned his head back. "God," he said, "I hate driving around here in the dark. How can you stand it?"

"Sonny's position keeps us safe. And, of course, we've lived here all our lives. We know the city like the palms of our hands. Do you want vodka as well?" Lena said looking at Sloan.

"Yes, please, not too much." Sloan thought Lena looked no older than eighteen. Her wide-eyed, open expression made her look like a child.

After giving Sloan her drink, Lena made one for herself and sat in a chair facing her guests. "I'm no good at casual conversation, and Sonny doesn't like me talking about the cause, so it's okay if we sit here and are silent.".

Charmed by the forthright simplicity of this his little speech, Sloan felt the tension leave her muscles. She glanced at Shimmer to take the measure of his mood. Either the vodka or Lena had calmed him down enough to loosen his muscles as well and allowed him to spread an arm on the back of the couch and cross an ankle over a knee. The three of them did indeed sit in peaceful silence until the front door opened suddenly and Sonny Caravaggio walked into the room. He had the kind of build that would never be slender, sturdy bones covered in hard muscle, not an inch of fat. He wore his blond hair combed back in neat, oiled rows. His skin was fair, and he had appealing light blue eyes. Only his strong Roman nose hinted at his Italian ancestry. A face anyone would trust.

"Glad you're here," he said in a Brooklyn accent so thick you could cut it with a knife. "But looks like you ran into some trouble on the way, though. What happened?"

"Is nothing. Wasn't looking and walked into a tree."

Still looking at Shimmer, Sonny didn't speak. Eventually, he continued. "We don't have much time. I'm on duty at eight. I've got the papers you'll need here in my pocket." He looked at Sloan. "I wasn't expecting you."

Shimmer straightened his back. "She is big piece of the resistance in Coleton. Plays a very big part."

Sonny looked her over. "Maybe we can get her in the family kitchen. If not, maybe the public one. Do you know anything about cooking? "

"I was a two-star chef in New York."

"Well, well. That could turn out to be very handy. I've got plenty of generic papers just in case. Maybe we can put a cheffy resume on one that would be plausible." He sat in a chair identical to the one Lena used. He leaned forward, his elbows on his thighs, his hands dangling between his legs, eyes on Shimmer. "This is what we have. Whitbeck is here, living in Blair House with his family. And not happy about it. His sons have basically turned into spies for Diamond. The wife is so beaten down she might as well have had a lobotomy. You know about Diamond's financial situation. He's found out forcing people into factories to work isn't very efficient. It takes a lot of manpower to make them productive when they don't want to be. That's why he has increased recruiting in small towns. The people are poor, never had much opportunity and are scared of H 26. They're happy to have jobs that pay decently, or almost decently, and, of course, they get the vaccine."

Lena got up and made her husband a glass of ice water and when she handed it to him, he smiled at her in a way that made it clear he adored her.

"So, Jamie, I've gotten you on the painting crew at the White House. You can start tomorrow. You won't stick out because of your spots. A lot of workers have had the virus. The president and everyone around him have been vaccinated and boosted to the eyeballs. The Nationalists like to have survivors working for them, so they don't have to waste the vaccine. Anyway, there's a guy in the painting crew you can trust. He will give you info about the plans for Coleton. He has access to many, if not all the rooms in the White House. The First… Lady is having the whole place repainted. She thinks the present colors are depressing and she wants to brighten everything up, make it look…"

"Like a bordello," said Lena.

Sonny glanced at his shoes and tilted his head so he could smile at his wife then straightened. "Like I said, Mike has access to just about everywhere, as does his crew. It's a great position for us." He studied Sloan. "Did Jamie tell you I'm with the Secret Service, so I have to stay close to the President? Can't go wandering around. But naturally, I hear plenty."

At first, she hadn't known who he was talking about then remembered Shimmer's real name. It seemed eons since she'd first met him.

Shimmer leaned forward toward Sonny. "How strong is the resistance here?"

"Not strong enough. If we could get Whitbeck on our side, it would make all the difference. Gobs of assets everywhere. Some in the kind of banks offshore you need retina prints to get to them. Plus, primo land just about everywhere. The Europeans would pay dearly for it. Factories in the middle east and Asia. Most importantly, he's rumored to be in bed with the Saudis." He stood up. "I need to get dressed for work. I'll be back around six in the morning and we can go over the papers."

No one had mentioned Rosemary.

# CHAPTER SIXTEEN

**S**onny disappeared up the steep, narrow stairs at the back of the hall. When Lena started collecting glasses, Sloan stood up to help her. The room spun and she flopped back on the couch. "Whoa, that vodka hit me like a ton of bricks."

Lena took the glass from her hand. "You've been traveling all night. I have a bedroom for you if you want to sleep."

Sloan nodded and without even looking back at Shimmer, she followed Lena upstairs. Like the other spaces, the room was long and narrow. The walls were royal blue, the double bed done up in white, pristine bedclothes.

"I expect you didn't pack any pajamas." Lena opened a drawer in a white dresser then handed Sloan a set of PJs. "Do you want a bath?"

Sloan could barely keep her eyes open. "Maybe later." After Lena left, she yanked off her clothes as fast as she could, put on the PJ top, which hung off her shoulders and over her hands, and climbed into the white bed. How strange it felt to lie on a real mattress between smooth sheets. Sloan rolled onto her side. Her body had absorbed the events of the last few days and took over her mind, stopped it in its tracks. She fell beneath the level of dreams and slept solidly in the absence of thought.

A sun, compromised by buildings and the humidity of DC, seeped through the window when Sloan woke to find Shimmer standing by her bed.

"Lena left us a note to help ourselves to whatever is in the kitchen. She's gone to work." It was two o'clock in the afternoon.

They ate bagels and cream cheese and orange juice. Sloan felt disoriented, confused. Too much had happened too quickly. She yawned and pulled her hair into a ponytail. "You didn't say anything about Rosemary last night. I thought we were here to get the brass tacks about her role in all this."

Shimmer poured more juice in her glass. "We must take things one step at a time. Do you want water as well? Is important not to get dehydrated."

"I thought she was the reason we came here. To ask questions about her. I thought we could trust Sonny."

"We can trust Sonny as much as anyone but things happen. Compromise is sometimes necessary. Remember, in this world no rules apply. Anyone is, as you say, fair game."

There are times when the universe arranges itself in a way that makes it hard not to believe in fate. When Sonny came home from work, he told them the head chef at Blair House had apparently run away. The Secret Service man's influence was great enough that the Whitbecks and more importantly, President Diamond, were willing to give Sloan a chance to take the errant chef's place.

The first day in Blair House, Sloan walked around in a sparkling blur. Diamond's takeover had started slowly, could even be ignored until suddenly it blazed over the big cities, burying all but the memory of what it was like to live in a bountiful democracy. Now, here at Blair House, the people were in good weight. Even the servants—some of whom had discoloration left from Hepatic 26—showed no sign of deprivation. Abundance was the word she thought of repeatedly.

Sloan spent the first day marveling at the kitchen where she now worked: fresh vegetables of all kinds, fruit taut with ripe juices, frozen Maine lobster-tails, langostinos, trout from Wyoming, rib-eye steaks aged sixty days, baby-back ribs from heritage pigs fed on acorns, beef rib racks the size of your arm, every spice Sloan had ever heard of and some she hadn't, a ten-by-ten pantry filled with jars and cans of every ingredient you could possibly think of. Yet, with all these riches, it was a simple clear broth Sloan turned to.

Mrs. Mary Whitbeck had stopped eating.

The word simple was deceptive. It simply meant that the ingredients were common, treated with the utmost respect and not hidden under spices, sauces, or unnecessary techniques. Roast a chicken with fresh sage and thyme in the cavity. Boil the carcass slowly for several gentle hours. Into this add chopped celery, carrots, onions, and Sloan's secret ingredient. Cook another hour, strain, let cool, scrape off the layer of fat.

It was this honest brew Sloan brought to Mary Whitbeck's bedroom. She was propped up on her pillows, looking out the window. Judging by the look of her, she hadn't eaten for quite a while.

Mary Whitbeck, having grown up with servants, didn't notice their existence. They were ghosts, robots that met her needs and kept the household running. If they dropped something or brought home the wrong merchandize, being a mild-mannered woman, she didn't get upset. She knew the next time she journeyed forth through the unfortunate place of mishap, all would be well.

Sloan joined the world of the invisible people, and she liked it fine. As she settled the broth on a breakfast tray and put it across Mary's lap, she sniffed a familiar smell. Rum. "Oh, excuse me," she said. "This bowl doesn't look quite clean. Let me get you another."

All the staff wore the same uniform: starched stiff white shirts, black linen slacks. Sloan didn't need to wear a chef's hat or a double-breasted chef's jacket. If she took off her apron, she could move around Blair House looking like all the other servants. With a bottle of furniture polish and a rag in her hand, she could go anywhere unnoticed. Slipping around when she'd had the opportunity, she discovered the liquor cabinet. Now, being sure no one was near, she draped the rag over a bottle of Mount Gay rum and after dropping a few drops into a new bowl of soup, she hid the liquor behind boxes of pasta in the vast pantry.

"I am so sorry about the dirty bowl," Sloan said as she once again placed the broth over Mary Whitbeck's lap. "I will make sure it never happens again." She then stood beside the bed, her hands crossed crotch level, waiting. Mary Whitbeck picked up the soup spoon and sipped the golden liquid. She frowned and licked her lips. As she filled the spoon again, she happened to glance up at Sloan, surprise blooming in her face. Sloan ducked her head, said, "I'll be back for the bowl," and disappeared.

Sloan didn't sleep well that first night. While she laid awake, she thought about how to get information without raising suspicion. The assistant chef's expression had been unreadable. Sloan couldn't tell if she was angry at not being promoted to head chef or not. Finding out could be a helpful way to start a personal conversation.

On the second day of Sloan's employment, she was sent to the open markets to purchase fresh ingredients. Her workday started at six in the morning and lasted until ten at night, maybe longer if there was a dinner party. No one, not even the other staff, seemed to find these hours extraordinary. She was allowed time off during the day when things were slow.

What amazed her was the difference between the people connected to Blair House and the people she saw on the streets, who were thin, discolored, ragged and sometimes bald. No one at Blair House was ravaged in any way. Spotted, maybe, but clearly, they ate well. She herself had been tested then vaccinated as soon as she walked through the door.

As she turned a corner and stepped into the hum of the open market, a lightning thrill went through her. Although everyone was masked, the personas could have been exchanged with the vendors in New York City. She hadn't realized how much she'd missed it: the fish mongers, loud and aproned, slapping fish into piles, the quiet, melancholy fruit and vegetable owners, gently stacking their wares in geometrical patterns.

It would be sea bass with lemon, garlic, herb sauce for dinner tonight, a good thing as it was one of Sloan's favorite dishes to prepare. The sons and a few guests were dining with Mr. and Mrs. Whitbeck. Sloan's driver helped her load her purchases in the back of the SUV.

Rose, the assistant chef, helped her unload and put away the food. Sloan guessed they were about the same age. Yesterday, she'd told Sloan she'd been there a month. Before that, she'd worked in a bistro. Lawrence, the oldest son, liked the food there so much he had persuaded the head chef at Blair house to hire her away.

Sloan had a thousand questions she wanted to ask but had played it safe her first day, mostly listening to Rose as she explained the kitchen, mealtimes, and what the family liked.

Today, they worked quietly for a while, putting the non-perishables in the pantry, filling the refrigerator. Eventually, Sloan said, "Listen Rose, I hope you're not mad at me for being given the head chef's job. I wouldn't blame you if you were."

"Oh no, I'm glad of it. I don't want all that responsibility. The other chef was terrified. That's why she run off."

Sloan dropped the fish on the counter. "Terrified? Of the Whitbecks?"

"The Whitbecks and just the whole situation. They're practically prisoners here. At least Mr. and Mrs. The sons spend a lot of time at the White House."

Sloan leaned back against the counter. "The situation? And what do you mean they're prisoners?"

"Oh, I don't know for sure. Susan, that was the run-away chef's name, was a bit daft anyway."

Sloan waited a moment before asking, "Do the sons work at the White House?"

"I can't say for certain?'

"And you? Are you frightened?"

"Not so much. I'm just a lowly employee. If things go wrong here in the kitchen, I can always blame you." Rose smiled, showing a deep dimple in each cheek. She had a naturally cheerful countenance: soft surplus weight, broad face, blue-green eyes, and pale curly hair pulled into a fuzzy ponytail.

Sloan thought she looked like a goose-down pillow with a belt around the middle, the kind of looks easily dismissed. "Fine with me," she said, smiling back at the girl. "What are they going to do? Fire me? Then I could go home."

"And where is home?"

Sloan hesitated a beat. "Nebraska."

"Wow, how did you get all the way here?"

"It's a long story." Sloan turned to face the counter, unwrapped a sea bass, picked up the cleaver and whacked off its head. She took a slender, sharp knife from the knife drawer. "I heard the Whitbecks are richer than God. Do they have any other children besides those two sons?"

Before Rose could answer, a maid stuck her head around the swinging door. "Mrs. Whitbeck wants to see the cook."

Terrified, terrified, terrified tolled through Sloan's head as she made her way upstairs. She had never been terrified in her life, semi-terrified maybe, when she had to flee New York City, but gut-wrenching terror, no.

She opened Mary Whitbeck's door and entered halfway into the room.

"I'd like another bowl of that soup," Mary Whitbeck said, never taking her eyes from the window.

Sloan looked at the ornate grandfather clock standing in the corner. Ten on the nose. "When would you like it?"

"Now."

Fortunately, there was plenty left over. It occurred to Sloan she had no idea how to behave like a servant. The closest she could come was the way she expected her staff to act. Exclaiming, "Yes, chef," obviously wouldn't work. She shifted her weight. No way would she use the word ma'am. She didn't think simply turning around and walking out was appropriate. The precariousness of her position struck her for the first time, along with the word prisoner. She imagined the bedroom door slamming shut. "Coming right up," she said and beat it out of there.

# CHAPTER SEVENTEEN

**M**r. Stirling Whitbeck didn't become one of the richest men in the world without being able to take the measure of people. He also knew enough about human behavior to know a child doesn't develop his/her own sense of right and wrong until at least eight. Up to that point, children do or don't do things based on a system of punishment and reward. Between eight and ten, they build their own moral compass. More or less.

By the time each of his boys turned ten, Whitbeck knew their moral compass consisted only of what gave them pleasure. In fact, it couldn't be called a moral compass at all since there was no empathy or compassion about it. He blamed this on his wife, though without malice.

Mary had been raised old school with a strict English nanny who made no exceptions to the rules and followed the established schedule decreed for a girl raised in the Victorian era. Being an easy-going child, Mary followed along without fuss. She did stand up to her parents when it came time to choose her college, however. She chose Cornell. Even though it had an excellent reputation and was considered almost Ivy League, it was still a state school. Mary told her parents that didn't matter; Cornell had the best hotel school in the world, and that's what she wanted to do. Manage a hotel. Since even her father couldn't object to that, he agreed to pay the tuition.

Cornell turned out to be as strict and demanding as her home life, only without any interest in her well-being. Mary was twenty when the bonds began to chaff. She started going to frat parties where the liquor flowed. That summer when she returned home, she continued the party scene. The nanny was gone, taking any curfew with her. Never having overseen disciplining Mary, her parents were at a loss about how to rein her in. She met Mr. Whitbeck at a jumped-up excuse of a social event where the main draw was the drugs, alcohol, and sex.

Why Whitbeck chose Mary over all the women he could have plucked from the vine, people had trouble fathoming. Yes, she was lovely in an English rose sort of way, with her naturally blond hair, porcelain skin, and China-blue eyes. But pretty girls were a dime a dozen. She was half his age, which counted for something. The simple truth was, no other woman made him feel so restful. Uncomplicated, cheerful, obedient, and surprisingly interesting in bed, she made coming home something to look forward to.

Mary loved being married and adored being a mother. Remembering her childhood, she insisted the nanny impose no rules. If the boys wanted ice cream for dinner, they should have it. In fact, Mary saw to it they received anything they asked for.

Mr. Whitbeck, as he watched his sons grow, saw what a disaster this kind of upbringing could be. By the time they were ten he disliked them, and being astute, knew he would never respect them.

When Rosemary surprised him and Mary with her arrival, he made up his mind things would be done differently this time. He fired the lazy, happy-go-lucky American girl in charge of his children and went old school by hiring the sort of nanny his wife had had. He made sure his daughter received gifts only on her birthday and Christmas. She ate lean protein, lesser amounts of starch, and heaps of veggies for dinner. Dessert only on special occasions.

Being a devout equestrian, he was thrilled when Rosemary displayed the same passion. Her brothers never even bothered to visit their ponies in the barn. As he watched this serious child develop, a strange feeling grew in him, and it kept on growing until he realized she mattered more to him than his own life. This frightened him. Not only for himself but also for her.

Always busy amassing and guarding his fortune, he was not home often and didn't have the lifestyle to dote on his children. Which was fortunate since doting was the last thing he wanted to do to Rosemary. The more he loved her, the stricter he became.

The dirtier, more corrupt and cruel he became in his business dealings, when he was tired, angry, or lonely or in any way doubted the quality of his life, he thought of Rosemary.

One particular incident reassured him he had managed to create something of real worth in the world. Something pure and good and so dear, he had to use his famous self-control to maintain his distance and objectivity.

When he had the time, he always went to his daughter's horse shows. Wilson Elliott the Third had turned out to be a wise investment and more importantly, his decision to give the horse to his daughter an even wiser one.

At sixteen, Rosemary was the top rider and Wilson the top horse in the Grand Prix circuit. At least some of the time. Another horse, Wise Child, and her owner/rider Emily Townsend, were neck and neck in the race to keep the top gun position.

At the penultimate show to decide the year's gold medal rider and horse, both girls and their horses were tied.

Whitbeck would never forget the day.

In the previous show a week ago, Wilson had cleared the course in more than his usual argy-bargied way, making Rosemary work hard to control his pace and keep him balanced. Both horse and rider were dripping sweat when they left the ring.

Unlike most riders at that level, his daughter walked her horse back to his stall rather than hand him off to his groom. Her father was waiting for her.

"Looked a little rough out there," he said.

*"He* was a little rough." To prove his rider's point, Wilson tossed in a few bucks and kicked out behind before Rosemary got him in the stall, where he promptly twirled around and whinnied loud enough for his whole section of the barn to hear.

"How much grain is he getting?"

Once again, unlike most top riders who let the trainers oversee the feeding routine, Rosemary knew exactly how much and what kind of grain and hay Wilson received every day. "No more than usual."

"You lost a few seconds having to fight him like that."

As it turned out, Rosemary and Wilson came in second to Wise Child due to those extra few seconds, putting them one point behind for the year end glory.

***

Rosemary combed Wilson's tail with her fingers while her father watched. "You have only one show to go to beat out that Townsend girl. Are you ready?"

"He's practiced very well this week and he's calm today."

Whitbeck said nothing. He believed encouragement would only make his daughter nervous. "It's probably the weather," he said eventually. They were in Florida. Rosemary's fluffy hair was even more woolly than usual. "Better use a lot of hair spray to keep that hair under your hat. Do you have a net?"

"Of course, I have a net."

"There are only six more horses to go before you're up."

"I know that."

A shadow fell across the aisle as Emily Townsend led Wise Child into the barn. The mare was a dark bay, her color all but black, the only brown a faint line around her nostrils. Where Wilson won by power, arrogance, and determination, Wise Child didn't seem to put any effort at all into winning. At 16.2 hands, she was slightly built with a demure, almost apologetic demeanor. She floated over the jumps, never seeming to hurry, but moving so efficiently she shaved seconds off her time. Even walking, she moved like mercury. Except today there was a bobble in the flowing liquid.

Wise Child was lame.

Rosemary and her father watched Emily led her horse to her stall. They had come in from the practice ring. The girl was as quiet as her horse until the stall door closed behind them. Then Rosemary could hear her competition crying. She looked at her father in a way she had never done before, then walked out of Wilson's stall and down the aisle to where Wise Child was stabled. Whitbeck stayed put, a little stunned.

Emily had her face buried in the mare's neck. Rosemary watched for a while then said quietly, "Emily?"

The other girl looked up, her eyelids swollen and her cheeks wet.

Rosemary shifted her weight. "I don't know if you'd want to, but if you do, you can ride Wilson today. If you want to. He's quiet today. I think it's the weather. And he's not as difficult as he looks. He's just full of himself. And he loves a clear round. If you just let him go, I think today he will behave."

Emily looked at Rosemary in disbelief, knowing she was the only thing that stood between this girl and the gold. They tended to avoid each other, not out of meanness but a confused and superstitious embarrassment. They only spoke in a subdued way to congratulate each other on their win.

After some persuasion, Emily did ride Wilson and she ended the year as top rider. Rosemary's father made no comment and successfully hid his aching love and tears at this display of his daughter's character.

Sloan's first dinner was a success. One of the waiters, slightly out of breath from trotting down the stairs, pushed through the kitchen door. "Mr. Lawrence said to be sure to tell the cook how much he loved the branzino. Best he'd ever had." The waiter dumped dirty dishes into the sink. "Said he might come down and tell you himself." He and Rose exchanged glances.

Sloan had refused to admit she was nervous about tonight, but now her shoulders and back relaxed. It wasn't truly branzino if you didn't serve it as a whole fish, but that could be tricky when serving a crowd and apparently the Whitbecks didn't mind. Anyway, she'd survived the first test.

After the waiter left, Rose picked up a dish towel and wiped her forehead while smiling at Sloan. "This is my favorite time of day. The cooking done, all has gone well, and we get to relax." She walked over to the sink, rummaged around underneath, and brought out a bottle of white cleaning vinegar. Next, she retrieved two water glasses from a top shelf, filled them with ice, and poured the vinegar over it. After handing one to Sloan, she helped herself to a long pull, shivered, sighed, and held up her glass. "Here's to ya."

Sloan sniffed her drink and burst out laughing. How many bottles of hooch, she wondered, were stashed away in this kitchen.

Rose hiked herself onto a stool. "So, Mr. Lawrence liked your fish. What do you think of that?"

"Is that a question?"

Rose drank more of her vodka. "Yes and no. The thing about Mr. Lawrence is, he's a man of strong desires. Food, wine, sailing, women." She had another swallow and eyed Sloan over the top of her glass.

"By that you mean he's a player?"

Rose nodded.

"No harm in that as long as he isn't a bully. I mean, he stays away from the servants, right?"

"Yeah."

"Should I be worried?"

"Yup."

The two women laughed. The heat of the kitchen, the alcohol, and the subject brought a bloom to their cheeks. Their faces glowed with a damp, youthful sense of the moment.

Sloan hopped onto the counter and looked around at the piles of dirty dishes, encrusted pans, and crystal goblets dimmed by grease. "So, who does the dishes here?"

"Not us, thank the Lord. A couple of house cleaners will be here soon, so drink up."

"He's not a rapist, is he? He's just a pest, right?"

"Ahh, Sloan, you seem to me to be the sort who can take care of herself."

While drinking, the two talked about the dinner they had prepared together. Rose topped off their glasses, threw hers back, and returned the gallon to its hiding place.

"I'm off," said Sloan. "Thanks for the help. You're a good cook, Rose." She hung her apron on a hook and used the kitchen phone to call a cab. She still didn't carry a cell.

━━✳━━✳━━✳━━

The night after her first day of work, everyone was in bed when Sloan returned home. She'd been disappointed, but tonight she saw a spot of light in the living room as she opened the front door.

Shimmer was lying on the couch, staring at the ceiling with an arm behind his head. The light drew attention to his curls, emphasized the high cheekbones and clean jaw line. Not for the first time Sloan noticed his sensuous mouth. He swung his feet to the floor, patted a cushion next to him. "Wasn't sure you'd be home tonight. Maybe you decided to stay in that famous house with the fancy new job and the fancy kitchen and the fancy extraordinarily rich people to feed. Must be nice."

"Shimmer?"

He moved off the couch and brought one of the upholstered chairs closer to it, sat with his legs stretched in front of him. "Oh, do not look so worried. I'm just playing. Tell me, how was your first day? You are looking tired but not sad, so that is good. You must have much to tell."

"Not really." Sloan sank into the couch and slipped off her shoes. "Well, actually I do. But first tell me what is happening at the White House."

Shimmer draped an arm over the back of his chair. "I don't know how to start. Some nasty things are going on there. I think they would upset you if I told them. But one very good thing. Mike is perfect. You should see him, just average in all ways, the kind of guy who can disappear in any crowd. He is like a cat. First, he is here and then next thing you know he is someplace else, or he just disappears. I've only known the guy two days and already I love him. Reminds me of me, except I am not average looking. Anyway, the important thing is, like Sonny say, being the boss painter, he can be anywhere. Or almost." He paused and regarded Sloan for a moment. "Your hours, by the way. They are terrible. How can you work like that? Is not human." Shimmer dropped his arm onto the arm of the chair. "At least is not forever, right. Me, my hours are perfect if you don't want to work so hard. Frankly, I wish they were more like yours, instead of nine to five." He flicked a hand and made a dismissive sound. "Bankers' hours. But Mrs. Diamond doesn't like to be awake early, and her ears are very sensitive, so no noisy painters before nine. Can you believe it? The place has 150 rooms or something like that, and she is afraid we will wake her up. And we must be out of there by five in case people are coming to dinner. Apparently, that is just about every night. Mike got me placed working on the staircase to the living quarters, which is perfect because so many people pass by." He threw back his arm. "Is huge spiral thing. Like in a movie."

Shimmer leaned forward and lowered his voice. "It is a terrible place, Sloan. Everyone walks around looking scared to death. Mike tells me this Rosemary search is very serious because Diamond is in great financial trouble. Mike says there even has been talk of water boarding to get Whitbeck talking and other stuff like what they did in Abu Ghraib. But how do you take a tortured person to a bank and get his retina scanned." He sat back and crossed his legs. "He wouldn't talk, anyway. That's what they say. So, Rosemary is the key because he would sing like a canary before letting anyone hurt her. If they haven't found her in a few days, they will send the big guns to Coleton. Not sure what that means exactly but it can't be good. This is all coming from listening and from other informers. Really, people like Diamond are so stupid. He is paranoid to the biggest degree but forgets to think about the painters. Maybe is because of Sonny. Mike says Diamond is crazy for Sonny. Thinks the guy walks on water. Would have him live there, but the wife says no, no way. Diamond has some weird habits; I won't go into that now. Sometimes he calls Sonny to come in at night. Is hard to figure which way he will go. But we don't need to…"

"Shimmer?"

"Yes?"

"What are we going to do about Rosemary and my mom and everyone else?"

"I was getting to that. We are meeting tomorrow night, here, as soon as you get home, Mike too, and we will make some decisions. We still have time."

"I thought you said in a few days. In a few days they will send in the big guns."

"I might have exaggerated a little. Takes time to get the big guns organized. And Diamond isn't bankrupt. He still can run the country for a while."

Sloan's adrenaline had drained away, leaving her stupefied and limp with exhaustion. A weird image went through her head. She pictured herself getting up and kissing Shimmer on the forehead and saying goodnight.

He stood and looked down at her. "Look at you, falling asleep sitting there. Go to bed. I will see you tomorrow night. And don't worry. We will get word to your mother."

"Have you told anyone where Rosemary is living?"

"Not yet. Maybe tomorrow night."

"Did you say you knew her?"

"No. Now don't worry. I know you will, but please don't." He picked up her hand and pulled her to her feet in front of him. "Go to sleep, Sloan. You have to be back at work by six."

# CHAPTER EIGHTEEN

**S**onny approached Shimmer, who stood at the drinks cart pouring a glass of ice water, and put a hand on his shoulder. "How you doing? Feeling okay?"

"I'm okay, but I think I should not drink anymore. The mornings are not so good."

"I'm surprised you lasted this long. After having the virus, most people can't drink at all."

"I will miss it, you know."

Sonny patted his shoulder. "I can't even imagine."

Sloan, Lena, and Mike were already sitting, waiting for the two men to join them. Everyone sat in a position so they could see each other.

Shimmer swirled the water in his glass. "I need to clear things up in my mind. About the monies and the fact that Diamond is supposed to be running out of it. Where I come from, the peoples think the U.S. can never run out of money. Most of Europe thinks the same. And Africa. America is the golden goose, right? So why doesn't she just lay more eggs, and while she's at it, give a few to us who are starving? That's what the poor say in Africa. And Europe."

Sonny cleared his throat and squared his shoulders. "The so-called advisors, intellectual elites in this country, the talking heads who don't come out from behind their desks, or the thugs running around grabbing power, say the same thing. The Fed can issue bonds and sell them, they say. They have no clue who's going to buy these bonds. The people who are hiding and starving? Or the slaves working for the government? The government tried to sell them to China, but China just laughed and hinted at calling in our debt. Which is huge by the way.

"Blow China off the map, the generals say. Okay. The nuclear warheads can wave to each other as they go from the U.S. to China and China to the U.S. So, then they tried to sell these bonds to Russia and Russia doesn't even bother to answer. Bonds aren't the answer. To get what he needs to run this country, Diamond must have cold hard cash and he will need to go to other countries to buy and sell goods. Well good luck with that. He's a pariah. And H26 has seriously hurt our own production.

"We're a failing country and the world knows it. Big business is dead in the water. The capitalist system is over. Whitbeck appears to have had the sense to move his fortune offshore, but until recently he stayed loyal to Diamond. Now… he won't let him get his hands on his fortune and Diamond is beside himself.

"Print more money, the know-it-alls in suits say. Have they forgotten the civil war and carpetbaggers? Runaway inflation? They have no idea what is really going on. If Diamond wants to do something, he needs to go into the factories, take a careful look at supply chains, instead of listening to other people's theories. But he's too lazy." A muscle twitched along Sonny's jaw.

Lena, sitting next to him on the couch, put a hand on his knee. "My husband must follow the President around all day, while keeping his face neutral. He even has to agree with him sometimes. When he gets home, he unloads, gets it off his chest." She smiled. "He's Italian, you know."

Sonny smiled at his wife. "She's right. But seriously, things are so much more complicated than these talking heads understand. I've always hated the theorists. Look at Greenspan. He came closer to ruining this country than any other man. Easy money for the rich, let the poor fend for themselves. Thank you, Greenspan, for the dot.com bubble and the subprime mortgage crisis. You can keep your theories. Jesus."

Lena said, "Sonny."

He sighed and leaned back.

Sloan hesitated before saying, "So, Diamond and his minions are pretending money isn't a problem?"

Sonny said, "Of course. They can't admit the trouble they're in. And they've got people lining up to agree with them."

Mike uncrossed his legs and laughed. "I heard someone the other day say congress should do something. Raise the debt ceiling or something. It was all I could do not to laugh. Do they really not know what is going on? Congress was a useless bunch of spineless windbags before Diamond took power. They sure as hell dance to his tune now. Raise the debt ceiling? Someone please explain to me what good that would do.

"And we do continue to make bonds and what's left of 'free' big business buys them, putting money into the government. It's just not enough. The thing is, Diamond has taken over so many corporations and they are now part of the system. He can take their profits, but the profits aren't that big anymore. He seriously underestimated how expensive it is to run a government based on fear and slavery."

Sonny sat forward. "Diamond doesn't have the manpower or money to keep forcing people into work camps like the Nazis did in Germany. The country doesn't support him the way Germany did Hitler. Europe is still free, unlike in World War Two. The days when troops can roll in and take over businesses and towns and their money are over, thanks to Switzerland, the Caymans, and the Rock of Gibraltar and history. This is America boys. Remember that. 'A Rabble in Arms' defeated the great British Empire. They'll have Diamond's head on a pike when things fall apart."

Shimmer heaved a sigh and said in as loud a voice as Sloan had ever heard from him, "*Stop*! All this talk, talk, talk. Why do we need to know what the peoples with eggs for heads living in tall white castles say? We know if Diamond is to succeed, he needs Whitbeck's monies. That is all we need to know. The rest is just bullshit talk. We concentrate on keeping Whitbeck from caving." He turned to Sloan. "So, my lovely, that is why you are so important."

"You're forgetting something."

Shimmer let his eyes stay on her face. "Yes, is true. We also must find out what Diamond's plans are for Coleton."

Sloan scooched forward on the couch. "And Whitbeck is being held hostage until they find his daughter for leverage. What *are we* going to do about what's going on in Coleton? Whitbeck's estate is near there. I understand a fugitive hunt for Rosemary is about to take place. What are we going to do about it?"

Everyone looked at her. She looked squarely at Shimmer, who cleared his throat, crossed his legs, and folded his hands in his lap. "We know where Rosemary is," he said. "She's living with Sloan's mother outside of Coleton."

# CHAPTER NINETEEN

**N**early vibrating with anticipation, Rose greeted Sloan as soon as the door swung open. "The Whitbecks are going to the White House for dinner, and President Diamond wants you to go along and help his chef. He doesn't like his cooking all that much." She popped up on her toes. "You could bring me along, I expect."

Sloan wasn't sure if she was pleased with this development or not.

Rose reached into the pocket of her apron. "Here's the menu.

*Vichyssoise*

*Small brownie trout*

*Standing rib roast with horseradish sauce, roast potatoes, Yorkshire pudding and micro greens*

*Individual blue berry galettes with fresh whipped cream*

Rose flicked a towel at the paper. "Mr. Diamond likes his food, now don't he."

"Are all the ingredients at the White House?"

"Sure. Do you know how to carve a roast beef, cause the president thinks it's beneath him. Doesn't know the host is supposed to do the carving."

Sloan had never carved a standing roast in her life. Where she had worked, they served thick rib steaks with the bone attached. Ordinarily she would object to this break in protocol, but it would give her a chance to observe the people at the table, all of them players in the drama that had become her life. Some culinary schools were devoted solely to the art of carving and the slices had to be cut with surgical precision. She'd have to fake it. Sloan doubted Diamond would notice. His looks made him appear the clown. Whitbeck was another story. "When is dinner served?"

"Seven. We're to be there at four."

"What does the White house chef think of this?"

"Knowing chefs, I expect not much."

"Why doesn't he or she do the carving?"

"He. And I'm sure I don't know."

"Rose, why is he asking for me? Don't you think it's strange?"

"Seems like Lawrence was braggin' on you. That's what the maid told me."

Sloan looked at the menu. "Not big on veggies, is he." She stared into the middle distance; her mind already focused on how to prepare the food should the White House chef let her. She wouldn't be able to track down Whitbeck today, which left her anxious and relieved at the same time.

As it turned out, Randy Close, Executive Chef to the President of the United States, was more than happy to have Sloan share the cooking with him. Tall, chubby, with greasy hair, he wore a perpetual expression of unease and anger. "The guy's a real bastard," he told Sloan. "Expects me to prepare a dinner for six extra people at the drop of a hat."

"Six?"

"Yeah, the Whitbecks and a couple of guys. Like I have rib roasts lying around the kitchen." Randy tied a bandana around his forehead because he was sweating. "I've got the roast in the oven and the Vichyssoise is in the fridge. How are you at Yorkshire pudding?"

"I happen to be famous for my Yorkshire pudding," Sloan lied.

"These trout have been flown in from Montana. Super special. I'll let you do those. They want a lemon and brown butter sauce to go with them."

Sloan wondered where he'd worked before and how he'd gotten this job. No surprise he didn't want to carve.

Randy began mixing flour, butter, and ice water to make a dough. "The man's a pig. Wants a full meal at two in the morning, two or three times a week. I keep Whoppers in the freezer and Tater Tots. He gobbles them right up."

"What's Mrs. Diamond like?"

"Wait till you see her. These goddamn galettes will be a pain in the ass."

"You've got the soup done and the roast cooking. That's more than half the job."

"He wants a goddamn gravy with the beef."

Randy, Rose, and Sloan fell into the easy rhythm of prepping vegetables, making dough, cleaning blueberries so they would be set for the mad rush that always started a half hour before service and continued throughout the meal.

Sloan was admiring the trout when the door flew open. Shimmer jumped into the room and flattened himself against the wall. "Diamond has gone off somewhere. Does not want to be disturbed. Come now and I will show you around." He grabbed Sloan's hand and pulled her behind him. They were gone before Rose or Randy could say a thing.

"Won't the secret service or someone want to know what we're doing?"

"I am a painter, remember. With an official card saying it is so. And you the famous chef who is here to help—" Shimmer flicked his hand. "Whatever his name is. I am showing you the dining room."

The questions of why a painter would be showing her the dining room, and why she would need to see it occurred to Sloan, but she let them pass. She was in the White House and even though the country was nothing like what it once was, being in this building still made her giddy.

Shimmer put his hand on the small of her back. "Besides, this place is very strange. In some parts, you get the feeling you will be thrown in jail if you look the wrong way; other places, no one seems to care what is going on. Like two different countries. I have heard Diamond is not so very smart. He's street but not so good at running things. That's a room for reading I guess, over there, and the dining room is right here."

Sloan plucked his sleeve. "Let's go see the Lincoln bedroom."

He looked at her quizzically with half a smile. "Am not sure we can explain why we are in that particular place, but we will see." Shimmer looked down the hall where two men stood stick straight and, except for their roaming eyes taking in the surroundings, completely motionless.

He showed her the dining room, living room, and was heading for the stairs when a door opened some distance away. Down a long hall, Diamond and a little girl with long, red-gold hair walked out of a door. She looked to be about seven or eight years old. Diamond had his hand on the crown of her head.

When Sloan saw the expression on the girl's face—dazed, bewildered, unspeakably shattered—water filled her brain and her muscles. She knew exactly what that look meant. She didn't know how she knew, but she knew. She felt herself slipping and became suddenly aware she had been removed from the world. The floor came up to meet her. She didn't have to do anything but lie there with her eyes closed, and the world could go on without her. When Shimmer gathered her up and began to trot, it didn't matter where he was going. When he entered a room and laid her on a fainting couch it felt perfectly natural. He started calling her name and patting her cheek, but Sloan didn't have to respond. She could stay removed for as long as she wanted.

But then her eyes decided to open, and she let them, even though she knew the world had turned upside down, changed direction, flown off into another orbit, and would never come back.

Shimmer pulled her to her feet. "Lock the door behind me." They were in a bathroom. He dragged her to the door, went out and shut it behind him, calling to her to lock it, so she did before returning to the fainting coach. How odd, she thought, to have this type of furniture in a bathroom. Perhaps whoever bathed in here liked company. Sloan imagined a man stretched out holding a martini glass. She began to shake violently. The new world, along with its knowledge, was threatening to take over when someone pounded on the door. Sloan made her shaky way to unlock it then Shimmer and Rose were on either side of her, holding her up.

"I don't seem to be able to stop shivering."

Rose reached into her pants pocket, pulled out a medicine bottle, opened it and put two tiny pills in Sloan's hand. "Take these. They will stop the shakes."

Sloan obediently swallowed them dry while Shimmer stared at Rose, who scowled at him and said, "What? A chef's work is incredibly stressful. Especially here. We all take them."

When Rose and Shimmer, still holding onto Sloan, returned to the kitchen, another man was helping Randy swab the stainless-steel counters. He too was plump but short. He wore his hair long and like Randy's, it looked greasy. His apron was covered with food stains.

"My sous," said Randy, then looked up at them. "What the hell? What's wrong with her?"

Shimmer surreptitiously put his hand in the middle of Sloan's back, forcing her to stand more upright. "Nothing, nothing. Occasionally, very occasionally, she has tiny fainting fits. She will be fine any second now."

"She'd better not have one while serving."

"No. No. Of course not. She only gets them once or twice a year. Now she's had one, it won't happen again for a very long time."

The pills took hold and Sloan got caught up in the frenzied scurry that goes with serving a formal dinner to a crowd. There would be eleven: the President and Mrs. Diamond, their three boys and the Whitbecks, plus two gentlemen on their own. Thoughts about preparing the food filled her head, leaving no room for ideas concerning the new placement of her world.

Directly outside the dining room door, another man in a dark suit stood in the now familiar soldier position, except his shirt was more formal than the others, with French cuffs, gold cuff links and a tie stud. He stepped toward Sloan and her serving cart. "You will serve the President first. He sits at the head of the table. Next Mrs. Diamond at the foot. You will start at the bottom on the right, move toward the president then cross to the left and continue to the foot. Do you understand?"

A modern-day butler. Why wasn't he carving? "Got it," said Sloan.

The first thing she noticed when she walked into the dining room was the plethora of stiff, darkly suited men lining the walls. The second was Mrs. Whitbeck, looking deathly pale and so frail it seemed she might float to the ceiling at any moment. Sloan wondered if her husband had a hand on her leg to hold her down.

The president ranked only third in her impressions. Even more grotesque than in his pictures or on TV, he sat like a buffalo ready to charge. If he remembered seeing her faint earlier in the day, he didn't show it, which didn't surprise Sloan since he was one of those people who didn't see servants. She pushed the cart toward him. One of the stick men peeled away from the wall, stretched out a stiff arm to stop Sloan three feet from Diamond. He reached for a plate with the presidential seal and held it toward the cart.

"How do you like your meat, Mr. President?" Sloan said. The inadvertent choice of words sent needles into her pores.

"Rare."

Sloan placed the knife directly in the middle of the glistening roast and sliced it between the bones. It went through the beef as though it were butter, the way only the highest quality knife sharpened to perfection could do. Sloan wondered how many seconds it would take to reach Diamond and plunge the blade into his carotid. Juices ran from the red flesh. She shaved a thin slice and put it on the plate. Before she could present it to the President, the man stepped forward and took it from her. He turned to the sideboard, cut a bite, and ate it. After a moment he nodded to Sloan. She made several cuts, and the suit placed them in front of Diamond.

When she turned to go to Mrs. Diamond, she saw the seat was empty. Without hesitation Sloan wheeled her cart to the bottom right and began to serve the table. No one spoke. Apparently, no one felt it necessary to keep her from attacking the other diners.

She'd served three people when the door opened, and, leading with her tits, a Hustler's hustle came into the room, wearing a dress so tight you could make out the anatomy leading to her legs. Somehow, she managed to walk without mincing to her seat, where she sat slightly sideways, legs crossed, and lit up a long cigarette.

Sloan started to roll her cart toward her, but the woman waved her away.

"Look at my beloved wife," said the president. "Isn't she the most beautiful thing you've ever seen? Well worth waiting for." He raised a glass. There were murmurs along the table while everyone else lifted their wine high.

Diamond smiled. "Here's to Corina, the most succulent piece of beef ever to walk on legs."

Mrs. Diamond blew smoke into the room.

# CHAPTER TWENTY

The pills had worn off and Sloan started to tremble again, though not as badly as before. Dishes stood stacked all over the counter, piled high in the sinks. Greasy pans covered the surfaces of both stove tops. In that murky world of sedatives and shock, Sloan would have been happy to move around in a distracted way, slowly cleaning up the mess, washing the dishes, cleaning the kitchen, but a housekeeping crew swarmed in, followed by a maid who poked her head around the door and said, "Miss, your cab has been called."

As soon as the driver closed the door behind her, rain erupted and pounded on the roof of the car. Sloan had been unaware of the signs of a storm as she'd waited outside the gates for her ride. The water pounded so furiously on the metal it felt as though they were under attack. As the driver pulled away from the curb, the lights from the car swam in the water running across the street. By the time Sloan arrived at Sonny's house, the hangover from the sedatives had worn off, leaving only shock, which she discovered to be an improvement. She walked up the porch stairs aware of the rain soaking her hair and running down the collar of her shirt, yet it didn't matter. She noticed, without feeling anything, the faint light in the living room, Shimmer standing up from his chair and putting a blanket over her shoulders then going into the kitchen. She sat on the couch, her reaction to what was going on around her like that of a mirror, untouched by emotion.

It was the same when he brought her a pot of tea and a cup and saucer. "Drink this," he said, filling the cup with steaming liquid. "I've put sugar in it. Sweet hot tea. Best for shock, or so my mother told me."

Sloan found the drink sickeningly sweet and too hot, but it didn't matter, didn't matter at all. She drank it down dutifully then handed the cup and saucer to Shimmer.

Upstairs, she undressed, slipped into the nightgown Lena had left for her and pulled the covers under her chin. She knew she wouldn't sleep but that didn't matter. She could stare at the ceiling all night long.

The rain, coming in sheets, filled the bedroom and rose over Sloan's head. Little fishes swam everywhere, across her neck and chest, along her sides, over her belly, down her thighs and between her legs. She launched herself into a sitting position, her back straighter than any of the men who stood guard at the White House. She panted, gasping for breath. Slowly, the sound of the rain, gentler now, formed a rhythm in her brain. White noise, she thought. The noise in the machines people bought for sleeping. She blinked several times, laid back down. She'd fallen asleep after all. The shaking began again, increasing until her teeth rattled. I'm going to fall apart, Sloan thought. I'm frozen to the core. I need Shimmer. But I can't go to him. Not like this. I'm not even sure I can get out of bed. A tentative foot on the floor then another, bringing her torso upright facing the wall. Sloan catapulted out of the room, ran across the hall, slowed so she could open his door quietly, but Shimmer sat up when she walked over the threshold. He moved over, made room for her on the bed, turned down the covers.

He wrapped his arms and legs around her, holding her tight against him to stop the shivering. He started singing in a language Sloan didn't understand. Possibly African. The odd lilting tune going from one minor key to another entranced, hypnotized, put her back to sleep.

At some point, feeling hot, Sloan moved away from him and rolled onto her back, allowing a black, hairy tarantula, as big as she was, to crawl on top of her and pin down her arms and legs. He sunk his mandibles into her breast then pierced her with one of his hairy legs. She woke from the dream with a cry of pain, flung herself to the side and onto the floor. Shimmer picked her up, one arm under her head, another under her knees and laid her back in the bed. When he pulled her close, she tried to move away, but he kissed the back of her neck and whispered, "Hush, is just me."

A sliver of sunlight from the one window in the room ran across the wood floor, up the bed and onto Shimmer's body and head, lighting up his speckles and dark curls. Still asleep, he laid on his side, facing Sloan, the covers under his arm and across his chest. He wasn't wearing a shirt.

Sloan wondered if he was naked. This wasn't the first time she'd slept with him, but that time had been chaste and platonic. Almost. She'd slept with other men too, but only because there was no place else to sleep. And those occasions had always been platonic. Always.

It's Saturday, Sloan thought, my morning off. She didn't need to be at work till noon. She ran her fingers from Shimmer's shoulder, down his side, under the sheet, over his hip and along his thigh. Boxers. He slowly opened his eyes, his thick lashes sooty with sleep.

"I'm not the same person I was yesterday morning," Sloan said.

"I know. I saw it happen when you noticed Diamond with his hand on the child with the same beautiful hair as you. You went white."

"What happened? I don't understand. I know I fainted, but why? I feel as though the world has changed in some nasty, humiliating forever kind of way."

Shimmer looked at her for a long while, his face serious. Finally, he said, "Where I was born, there was much violence. Toward men and also girls, sometimes little girls no more than five. Some disappeared, vanished forever, sold into a big traffic business. Some were raped and killed, left on the side of the road. Others were raped in front of their families then left to live or die. Sometimes these girls never left their houses ever again. I know two women who killed themselves because they could not protect their children. Often the girls went into prostitution."

"Why are you telling me this?"

"Maybe something like that happened to you."

Sloan popped up on an elbow and stuttered out the words. "That's disgusting… you… you're wrong. Absolutely wrong. I'd remember if it did."

"Maybe." Shimmer used a finger to tuck a wayward strand of Sloan's hair behind her ear.

She waited for the tsunamis of panic to hit her and send her running out the door. Nothing like it happened. This close, his face looked perfect. The defined black brows, his calm expression, even the speckles. "You have the most beautiful eyes I've ever seen," she said.

Shimmer smiled. "Now you are teasing me."

"No, not at all." Sloan leaned forward to kiss him.

Shimmer drew back. "I have never wanted to be with a woman as much as I want to be with you right now." He touched the round end of her clavicle under her neck. "I am thinking it would be beautiful for me but not so good for you. Not now."

"But why? I haven't gotten this close ever. Not my whole life. Until now."

Shimmer smiled again and put his arm around her shoulder, pulled her next to him, and laid his chin on her head. "Let's not ruin that. With luck and the good Lord's help from above, it will last." He moved so he could kiss her hair line.

The front door opened and closed. "Jamie, Lena, Sloan," Sonny called from the bottom of the stairs.

Shimmer kissed Sloan quickly in the same place and scrambled out of bed. "Diamond made Sonny spend the night last night. He does that sometimes," he said as he pulled on his jeans. He shrugged into his t-shirt, didn't bother with his shoes before he bounded down the stairs, Lena right behind him. Sloan thought about it and decided to go down in her nightgown instead of taking time to dress.

As she ran down the stairs, she heard Sonny say, "Sit down." Lena and Shimmer sat on the chairs, Sonny on the couch. He looked up and nodded at Sloan. She perched on the other end.

Sonny leaned forward, forearms on his thighs, hands clasped. "Diamond made the whole family stay after dinner. He put them in a small, square room with a big table and wooden chairs—have no idea what it's used for. It had two doors, one on each end, and he locked both of them. I was there with two other Secret Service men. He didn't waste any time. He told Whitbeck if he didn't either give him access to his money or hand over the girl in five days, he would send the heavy artillery to Coleton. Said he was being generous because Whitbeck had given so much money for the takeover.

"Whitbeck said the girl wasn't in Coleton. She'd gone overseas. Would never be found. Diamond laughed then puffed out his lips the way he does then sucked air between his teeth. Said he thought Whitbeck was smarter than that. 'There isn't an airport, ship, blimp, drone, you name it, I haven't covered for weeks. Radar on every border of the country. That girl of yours is still in this country. And don't bother telling me she's squirreled away in the Rockies somewhere. I've got buses and trains covered. And all the security monitors on the highways are covered too.' Whitbeck told him he was bluffing. Diamond looked at him with those slit eyes he uses sometimes and said, 'Try me.' Mrs. Whitbeck starts to cry. Those kids of hers, those worthless fuckers." Sonny glanced at his wife. "Excuse me, honey, Sloan, you too."

Sonny sat back against the couch. "So, the long and the short of it is, we've got five days."

"To do what?" said Sloan.

"I don't suppose you'd consider giving Rosemary up."

"No!" Sloan and Shimmer spoke at the same time.

"Didn't think so. We could get her here, but I don't think it's safe. I'm surprised Diamond hasn't already sent someone to check out this house."

The universe shifted, arranged itself, and someone knocked on the front door. Lena opened it. A man dressed in the Nationalist uniform tipped his cap and walked into the living room. "Good morning, everyone. Just thought I'd stop by and say hello."

The toss wasn't that bad. Officer Richard Mosely was joined by another Nationalist ten minutes after he arrived. Together they ran their hands over all the door frames, the crown molding, under every stick of furniture and under and over all the cabinets.

They didn't pull drawers out of bureaus and throw the contents on the floor. They didn't cut open the upholstered furniture or mattresses. Charmingly apologetic, Officer Mosely explained they would have to take every device that could be used for communication with them. "We just have to check them for viruses in case you've been hacked. You understand." He explained to Sonny, President Diamond was terribly sorry about the inconvenience. It was just routine. And they had been strictly told not to make a mess. President Diamond was extremely fond of Sonny and trusted him with his life, but you could never be sure about the people who visited his home. They could hide cell phones or bugs while Sonny was in another room… to be used at a later date. You just didn't know these days. Did Sonny have any people over without security clearance? No. Well, that was smart.

When Sonny let them out, Officer Mosely said in a low voice, "The president is gearing up for a massive military tactic. Everyone is on high alert. And believe me, no one is an exception to his scrutiny."

Shimmer understood the Nationalists hadn't come to search but to plant.

Sloan, Shimmer, and Lena stood in a miserable cluster in the living room waiting to hear what Sonny had to say. He waved them through the kitchen and out the back door. "We can't say anything, anywhere in the house," he said when they were outside. "You can bet the house is now crawling with bugs. A minor setback." He sat on the arm of an Adirondack chair. "I've got the day off. I'll drive around and see if I can find any of our people who can get someone to Coleton."

"Someone?" said Sloan. Panic flew across her face.

"We may need you at Blair House for a few days."

"I'm not going to warn my mother?" Her voice caught.

"Shimmer can do that. Plus, he knows the resistance there. Now let's get back in the house and act normal or someone will get suspicious about the silence. We'll make breakfast. Shimmer, when do you need to be at work?"

"Nine. So, I will not be having anything to eat but be on my way."

"I've got until noon," said Sloan. She held Shimmer's arm while Lena and Sonny returned inside. "I don't like this. I should go with you."

"Indeed, no. Is very important you stay at Blair House. I will get to your mother as soon as possible. You must trust me on this. I will talk to Mike, and he will keep an eye on your safety."

# CHAPTER TWENTY-ONE

**D**uring their morning briefing, the Sargent, or Sargent Master, or whatever you called him, told Luther and the other recruits they wouldn't be learning the city today. Instead, they were going into the countryside. "Your captains will explain the details. There will be a local man in every vehicle."

The same group Luther had been riding with since the first day gathered in the parking lot next to their SUV. Captain Riddick was, as it turned out, indeed a local man, so no need to exchange personnel.

"Now listen up," said Slater. "Some info has arrived that an essential person is located somewhere in this area, and at this moment, finding her is our priority. She's eighteen or nineteen years old. Rumor has it she's most likely to be in the countryside rather than Coleton. I can't emphasize enough how time sensitive this is. So, take notes, just like you've been doing, only better. There are few street names to go by. We will do a general sweep, nothing to alert the locals, just driving around to get the lay of the land. But we are expecting more info anytime and soon we will be kicking ass and taking names. It is essential you come back with a working knowledge of a thirty-mile radius. If you get distracted or don't notice something, tell us and we will go back."

With that said, everyone piled into the SUV. The chicken breasts Henry had brought Luther turned out to be an immense help. Also, he found he could tolerate scrambled eggs. He was slowly getting over the effects of the virus and though only about sixty percent, he no longer felt weak as a kitten. He liked the idea of going into the country. He didn't think he would have trouble taking the lay of the land since he had grown up in rural Idaho, which didn't have street signs to navigate by either. He wished he had a window seat.

The morning was cool, crisp, about sixty degrees with a forecast of mid-eighties. An unusually nice day for this time of year in the Allegheny Mountains. It smelled like spring, warming soil giving off a musky scent, the spice of foliage uncurling on the trees. Luther sighed and leaned back in his seat.

They drove along a railroad track through a seedy part of town and then suddenly there were no more houses, just Will's Creek on the right and a steep mountain on the left until the topography opened into fields where small businesses—a car repair shop, restaurant, insurance building, hair salon and palm reader—spaced themselves loosely along the road, separated but visible to each other. Luther had memorized the directions to Sloan's farm and noted she had described something like what he was seeing.

Slater turned off the main road, passed a Sheetz lit up like Disney world, and kept going down a narrow, badly maintained macadam road. Sloan had said something about a Sheetz, but Luther couldn't remember the context. Sweat pricked his pores.

They came to what passed as a village. Small, not too sturdy homes, with little space between them, sat so close to the road it seemed they were clinging to it. In front of a tiny post office, a small sign with a white background and black letters stood out from its dull background. WELCOME TO SAVAGE. Luther's muscles turned to steel and his skin tightened around them. The town of Savage was on the way to Sloan's. And not too far away.

He couldn't take his eyes off the scenery around him to take notes. A struggle to memorize what he was seeing and not give himself away ensued. He wanted to lean forward to see around his companions but controlled himself. He swung his head from side to side, taking everything in.

The cluster of houses disappeared, followed by empty fields with an occasional barn sitting back from the road then another turn onto an even narrower road. Houses appeared again, modest but neat with large, well-kept lawns.

Luther's breath roared in his ears and the thumping of his heart nearly choked him. And then there they were. The bales of clothes brought in by semi-trucks with the idea of setting up a small business selling them at vastly reduced prices. However, the entrepreneur—a man who had never worked a day in his life—gave up when they didn't sell and left them unprotected from the elements. Cockroaches and silverfish soon began to thrive in the tightly packed material. Families from the Holler stole a few articles and sent their children to school in them. The health department had been trying for years without success to have the bales declared an environmental hazard.

Sloan had told this story to Luther one night after service while they were swabbing down the steel counters and laughing about how quaint, even ridiculous, their homes of origin were. These eternally damp, smelly bales bordered her land.

The SUV passed the teeming mixture of clothes and pests. Behind a stand of cedar trees, board fencing appeared, enclosing what Luther thought might be a pasture. It was at least ten acres, but the grass had been eaten to stubs. At the end of this field a huge bank barn stood on a knoll, the red paint faded to patterns of rose and salmon pink. Just under the peaked roof was the declaration VALLEY FARM 1812.

A driveway next to the barn led straight to another large building, though it was clearly not from the same era. Newish, it appeared to Luther to be a stable with a shed extension where horses could be tied for grooming. This building gave off an aura of prosperity, the kind of prosperity that comes from arduous work and enough money.

In front of it, the driveway took a sharp left and headed toward a quintessential Pennsylvania farmhouse: red brick, two stories, the rooms upstairs the same size and shape as those downstairs. The kitchen would be in the back. This time Luther craned his head for a better look. No signs of activity; no one in the stable or around the house. Not any horses, except maybe one behind the stable. The pastures stretched for miles, all of them poor.

Slater and Riddick had been pointing out landmarks along the way. Now, Riddick pointed at the farmhouse and said, "That's Clare Raffiene's place. She's supposed to be a witch."

Slater snorted.

Tears came to Luther's eyes. He blinked them away rapidly.

Past this farm, they drove for miles. Luther noticed nothing. He managed to get his breathing back to normal and rode along with the others, the frantic thought, *how do I get back here*, beating a tattoo inside his head. A man behind him said, "God, we're in east Jesus. There's absolutely nothing here."

"I grew up in this kind of place," another man said. "Only without the mountains. Where I grew up you could see corn fields for miles and miles. Don't know what you'd do with this land here. Not even sure why we're here."

After several more miles they came upon more fencing. Instead of wooden boards this was made of barbed wire. Luther thought absently about how much he hated barbed wire due to the harm it could do to livestock.

"What's this?" said Slater. Behind the fencing, the fields were lush and a healthy green. "Looks like someone has some money. Now where do you suppose they would get it?"

"You think they might've gotten it from the governments?"

"Where else?"

The barbed-wire fencing continued as did the rich fields.

"We're definitely going to have to look into this." Slater twisted his head, yelled toward the rest of the men. "You boys better know how to get here." He faced front again. "Why haven't we heard about this?" Just then a horse-drawn buggy appeared from around a corner. As it drew closer, they could see a man and a woman, both in black, sat side by side.

"Amish," said Riddick.

"Oh, hell," Slater answered.

Riddick watched the buggy pass by. "I heard they've got money stashed in their mattresses cause they don't buy any expensive equipment."

"We need to get that land. Grow something besides grass."

Riddick chuckled. "Good luck with that. They don't consider themselves part of this country. Don't even pay taxes."

"You think they'd hide a girl there?"

"No way. They don't want anything to do with 'them English.'"

"Yeah, I saw that movie too. Still, there's a new sheriff in town who wouldn't mind going in there with a few AK47s. And that witch's place? Just ripe for the plucking."

Luther closed his eyes.

# CHAPTER TWENTY-TWO

Luther imagined smothering Henry with his pillow. Instead of turning off the TV after the ten o'clock news and going to sleep, Henry started flipping through channels and kept on doing it. Finally, Luther said, "Hey, do you mind shutting that thing off? I'd like to go to sleep."

"In a minute."

The minute stretched to fifteen.

Luther didn't think he'd ever been so angry at someone. "Look, I've got a splitting headache. Do you mind?"

Henry turned to look at his roommate. "You're not getting sick again, are you? You were doing so well. Was it the meatloaf?"

"Maybe. Or the pollen. Did you notice the SUVs are covered in a fine yellow dust?"

"Yeah. Are you allergic to anything? I've no idea what grows around here."

"I don't know either, but do you mind if we go to sleep now?" Luther switched off the light by his head.

Henry turned the TV and his bedside lamp off. Luther could hear him rustling around in the covers for what felt like an eternity. When Henry finished rustling, he punched his pillow several times before at last putting his head down and holding still. "Maybe it's the ride in the country that's got me all stirred up," he said. "All that fresh air."

"We never got out of the car."

"Maybe it's just the weather in general. You've got a headache, and I can't sleep. Must be a low front coming in. Or maybe it's a full moon."

"It's not a full moon." Luther had no idea if the moon was full or a crescent, but the last thing he wanted was Henry getting up and looking out the window. He turned his back to the other man and made sleeping noises: slow breathing, faint snoring sounds, deep slumbering breaths. Stiff with anticipation, he waited for Henry's snores. When at last they came, he slid out of bed and put on his street clothes with the stealth of a cat burglar. He held his shoes in his hand, opened and closed the door so carefully any noise it made fell below the range of human hearing.

He tiptoed down the hall to the stairs and crept down them to the bottom floor. *Damn.* A young man sat at the made-over reservation desk. Luther turned around and headed toward the neon exit sign. The door under it was locked. There were four exits and all of them were locked. Was this intentional? Were they really being held prisoners in this wretched Holiday Inn? Locked in at night? He leaned against a wall. He didn't remember seeing any fire escapes on the outside of the building. Could he climb or jump from his third-floor room? Yes, he thought he could, but there was the minor problem of waking Henry. He wondered how long the young man would stay in the lobby and why was he there at this time of night. Luther decided to see if he could find the stairs to the kitchen below.

"Where you headed, soldier?"

Luther snapped around. A man in a Nationalist uniform stood behind him. "Going somewhere, recruit?"

"Ah… I couldn't sleep, thought I'd get some fresh air."

"You didn't get enough fresh air today?"

"We stayed in the car."

"You'll get plenty of fresh air tomorrow. Now I suggest you go back to your room. Busy day tomorrow. You'll get all the exercise you need."

Luther lay clenched in his bed. He would get to Sloan's. There was no question of that. How was the question. Any farm boy worth his salt could hotwire a vehicle. But the SUV would be missed as soon as everyone went outside in the morning. He was certain he didn't need the car and could walk to her place. He felt stronger every day. But he'd be missed sooner than the vehicle. Would the Nationalists put together yesterday's trip to the country and his disappearance? God, it would be awful if he led them right to her. Maybe he could write a note saying he was going home. Better not take a car. They'd be sure to go looking for it. He'd leave as soon after dinner as possible, so he'd have the night to get to Sloan's.

Luther mulled over his possibilities. He decided tomorrow morning before roll call, he'd find the kitchen. After all, Henry knew where it was. He could just ask him, then do a quick reconnoiter so he would be able to get to it easily after dinner. Once there, while the kitchen crew was busy cleaning up, he'd slip quietly out the back door. He was sure it wouldn't be locked. Chefs were always stepping outside for cigarette breaks or a snort of cocaine.

When the knock came, along with a voice on the other side of the door calling out, "Rise and shine porcupine," he was still awake, nattering over details. He hadn't slept a wink. Jacked up on adrenaline, and the need to do something, anything, to protect Sloan, he wasn't tired at all. "Hey, Henry", he said, "how do you get to the kitchen?"

"Why do you want to know?"

"I thought I'd ask for poached eggs for breakfast. Easier on my stomach than the greasy scrambled eggs we usually get."

Henry sat up. "Geez, I hate getting up this early. So, you want poached eggs, do you? I think the chef will go along with that. I'll take you to him. It's easier than telling you how to get to the kitchen. Besides, he likes me."

Henry was right, the chef didn't mind, seemed to get a kick out of a big boy like Peter Jones wanting poached eggs. He even brought them to the dining room himself, making Luther cringe.

During roll call, the Master Sargent announced, "You girls are in for a treat today."

Luther felt gut punched.

Another Nationalist began handing out foot long batons. When everyone had one, the Master Sargent held his in his fist, snapped his wrist and it jumped to three feet long. "That's how you do it, boys. A girl could do it. Now give it a try." The room filled with the sound of snapping.

"See, easy as pie. Now get in your groups. You're going hunting. For men and women. Healthy men and women. Even better, find some obvious survivors. You know. Spots, hair loss, thin but otherwise healthy. Stay away from anyone who looks remotely sick. It'll be five of you to one or two of them. These billysticks will be more than enough to subdue them. Why not guns, you might ask. You'll get them in due time. Once we feel it's safe to arm you. You'll be riding in vans today with a place in the back for prisoners."

The new vans took up most of the parking lot. They must have arrived in the night. The fronts looked like regular SUVs, similar to those they had been riding in since the first day. But wire mesh separated the fronts from the large, covered backs where there were no seats, just a metal floor. The vehicles were huge. Luther wondered if they had been designed by a motor company for the Nationalists with a specific purpose in mind.

Luther looked at his fellow recruits. The faces of some were lit with excitement, others looked unsure, their faces tight and anxious.

"Aren't they even going to give us some training?" Henry said, nervously tapping his baton in the palm of his hand.

Captain Slater smiled unpleasantly. "This is going to be as easy as shooting fish in a barrel. You'll train by doing. Great way for us to find out if you've got what it takes."

"Captain, where will we be going?" Luther knew it was a reckless question but couldn't help asking.

Captain Slater looked at him long and hard. "Today it will be here in town. I'm telling you this because I'm in an especially good mood this morning. Don't question me again, recruit."

"Yes, sir." Luther saluted. The burst of relief that they weren't heading to Sloan's made him temporarily giddy.

Captain Slater didn't salute back. "What's your name, soldier?"

Luther almost blurted out his real name but caught himself. "Peter Jones, sir."

"I don't think I like you, Jones. We'll see if I do by the end of the day."

Heavy clouds hung low in the sky, forming an opaque cover over everything. A light mist fell, so fine it might be ignored, yet it turned the red brick buildings of Coleton a dark, flat brown and the damp sidewalks and cobblestones a dull gray. A block away from Main Street there wasn't a soul in sight until the van made a left turn, crossed the railroad tracks, and came on a slightly built man, walking down the sidewalk, hunched against the damp, hands in his pockets, head down.

Slater sped up to get in front of him then made a sharp left onto the sidewalk blocking the man's way. "Bring him down," he said.

Luther was the last recruit out of the van. Two others had opened the doors and jumped practically before the vehicle stopped. The young man turned and ran in the opposite direction. But the well fed, well rested Nationalists soon had him by the upper arms and yanked him around to put on cufflinks. Another Nationalist opened the doors to the back of the van. The two holding him pushed him in, where he fell on his face before scrambling onto his side then into a sitting position. Luther noticed he was just a boy, seventeen or eighteen at the most.

Everyone high-fived and shouted "Yeah" as they settled into their seats. Except for Luther, who looked out the window avoiding Slater's eyes.

The streetlights had come on along Main Street. It's the gloom, Luther thought. The shop window fronts were dark except for two, where dim lights faintly shone. Slater parked in front of one of them. He turned to the men behind him. "Jones, Henry, Gilbert, go inside. See who's there, corral them, and put them in the back.

"What if they outnumber us?" a recruit asked.

Slater adjusted the rearview mirror so his face could be seen by those in the back. He cocked an eyebrow. "Seriously?"

Henry leaned forward. "What if they're old? Or children?"

"Unless they're crippled, bring them out. They have that light on for a reason. Leave any kids under ten behind. You other two, get out and stand by the door for back-up."

The thin, yellow-spotted couple behind the counter already had their hands up when the recruits entered the shop. "It's just us," the man said. Luther watched as the couple came out to stand in front of them, their hands still in the air.

"Jones, you cuff 'em," Slater said. Luther hadn't noticed him come inside.

The cuffs were too big for the thin wrists. The dry, loose skin moved over bones when Luther clicked the metal shut.

"I love you," the man said to his wife.

"Shut him up," Slater said.

Luther touched the man's back with his baton.

Inside the van, the boy had his head on his knees. Luther could hear him crying. He and Henry half lifted; half pushed the couple inside. The ceiling, too low for them to stand, forced them to crawl forward on their knees. "Sit," Henry said, pushing the man's shoulder.

Luther waited a moment. He knew Slater was watching. He helped the man and woman to a sitting position anyway.

The Bell, named for the shape of the highest section of the city, was where the rich and fashionable people lived. The houses, built by expensive architects, were arranged in picturesque positions on large lawns with big, old trees and established gardens. Each house was different: stucco, clapboard, brick, cedar siding gracefully turning silver, and ivy-covered cottages. Most of the people who lived there were in their late thirties to mid-fifties, their children old enough to have been sent off to college or prep-school.

Half the residents were Republicans and had already contributed to Diamond's takeover either with money, information, or their sons and daughters. The other half no longer sent their children to public institutions but to remote vacation homes where hopefully they would be overlooked. Sometimes the parents joined them, but more often they stayed in their homes, trying desperately to keep their businesses going. Each week increasingly more stopped going to work, stayed inside, and became customers of the underground economy and, like the resistance, used the barter system as a means to exchange goods.

The Bell, as far as the Nationalists were concerned, was a gold mine. Houses filled with riches and adults past their prime, soft and easy to overcome yet with potential to be useful.

Slater drove the van slowly up the hill. A few people worked in the gardens in front of their houses. Two men washed cars in their driveways. One looked up and watched the van making its slow climb. He stood still for a moment then pointed his finger at a home across the street two houses up. White stucco, green shutters, overgrown lawn.

The owner of the house looked to be in his early forties. His wife, tall and thin, slipped away to another part of the house as soon as the Nationalists walked into the front hall. The husband had the physique of a man who took exceptionally diligent care of himself: flat stomach, large back and arm muscles, thighs like trees, excellent posture. Though hopelessly outnumbered, he gave the recruits a run for their money. He threw two on the floor, head locked another and socked him in the face. Finally, Slater, who had been watching, barked, "Finish him off, girls." Henry smacked the man over the head with his baton and he crumpled to the floor, out cold.

"Now go find the woman and hurry up about it."

Luther stood in the doorway of what he assumed was the master bedroom. It was entirely white: the walls, the carpet, the bed covers. Even the brick fireplace was painted white. He wondered idly if the owners ever made love in this pristine fairytale room. He stared at the white brick, unable to pull his thoughts together until he noticed some small flecks of soot on the floor. He walked over, kneeled, and looked up the chimney. Something blocked the light. Maybe the flue was closed, except Luther could see it wasn't. He waited; his head as high up the opening as possible. Nothing but black. Then the slightest thump. A few specks of charred material fell around his head and onto the white brick floor. He heard footsteps coming down the hall, stood and dusted himself off just as Gilbert walked through the door.

"Nothing here," said Luther. "Did you check the attic?"

"Some others are doing that."

They couldn't find the woman, but Slater didn't mind. When they left the Bell, the van held eight prisoners squeezed in the back, four on each side, half of them survivors. Slater was a happy man. At the bottom of the bell, Luther saw the same girl he had seen on his first trip through Coleton, her ponytail flying as she ran into an alley. Slater stomped on the brakes and shouted, "Go!" Two men jumped out and grabbed her in less than a minute. Like shooting fish in a barrel. The two recruits threw her face down on the eight other captives' feet, not bothering to cuff her.

Slater had to look for a parking place. Along with the SUVs they had used before today and the new vans, what looked like regulation army trucks, with their exteriors painted in camouflage, filled the Holiday Inn's parking lot. He finally pulled into a spot on the edge next to the woods. "Unload and go around to the back with our friends. Captain Riddick and I will go with you. Use your batons if you have to." Slater opened his door.

Luther realized he had forgotten the captain in the passenger seat. Riddick hadn't spoken a word during the whole trip.

Only the girl fought them. She bit two recruits, scratched another, and kicked them all. Luther managed to be the one to finally handcuff her and whispered in her ear not to struggle. He said this with his head bent as he clicked the bracelets shut. He flicked a quick glance at Slater, who stood watching him, his face hard. Luther roughly shoved the girl two steps then grabbed her shirt collar and yanked her toward the back of the building. The last thing he wanted was to have Slater or any Nationalist thinking he was soft or worse, that he sympathized with the captives. He would find a way out of this hell this evening. He wished he could take the girl with him, but he couldn't.

He planned to slip into the kitchen after dinner when he could be just one of the men who filled the halls and elevators on the way to their rooms while others lingered, talking, in the dining room over cooling cups of coffee.

Henry was always one of the coffee drinkers, affably going over the events of the day. He'd have a mouthful to talk about this evening. Usually, Luther sat with him. Tonight, he would say, "I'm done in. I guess I'm still a little under the weather. I'm gonna hit the hay early," then he would go upstairs and arrange the pillows on his bed to look as though he slept soundly under the covers. Timing would be tricky. It needed to be dark when he slipped outside. He hoped the chef wouldn't notice him or even better would have already left. He couldn't worry about the rest of the kitchen staff.

## CHAPTER TWENTY-THREE

Luther fell in with the stream of recruits and prisoners walking or stumbling to the back of the hotel where they found a large metal corrugated building. The door, split in the middle, had large wide sides and a heavy bar holding them closed. He noticed a round cupola on the roof, the kind with a fan designed to pull air from the inside out. Slater, who had somehow gotten there before them, unlocked the padlock. The structure looked newly built, and Luther wondered if it had been made for the singular purpose of holding prisoners. When he forced the girl inside, he saw a sea of faces in various forms of anguish. The faces of the recruits didn't register. He turned to the girl. "Don't make trouble. It won't do you any good."

She stared into his face. "Let me go."

Luther removed his hand from her shirt collar. She shook her shoulders to loosen them and looked around. Luther saw her face harden with grim determination and felt stung with shame. If he had half her gumption and savvy, he wouldn't be in this God-awful mess, wandering around confused and sickened by a half-baked plan to escape. He recognized in her not only the will and strength to survive, but the steely character to endure what she needed to endure without wasting energy on self-doubt.

At Slater's direction, the recruits shoved their prisoners toward the back of the building. The sides were steel, and Luther took note of the lack of windows. The day had remained overcast, the sun well hidden, but when the clouds burned off, this place would turn into an oven. He looked down at the cement floor.

"Listen up." It was Slater. "You boys don't need to do any more today. Just keep your catch as far toward the back as possible. Don't want anyone slipping free."

Luther turned and looked over his shoulder. Men in uniforms strong-armed a variety of men, women, and young adults through the door. He guessed this was the last of them.

Slater stood to the side and watched the people pass. "Okay. Not bad for a first day's work. Now clean up and get ready for dinner." Not being allowed to change out of their uniforms, cleaning up meant washing and disinfecting their hands, scrubbing their faces, shaving, and combing their hair.

He stayed put for a moment, surreptitiously looking for a source of water. At first, he couldn't find one then he noticed on the right side toward the back of the building a faucet sticking out of the steel. At least these poor souls had water to drink. Being careful to avoid Slater's eyes, he followed the other recruits heading toward the door.

The reception room teemed with men, some in uniform, some not. Most of them Luther didn't recognize. A group carried what looked like metal bed frames toward the hall.

"Who are all these people and what do you think those things they're carrying are?" Henry said, suddenly by Luther's side.

"They look like bedframes. And I have no idea who these people are."

"Why bring in new beds? Jesus, you don't think they're bringing in new men, do you? I'm sure as hell not going to share our room with someone else."

"They said that might happen, remember?"

"Come on. Let's go look."

Walking to their room, they passed two of the new men, dressed in t-shirts and jeans, heading toward the elevator. "What do you think they were doing up here? They'd better not be putting beds in our rooms."

"I've no idea, and why are you so rattled? So what if we have an extra guy in the room?"

Henry quickened his pace. He slid the key card in the slot and flung the door open. Sure enough, a small metal bed lined up between Luther's bed and the window. A pillow, blanket, and sheets lay stacked in the middle of the mattress. "Oh, my God, oh my God," Henry said, and threw himself onto his own bed, rolled onto his back and stared at the ceiling, one arm under his head. "I'm not putting up with this," he mumbled.

The captains and sergeants never sat with the recruits during meals. Luther thought this foolish on their part. After the first night, the same men sat at the same tables and a camaraderie developed, allowing words of dissent to be spoken by some men. They mocked or complained about their captains, the accommodations, or the lack of information about the purpose of this mission. In Luther's opinion, if left unchecked, this atmosphere could lead to a subversive sub-group. Not that that was a bad thing. He was merely surprised the officers hadn't thought of the possibility.

Anyway, it had nothing to do with him. He just wanted to keep a low profile and never responded to the negative remarks. Brass around or not, he knew better than to disparage their situation to anyone. Grumbling to each other could seem harmless, but you never knew.

Tonight, no one said a word. Even the usually affable Henry didn't talk. He'd been silent in the elevator on the way down as well, looking like the stuffing had been kicked out of him. Luther whispered, "You really gonna talk to someone about the bed?"

Henry didn't answer.

Around the table the faces were blank, eyes averted. An eerie hush settled over them all and the dining room was quiet, the sound of silverware touching plates the only sound. Everyone kept their head down and concentrated on their food. God, what have we done, Luther thought. It was extraordinary to him that men could be turned into thugs so easily. Or, if not thugs, be persuaded to act, at least for a day, like brutes. He couldn't get his mind off the girl he had violated. That was the way he thought of it. He had grabbed hold of her, imprisoned her, thrown her into a cage and left her there… at the very least to suffer alone with no idea what her future would be or worse, to be raped and/or killed. He struggled in his mind to find a way to take her with him, but nothing worked, the impossibility a solid wall he couldn't break through.

"Will you look at that," said Henry.

The new men, still not in uniforms, filed into the dining room, all of them carrying backpacks. Luther noticed for the first time extra tables had been set up. He'd missed this in the muddled haze of planning his escape and worrying about the girl. These new men didn't look like the original recruits. They moved with authority, not one of them looked around trying to figure things out. They found seats and waited to be served as if they had been doing it all their lives. Luther made special note of the backpacks.

Words in a hushed tone hummed around the table. The men looked from one to the other, their eyes bright with questions.

One of the sergeants stood. "We have some new soldiers with us. They will be sharing your rooms. Make them welcome." He sat down.

"That was short and sweet," said Gilbert.

"I am not, I mean I am *not* sharing a room with anyone but Luther." Henry glared at the other men.

Luther had never trusted his roommate, but this commitment to their connection touched and saddened him. Little does he know, he thought. Another person betrayed.

"Good luck with that," someone said.

Henry looked around the table. No one met his eyes.

"I wouldn't make a fuss," another man said.

Henry stared at him. His face had gone blotchy with anger. He turned to Luther. "What do you think about this?"

"I don't know. Maybe we should just wait and see. I mean, we don't have much to say about it. Don't go getting yourself in trouble. Let's just do nothing until we find out what it's like."

Henry grunted and looked away.

Luther took another bite of steak, slid the steak knife into his pocket then asked to be excused and left the table.

I will not feel guilty, he told himself as he closed the door to their room behind him. He couldn't believe his luck. Or perhaps he could. The confusion created by the arrival of new Nationalists could be a sign, he reasoned, a sign from God telling him not only was it his mission to warn Sloan, but God himself would make it easier. Originally, Luther had thought if he took his backpack, it would be an instant give away. He'd have to go without it, leaving him with no change of clothes, shoes, or basic toiletries. Now he'd fit right in. He removed his uniform, changed into a t-shirt and jeans, and stuffed the military clothes into the pack to be thrown away later. He added a change of clothes and sundries then wrote a quick note for Henry, saying he was going home. He hurried out of the room. His only problem would be running into someone who knew him. Praying, he pressed the elevator button, thought better of it, and turned toward the stairs. He heard the doors swoosh open. His luck or God's intervention held, and the elevator stood empty.

The halls were filled with men, originals and new. Head down, Luther slipped to the stairs leading to the kitchen. He straightened his shoulders, put on an impassive face, and looking straight ahead, walked through the swinging door past the people cleaning up and out the exit. The corrugated building rose black and solid in the long shadow of the woods. Luther refused to think of the girl, refused to wonder how he would find his way when it turned dark in two hours. When he came to the parking lot, he refused to look at the vehicles parked there. He refused to wonder if people gathered or walked among the cars. He stayed under tree branches, not venturing into the woods for fear of getting lost. He slowly let out his breath, which he hadn't realized he'd been holding.

Halfway to the road, Luther thought he heard a noise. A rustling. He froze. Silence. Then the noise came again. He didn't know if he should run or stay silent. His question was answered when a skinny redheaded boy burst out of the woods. He looked past Luther toward something behind him. The something turned out to be Captain Riddick.

"Who's this," demanded the redhead.

"A new recruit," Riddick said mildly.

"Why's he out here? You're supposed to come alone." The boy swayed and jerked, his eyes darting left and right.

"Good question," Riddick walked around to face Luther. "You want to tell me what you're doing out here with your backpack."

Luther said nothing.

"You wouldn't be thinking about leaving, would you?"

"Shoot him," the boy said distractedly. With his swaying and jittery behavior, he looked like he might streak back into the woods any second.

Riddick watched Luther's face. "You're Peter Jones. You ride with Slater and me. Somehow you don't show the same enthusiasm as the other boys do."

"No?"

"Uh-huh."

The men took each other's measure. Finally, Riddick said, without taking his eyes off Luther, "Rusty, this is a reluctant recruit who I think is planning to leave us tonight."

"To go home," said Luther. "My parents are very sick."

Riddick sighed. "You're already in deep trouble. Why don't you just tell me the truth?" He turned to Rusty. "A major move is taking place. Men are being brought here plus drones with the ability to detect human activity from the air. There is talk of helicopters. A sweep is going to happen, looking for some girl who is connected to Whitbeck. Tell your compatriots to be extremely careful. To lie low, go into deep hiding. We've been out to Will's Creek and Sommerset County. They definitely plan on going back. Make sure your buddies know that."

Rusty nodded and started back to the woods.

"Wait a minute, son. Maybe you could escort this reluctant soldier somewhere away from here."

"Okay," said Rusty, and he whirled into the trees.

"Go," Riddick said, "before he leaves without you, or someone sees you."

Luther vanished into the woods where he at once saw the red head climbing onto an all-terrain motorcycle he'd recently stolen.

"Where you want to go?" Rusty said, grabbing hold of the handlebars.

"Out past Savage."

The boy started the engine and hit the gas while Luther was putting his leg over the seat. He grabbed Rusty's waist as the cycle bucked and leaped forward.

# CHAPTER TWENTY-FOUR

Shimmer returned to Georgetown at five-thirty that evening. Sonny met him at the door, took his elbow, and guided him down the steps and up the inclining sidewalk. They walked to the end of the block, turned left, then at the end of Lafayette Street, turned right, walked two blocks, made another left then through an alley that ended in a waist-high stone wall. Shimmer enjoyed looking at this particular part of DC with its deceptively modest, tall, narrow brick houses, old trees, wrought iron fences, and the brick sidewalks through which small tufts of grass grew. Sonny sat on the wall.

Shimmer sat next to him. He waited.

Sonny sat up straight, crossed his legs, and folded his arms. "We gather info here; we gather info there. We try to put it together and try to make sense of it then pass it along to the people who need to know and maybe save some lives."

"Yes, that's pretty much what we do."

"But we're not really changing anything. The United States of America is broken. The 'great experiment' is over.

"Saving lives, this not a small thing," Shimmer said, slightly offended.

"I don't mind telling you, Jamie, I'm discouraged. I hate what this country has become. And I hate Diamond so much I'd shoot him in the heart, up close and personal, if it weren't for Lena. I might be able to get away, it's not impossible, but it's unlikely. Besides, he was elected president. The operative word being elected. Half the country is behind him. They have the same bigoted, hate-filled mind he does. And they're too stupid to realize he doesn't give a rat's ass about them. All he cares about is power and money." Sonny sighed.

"We are putting much effort into keeping this girl away from his fists. Presumably, Whitbeck's monies is of great importance. Without it, would the tyranny of Diamond fall?"

"I don't know if it would fall. But we'd probably go from the inflation we have now to a serious depression. I'm just a hired gun. What do I know about the flow of money? What I do know is Americans are brave, violent, pig-headed, and ruthless. They will not be contained or compelled for long. You've heard the expression 'like herding cats.' Keeping this country under autocratic rule isn't like herding cats, it's like herding wild water buffalo; a more dangerous and unpredictable creature it would be hard to find. It's costing heaps to pay the workers enough to keep them satisfied or paying guards to control them. And Diamond's pretty much broke. The Fed can't help. Printing more money is a waste of time. There's a story about what it was like after the civil war. A woman carried her money to market in a wheelbarrow to buy a loaf of bread. She got distracted and when she turned around, someone had stolen the wheelbarrow, leaving the money to blow away. But we've talked about this before, haven't we? And you're right. It's just talk."

"So, this president is no Hitler with the smarts to organize all those peoples and wage a world war. Thank God, right? Hitler had money from other countries too. Not Diamond. People in other countries hate him. I think everyone hates him except these stupid Americans. This is all good for us." Smiling, Shimmer cuffed Sonny lightly on the shoulder.

Sonny frowned at him. "Diamond's smart enough to seduce the military, intimidate Congress, stack the supreme court, but you're right, he hasn't a clue how to keep the supply chain rolling. He's not only a moron when it comes to the running of a country, but it bores him, so he delegates and doesn't bother to follow through. Can't think beyond his nose or dick."

"This is all good for us. So, cheer up. Your face is all tight." Shimmer kicked his heel in a staccato against the stone wall. "Do you really think the daughter is all Whitbeck cares about? He has other children, no? A wife. Diamond could easily do them harm."

Sonny stared at his friend. "You know he's a pedophile, right? And apparently, is very democratic in his perversions. Little girls up to late adolescents. As long as the teenagers aren't fat. I've seen pictures of Whitbeck's daughter. Stick thin with cantaloupe boobs that look like they've been super glued to her. He likes boys too, until they come close to puberty."

"I thought pedophiles only had certain preferences."

"Not always. There are several types."

"How is it you know so much about it?"

"FBI. Used to work there then switched over to the Secret Service. Little did I know." Sonny put his hand on Shimmer's leg. "Would you mind? Stop kicking the wall. It's driving me nuts." He pulled his hand away quickly.

"It helps me think. I don't like sitting still. This Rosemary? How old is she?"

"Sixteen, I guess." Sonny watched a woman walk by. Her skin was clear, and she was in good weight. He waited till she had turned the corner. "I guess Whitbeck doesn't care that much about his wife, poor woman. Must be awful knowing your husband's money is more important to him than you are. No leverage there. And the sons are up Diamond's ass."

Shimmer started thumping his heel again. "You are saying the country elected him. They think same as him. But I am certain they don't like the not having supplies, food, buying everything in government stores with prices to the sky. Some, many, will have changed their minds about this president. And do not forget there is the other half of the country. The ones that didn't vote for him."

"It's not like there is going to be another election to vote him out. And the other thing, Jamie, those people are afraid to use the air waves to communicate. This gives the Nationalists a huge advantage. Huge."

"Yes, this is true. That is why we continue to run around delivering messages." Shimmer gave a Russian-esque shrug. "Besides, the generals are starting to turn." He slung his arm around Sonny's neck and jostled him. "Don't be so gloomy. Does no good. Come on, smile."

Sonny hopped off the wall. "Let's keep walking. I don't like that woman passing by us. I've never seen her before. She's nicely dressed. Obviously, pro-Diamond. I don't like it."

Shimmer looked where she had gone.

Sonny put his hands in his pockets. "Everyone in this neighborhood is pro-Diamond or they pretend to be. Successfully. Like me. Turn here." They walked in silence for a minute then he continued, "How did your day go?"

"Slow. Everyone keeps their heads and eyes on the floor in front of them. They are scared. Nobody's talking. I only saw Mike for a little bit. He say all hell is breaking loose. The Whitbecks are locked up in Blair House tighter than ever. No word in. No word out. Why does the President ask you to stay the night?"

Sonny laughed. "He's a big baby, really. Like all bullies. The idiot tells me everything he's thinking when we're in his bedroom alone."

Shimmer studied Sonny's profile. With the dark blond hair neatly swept back in a wave, the beautifully proportioned forehead, Roman nose, clean jawline, and strong chin, he could have been a Roman gladiator. Yet his light blue eyes were kind. No wonder Diamond trusted him.

"Turn here." Sonny nodded toward another alley on the right. "He's so frustrated by Whitbeck's disloyalty it practically makes him cry. You should see him. Plus, he's desperate. He's putting all his hope into finding that girl in Coleton. But it's not just about saving the economy. He can't stand the fact he can't force Whitbeck to talk. He's like a four-year-old having a tantrum." Sonny paused then continued. "I managed to talk to four people today. We can get you out as soon as it's dark."

Shimmer looked up. The air had the blue cast of an East coast early-summer evening. The gloaming, people called it.

Sonny glanced sideways at his friend. "I'm sorry about Sloan."

"Yes. Is too bad. Tell her I am sorry. She will understand, I think. Perhaps not. Is hard to say with women. I hope she does. Be tender with her. How long before you can send her back?"

"We'll get her to Coleton as soon as possible. She's a huge asset in Blair House, though."

"I know this."

Sonny stopped walking. "There's something else. Without her six-week booster, the vaccine is much less effective."

"Sloan will not stay here another five weeks."

Sonny didn't respond. They walked another block in silence until Shimmer asked, "Would you regret it?"

"What?"

"Killing the president."

Sonny snorted. "No. No, I wouldn't. Not for an instant. I'm Catholic. I believe in the merciful Lord Jesus Christ. I believe it is a mortal sin to murder. I don't know of any absolution for it. But I'd do it anyway, every day of the week and twice on Sunday. Now at the end of this block, take a left, at the end, turn right and keep walking. You'll come to my house. I'll meet you there. I really don't like that woman walking by us like that."

The minute Sloan walked into the kitchen, Rose said, "Mrs. W wants you upstairs right now with her soup."

Sloan started for the refrigerator.

"I've been keeping some warm here on the stove."

Sloan stared at her for a moment. "Can you get the turkey out of the fridge?"

Rose reached into her apron pocket and pulled out the bottle of rum. "This what you're looking for? Or did you really want the turkey?"

Sloan's eyes grew round. Then she laughed. "Nothing gets by you, does it."

"Nope. I'd put in a hefty amount if I was you. She's been wailin' all night and half the morning."

Mrs. Whitbeck had been frail when Sloan first met her. Now she looked as though she had been dead for three days and was more than ready to pass to the other side. Her blond hair had gone white.

Mr. Whitbeck, dressed in a golf shirt and khakis, stood at the foot of her bed. His posture, the thrust of his jaw, the downward turn of his mouth and the knife sharp crease in his slacks all screamed military, though Sloan knew he'd never served. He'd always been too busy making money. She carried the bowl to a dresser across the room to keep him from smelling the rum. Hopefully, he would leave soon. She squared her shoulders and folded her hands in front of her as though she were standing in the aisle waiting to take communion.

"Please! Bring the soup to me," Mrs. Whitbeck said, an edge to her tone.

Sloan went back to the dresser, gathered the bowl between her hands, passed the man, and placed it on the breakfast tray already across the spectral woman's lap. Having done this, she didn't know what to do next, so she nodded briefly at Mrs. Whitbeck and turned to leave.

"Don't go. Stay with me for a while."

"I've got a turkey to prepare for dinner tonight." Sloan glanced at Mr. Whitbeck. "I'll come back later. Now I'll give you and your husband some privacy."

"Don't!" Mary snapped.

Sloan tried to make herself invisible or at least to vanish into the pale pink wallpaper. The air grew heavy until Mr. Whitbeck barked, "Are you the head chef?"

"I am. Yes." Don't, Sloan told herself. Keep your hackles down and your voice neutral. Do not pick a fight with this man.

Mrs. Whitbeck raised the bowl to her lips and finished off the broth. She leaned back against her pillows. "Sit next to me, Sloan."

Mr. Whitbeck pulled the upholstered chair next to his wife and commanded Sloan with his eyes to sit in it. "What are you putting in that soup?"

"What?"

"You seem to have bewitched my wife. She's through with the rest of us, but you she wants to sit by her side."

"Well, it's important how you poach the chicken. You must keep the water just below the boil. Then the veggies must be treated gently as well, just sautéed long enough to sweat them. You don't want any brown. Now the spices and herbs…"

*"Stop it!* That's not what I mean, and you know it."

Much to Sloan's surprise, he sat on the side of the bed, his shoulders slumped. "You live with Sonny Caravaggio, don't you? Sonny and his wife… Lena, I think it is."

Sloan hesitated.

"Oh, don't worry. I'm not spying on you. I know he's a favorite of the president. Anyone who Sonny speaks for gets a free pass. Everyone knows that. Even me here in prison. Cut off from the world. I'm just wondering if you're aware of the mess I've gotten myself into. Do people talk about me? How much do they know?"

"Not much." Sloan almost said sir before she caught herself. She'd never thought of using that word with any other man.

"Who else lives there?"

"One of the painters."

"One of the painters. I see. Another friend of Sonny's, I suppose." Whitbeck sighed deeply. "Here's the thing. I've gone as far as I can in this brave new world. It has pushed my moral compass to the breaking point. Diamond has given me an impossible choice. A lose, lose situation. I'm rotten to the core, have broken all the commandments." Mary stirred under the covers. "But there is one thing, one true and fine thing that has come out of this cesspool I have made of my life. And that's my daughter. She is innocent of malice and greed and the dreadful things people do to achieve power, doesn't even think about them because she isn't aware of their existence. And I've set her loose, abandoned her, left her behind." At this point Whitbeck bent his head, put both index fingers to his eyes and began to sob. Horrified, Sloan looked at Mary.

Whitbeck's wife hadn't raised herself from the pillows. She stared ahead as though nothing was happening.

Sloan hadn't been this unsure, this confused throughout the entire takeover. She rutched in her chair. The sight of this powerful man crying made her feel ill. She couldn't think of a thing to say or do.

Finally, Whitbeck raised his head and ran the sides of his fingers under his eyes. "You see, I don't even know where she is. I left her in the safest place I could think of… but all alone." He began to cry again, the tears running down his slack cheeks. "It all happened so fast; I couldn't get her out of the country with people I know and trust. But I'm a prisoner here. I have no way of communicating with anyone."

"Are you thinking I could maybe help? Get word out for you?"

Whitbeck stopped crying. "Could you?"

"Yup."

He eyed her suspiciously. "You really think so?" It was a testimony to the man's distress that he would consider, even for an instant, taking help from a young woman, let alone a subservient one.

"Yes, I do, I really think so."

Whitbeck turned away from her. "This is absurd. How can you be of help?"

A spark flamed in Sloan. She couldn't stop herself. "I know where Rosemary is," she said. Her skin instantly stung all over; sweat prickled at her hairline. Jesus, her temper was going to get her killed one day.

Whitbeck looked as though Sloan had stabbed him with a dagger. He opened then shut his mouth. For a moment he appeared stunned into helplessness. A void hung in the room until finally he collected himself and looked at Sloan with hatred. "You're lying."

"All right. If you want to think that, it's no skin off my nose." Sloan stared back at him, her green eyes flat and hard. Go ahead, she thought. You see me as nothing, a speck, something you would step on if it were in your way. Go ahead and think I'm lying. She looked away. As mad as he made her, she was sweating with relief at his dismissal of her slip-up.

Mary struggled off her pillows and grabbed Sloan's wrist with the strength of the living dead. "If you know where my daughter is, you *will* tell me."

Sloan had known since she entered the room, this woman wasn't going to make it. What was it like to have a daughter disappear? Look how her mother suffered over Annie. And she was just a friend. Sloan winced. Just a friend. What a despicable thing to think. But losing a child. There was no greater hell. She leaned forward and under the guise of removing the woman's hand from her wrist, got in close enough to whisper in Mary's ear, "She's safe. Diamond won't find her."

## CHAPTER TWENTY-FIVE

**W**hitbeck rose and squared his shoulders. "Come with me. What's your name, anyway?"

Sloan couldn't remember if she'd told him or Mary her name, and if she did, what it was. She blurted out Sloan Rafferty, a nice compromise.

"You, come with me."

Sloan followed him out the door, down the stairs, and into what she assumed was the living room. Whitbeck walked to the drinks table and poured three fingers of single malt. He turned to Sloan. "Sit," he said, and she did. "If I thought there was a five percent chance you knew where my daughter was, I'd have it out of you before you left the room."

Sloan waited.

"But how would you possibly know anything about her?" He took a deep swallow and stared into space. The man's shoulders sagged again and the loosened flesh on his face created deep folds around his mouth. He sat in a chair opposite Sloan. "Where are you from?"

"Nebraska."

"Where in Nebraska?"

Sloan didn't know a city in Nebraska. "Billings."

"There's no Billings in Nebraska."

"No, I meant Billings, Montana."

Whitbeck lifted the glass to his lips without taking his eyes off Sloan. After he swallowed, he said, "You said Nebraska."

"No? Did I? I meant Montana."

"You're a lying little guttersnipe."

Guttersnipe. That was a new one. Sweat ran down her sides.

"How did you get to the White House?"

"I went to the CIA, you know, the cooking school. Not the spy agency. And then I found a job in DC. I met Sonny and Lena there, and this job at Blair House came along, and Sonny recommended me."

"What restaurant did you work at here in DC?"

Sloan hesitated. Whitbeck wasn't allowed any form of device where he could Google something. "Sally's Sauce."

"Why did you tell me you knew where my daughter was?" Some of Whitbeck's presence had returned. Sloan could see how he could intimidate people around a boardroom table.

"I was scared. I just blurted it out to distract you."

Whitbeck looked genuinely surprised. "Distract me from what?"

"The rum. I put it in your wife's soup. It helps relax her. She knows you wouldn't like it, being she's an alcoholic and all."

For an instant, the man appeared dumbfounded. Then he turned angry. "Does she really think I care if she drinks herself to death? For God's sake. How would I know if you were putting rum in her soup, anyway?"

"You could smell it. At least, I thought so."

"You really are a sneaky little thing, aren't you. I'd fire you if I could, but I have lost control of everything. Does Mary know what a liar you are? I could break your arm. They'd have to let you go then. Or better still, your knees." Whitbeck stood and walked toward Sloan. He looked around the room. His eyes settled on an obsidian bust, three feet tall, shaped roughly like a baseball bat, on the mantle over the fireplace next to Sloan.

What would my mother do now, she wondered. The answer was clear. The man was split in two. His precious financial empire on one hand, the only good and fine thing that could possibly redeem him, on the other. Sloan stood up. "I'll be going now. I've got a turkey to prepare for dinner tonight," she said into the yawning emptiness between those two illusions.

Rose was all atwitter about Mary and her terrible cries the night before and early this morning, so loud they could be heard even in the kitchen. She peppered Sloan with questions, but only received vague, distracted answers, so she stopped and helped Sloan in silence as she prepared the turkey for the oven.

Sloan chopped and ground the herbs and spices, made a compound butter with them, and slathered it under and over the bird's skin, sautéed celery and onion, seasoned hand-pulled bread cubes and stuffed the turkey, all in a haze of anxiety and dread. When she shut the oven door, she prepared a glass of *English Afternoon* tea with ice and a teaspoon of sugar and carried it upstairs to Mrs. Whitbeck's room. She knocked on the closed door, heard a surprisingly strong, "Come in," entered to find the woman sitting bolt upright, eyes huge in their deep, shadowed sockets. "Can you help me find my daughter?" she asked.

Sloan placed the sweating glass of tea on a tray by the bed. "I've brought you some iced tea. There's no rum in it. Yes, I can help you find your daughter, but you are going to have to help me as well." She sat on the edge of the bed, holding up her hand when Mary started to speak. "Let me finish. To help me, you must be functional. I will still bring your rum, but not as much. Your husband, by the way, will fire me on the spot if he finds out I'm helping you drink." There was no point in letting the woman know she had free rein with the alcohol.

Mary started to wail. This time it was Sloan who grabbed a wrist in a vise. "If you want to see your daughter again, you will listen to me. Now stop all this caterwauling and think. I need to know exactly what your husband is doing day by day. He has five days before Diamond goes looking for your daughter." Sloan dropped Mary's wrist and moved her hands, palms up, mimicking a scale. "His money or his daughter. You need to get out of this bed and this bedroom and go downstairs and find out."

"He won't talk to me."

"Apologize for your behavior. Tell him you'll do better, you're on his side. You want Rosemary back as much as he does. You'll think of something, for heaven's sake. You've been married to him for forever."

"I don't think I can do it."

"You do it or you'll never see your daughter again."

The two women stared at each other. Sloan said, "You need a bath. I'll wait. Wash your hair. And hurry up before he comes in and finds us talking."

When Mary came out of the bathroom, Sloan gently combed the snarls out of her hair. She dusted the faintest pink blush under her cheek bones. No eye make-up, no lipstick, certainly no foundation. Sloan suspected Mr. Whitbeck was the kind of man who could sniff out a mercenary seduction better than most, and would be meaner than most when he did, even if it was his wife. She went to the closet and picked out a simple blue cotton frock. "Now get dressed and go downstairs. If you get too anxious, have a drink, just enough to take the edge off. If you are tempted to drink more, just think of Rosemary. Go to dinner. I will try to get a peek to see how you're doing. Don't talk about me to your husband. He'd have me drawn and quartered if he could."

Sloan followed directly behind Rose on her way to the dining room. She'd been unsure how to play this out. Would Mr. Whitbeck be aroused at seeing her again and say something or even kick her out? If she sent Rose, would he question why? She talked to the girl and then decided Rose would go first and if anybody asked where the chef was, Sloan would step in and carve.

When the door opened, Sloan peeked over Rose's shoulder. Mrs. Whitbeck was sitting upright, listing neither to the right nor to the left. She didn't appear out of control. She did look frightened, but then so did her husband. The door closed behind Rose. Sloan waited. There were no raised voices, and Rose did not appear back in the hall for about ten minutes then came out smiling. "No one noticed me at all."

"Thank god for the eternally rich," Sloan said. "We're interchangeable parts to them. Most of the time."

J. Compton-Case

## CHAPTER TWENTY-SIX

That night Luther entered another orbit, one that had little to do with gravity, the laws of physics, or earth's deadly coil. Rusty never decelerated when he reached the summit of a hill. He either flew down the other side or hovered in mid-air like a cartoon before landing with a crash in the middle of the next mountain. At times Luther's buttocks were two feet off the seat, his mad grip around Rusty's middle the only thing connecting him to the bike. Rusty whipped around trees, slinging Luther left and right. Small branches slashed his face, the bigger ones came close to killing him before he could duck. They came to a rocky spot, the bouncing cycle nearly causing him to bite off his tongue. All sense of time left him. He wasn't afraid but was aware he didn't want to die. All his thoughts focused on what was directly in front of him. As night approached, the trees turned to silhouettes. Rusty turned on a dusty light, narrowing Luther's attention even more as they hurtled behind it. Suddenly the cycle's roar stopped, and the rear wheel skidded to the right. They were engulfed in a silent dark. Rusty hopped off the seat and somehow managed to duck around trees and trotted out of the woods. "Stay here," he called over his shoulder.

Luther listened to him disappear then dismounted, put his hand on a tree trunk, bent over and vomited. When he was done, he straightened up and walked through the woods, feeling his way to a clearing where Rusty trotted toward a large, irregular black form. The full moon made it possible to see it once you were outside of the trees.

Rusty stopped in front of the black presence and jerking and swaying communicated with whatever it was. As Luther's eyes adjusted to the dark, he made out a horse with a human standing nearby. Rusty gestured urgently then turned on his heel and ran back toward Luther. As he passed him, he said, "That's Clare Raffienne. I told her about you. Go."

The cycle roared to life and Luther walked forward on his own. The woman—he could make out the person's sex now—ran her hand over the horse's back, down the long haunch, along the dip before the hock, over the hock, hesitated then continued down the bottom of the leg, around the fetlock and rested on the hoof. She leaned her shoulder onto the side of the horse, lifted the hoof, and began doing something to its underside. She carefully returned the hoof to the ground, straightened, and faced him. Sloan hadn't talked much about her mother, but what she'd said left Luther with a feeling of uneasy admiration.

Now as he walked toward her, her absolute stillness made him want to run in the opposite direction. He tried to remember exactly what Sloan had said about her, but his mind was blank. The horse began to nibble at the sparse grass.

It became harder and harder to approach the dark figure, but he forced himself, putting one foot in front of the other. When he finally reached her, the moon gave off enough light to cause his mouth to go dry as he looked into the woman's inscrutable face. He managed to ask, "Did the redhead tell you who I am?"

"Rusty. The redhead's name is Rusty. He told me a little. You're not from around here, and Riddick said to bring you to my farm."

"Right. I was Sloan's sous-chef in New York. When we had to run, I went to Idaho where I grew up. When I got there, I found out my parents and my brothers had died from the virus. I got the virus too, so you don't have to worry about me infecting you." Luther paused and when the woman said nothing, he continued. "I decided to come here to find Sloan. She gave me her address. But I got caught up by the Nationalists in Coleton. They thought I was one of them and I had to go along with it. Until tonight, when Captain Riddick sent me here… so, here I am. Looking for Sloan."

Clare rested her hand on the horse's withers. "Sloan ain't here. She's gone off to DC to get information."

"DC?"

"Yeah. She went with Shimmer. He's in the resistance. Knows people everywhere."

The skin around Luther's eyes tightened. "Shimmer?"

"That's his nickname. Can't remember his real one. He's been here a while but comes from some place in Europe, I think. He's got an accent."

"Huh."

"Rusty said you had information."

Luther straightened his back. "Yes. Diamond's gathering forces to come here. In fact, a bunch of men came in tonight. To the Holiday Inn, where we are staying. They're supposed to be looking for some rich man's daughter so Diamond can torture her until this billionaire signs over his money to him. Sounds like a movie, doesn't it? Diamond's broke."

"Shimmer told us the troops would be here in a few days."

"Really? Well, they're bringing drones and helicopters too. Also…" Luther squared his shoulders and held his head higher. "They know about *this* place. I was with them when they drove by. Captain Slater said he was coming back to get your land. I'd already planned to leave to warn you tonight. Riddick caught me in the parking lot along with the redhead and told him to bring me here." He dropped his backpack on the ground.

"Rusty. The redhead's name is Rusty."

"Right."

Clare looked up at the moon, ran her hand over the horse's back, and turned her attention to Luther again. "You can stay here if you want and sleep on the couch. Or in Sloan's stall. She likes sleeping outside. It's clean and there's a mattress and sheets. The bed's made. Sloan always makes her bed."

Luther tried to absorb this. Did the women not understand the danger she was in?

"Do me a favor." Clare handed Luther the horse's lead shank. "Trot him in a circle around me. You ain't afraid of horses, are you?"

Luther clucked to the horse and trotted alongside him. Clare followed their movement with her eyes. "Okay, you can stop. He's got a bad hock," she said. "Hopefully rest and cold-water compresses will fix it." She paused, looking momentarily lost, then shrugged. "Course, we probly won't be able to do even that." She unbuckled the halter and pulled it over the horse's ears and pushed him gently away. "Go on, get something to eat."

"Won't he run off?"

"No, he'll stay close to the barn. So, where do you want to sleep tonight?"

Luther knew he couldn't sleep in Sloan's bed, inside or out. Not without her. "I'll sleep on the couch, thank you ma'am. Do you know if Sloan's okay?"

"She's all right. Let's go inside." She turned abruptly and started walking toward the house. "By the way, that girl you're talkin' about… she lives here."

Luther stopped in his tracks. "What girl do you mean? The one they're looking for?"

"Yeah, I thought they wouldn't find us."

Luther couldn't see a thing in the unlit kitchen until he heard a match strike and a candle flame flickered.

"You thirsty?"

"Sure."

Clare retrieved a tin pitcher from the refrigerator and filled a glass with water. Luther drank it straight down.

Clare refilled his glass. "You hungry?"

"No… um, maybe a little. Don't want to put you out, though. I know food's scarce."

"Bear jerky or biscuits? I made the biscuits early this evening."

Luther's stomach rolled at the thought of bear jerky. "Biscuits would be fine."

Clare put a plate covered with a cloth on the table and sat down. Luther sat across from her, lifted the cloth and picked up a golden-brown-craggy piece of cooked dough very similar to what his mother used to make. He nibbled at it. The biscuit melted in his mouth.

"You can have another."

"No, thank you. One's enough." He stared at Clare. So, this was Sloan's mother. There was a physical resemblance, though the coloring couldn't have been more different.

"Didn't your mama teach you not to stare." Clare smiled.

"You really have that girl living here? Aren't you terrified?"

"I told you; I didn't think they'd find us."

"What are you going to do?"

"Hide."

Luther looked around the kitchen as if he could find an answer. "Where?"

"These mountains stretch a fair distance. I'm not sure exactly where." Clare's voice didn't sound as friendly as it had. She went to the cupboard and brought out a bottle with brown liquid inside and filled his water glass halfway. "Drink this," she said, handing it to him. "So you can sleep."

Luther sniffed it. Liquor of some kind. "I don't think my liver can handle it."

"Sip it then." Clare left and returned with a pillow and a sheet, which she dropped on the couch. "I'm going to bed," she said.

Luther listened to her walking up the stairs then placed the pillow against the arm of the couch and pulled the sheet over himself. The world's gone mad, he thought, as though he'd just realized it.

# CHAPTER TWENTY-SEVEN

**C**lare knew the land around her so well she could find her way in the dark. Even so, she brought the little horse out of the barn to tack him up in the moonlight. Narrow through the chest and ribs, slab shouldered, thin muscles in the rear, a weedy, unattractive creature who before the takeover would have been little more than worthless. Now those same features raised him to the top. He could get fat on rocks. Of all the horses in her care, Spec had lost the least amount of weight and vigor.

Clare would have ridden bareback, but it was going to be a long haul. She laid a racing saddle she'd gotten in a trade behind his withers, slipped the softest snaffle bit she owned into his mouth, gathered the reins, and mounted. Her feet hung below his belly.

Small and keen, his ears pricked forward, and Spec started off at a trot. Clare pulled him back to a walk. "It's going to be a long ride," she told him. The little horse had a good forward walk, his hind legs tracking up. Feeling no need to hide, Clare took the usual path. As they started up the mountain, the horse fell into a comfortable rhythm and the feeling Clare always had when on a horse settled over her. Her muscles and mind relaxed, she became acutely aware of the horse's movement underneath her, the sound of his hooves hitting the ground, the position of his ears and beyond that the sliver of sun rising over the highest mountain range. She felt the air change from cool to warm.

They traveled beyond the dirt path onto rocks. Nimble little Spec found his way more easily than most. When they came to the clearing that had once been Clare's home, her mind changed, sharpening her eyes. Grass and weeds had taken over what had been the yard and nearby pastures. The house she'd grown up in had shed many of its clapboards. The left side corner of the roof had collapsed, leaving the part of the house underneath exposed to the elements. She circled it then rode to the barn she and Annie had built. Its roof was still intact. She dismounted and walked inside. Open stall doors, looking like they had given up, hung from hinges rusted to uselessness. Cobwebs caught in her hair and the building smelled empty and raw. A rat or squirrel scurried over the side of a stall and disappeared. Weeds grew in the aisle.

Outside, she picked up Spec's reins and looped them over the hitching rail then walked to the pump next to the house, her heartbeat distinct under her ribs. She thought if she stopped and listened, she would be able to hear it pounding. She disciplined herself to feel no hope.

The iron pump carried a patina of rust but had kept its integrity. The handle felt heavy but not so heavy she couldn't move it. After years of disuse, Clare knew it would need to be primed, and priming it would be nearly impossible.

The hinge screeched and dropped flakes of rust. Clare hadn't thought whether she'd lost strength during years of deprivation but as she struggled to lift the handle, she felt stronger than ever, adrenaline replacing the loss of muscle mass. The handle reached its zenith at a sixty-degree angle. Clare used all her body weight to push it down. A sickening hollow sound followed its movement. She raised the handle again, then again and again. The hollow sound accompanied each stroke. On the fifth try, the sound changed. It became harsh, complaining. On the next stroke, Clare swore she heard a gurgle. Sweat forced the hair she'd pulled into a ponytail to spring loose and curl around her head. Her shoulders ached but she lifted the handle once more. This time, she was sure. The definite noise of water responding to the pull of a vacuum. The pain in her shoulders vanished as she pumped then returned when the sound didn't change. She stopped, took a deep breath, and pumped one more time. A brown spray spit from the nozzle. Clare doubled the rate of her strokes. The spray turned a rusty color. "Goddamn it," Clare said, "you will work if I have to do this all day." It seemed she might have to. Each time she leaned onto the handle, she prayed for water, ignoring her screaming muscles. And then it happened. The color turned toward red. For six strokes the color of the water stayed the same and then suddenly the spray turned into a stream and the stream began to lose color until the water ran clear. Clare leaned on the pump, panting. She didn't believe in God, but she did believe in the force of the universe, and she sent a silent thank you. Nothing short of a miracle had raised the water and pushed it up from the ground and out of the pump. Now she could look through the house. It didn't matter so much what condition it was in. With a source of water, her old home became a possibility.

The door to the kitchen hung from one hinge and had gotten wedged against the opposite side of the frame. The handle had survived, even if loosely. Clare took hold and pulled. The door moved an inch. Sore from working on the pump, she decided not to go through that again and threw herself backward while still holding onto the knob. The door flew free, knocking her down the stoop and landing her in the grass with the door on top of her. She pushed it off, stood, brushed herself off, and marched into the house. The kitchen floor was covered in leaves, debris, mouse droppings, and little mounds of indefinable shreds Clare figured were mouse houses. The cabinets and sink were amazingly intact, but the windows had no panes.

Clare walked into the living room and looked out of the destroyed corner to what had once been her home before she and Annie moved their business to Valley Farm. The floor under the collapsed roof had given way, and she peered into the cellar with its dirt floor and rock walls. She liked being both inside and outside.

The stairs held firm. What had been Sloan's bedroom was all but gone. Sunlight filled the space. She poked her head into her former bedroom and decided it was salvageable.

Clare spent less than ten minutes inspecting the house.

She glanced over her shoulder as she rode away. More than the damaged roof or the big gaping holes, it was the clapboard hanging from one or two nails that drained the house of life and made Clare wish she'd never returned.

She rode Spec through the wild grass and weeds to the path and stayed on it until it disappeared into the trees. Three years had passed since she'd made this trip and Clare wondered if she'd remember the way. It could have been yesterday, so clearly did it come back to her.

Green, vibrant grass filled the little clearing. Other than the farms in Somerset, Clare hadn't seen grass this healthy in over a year. She reasoned it must be the nitrogen in the soil from Unc's fire pit. That and the lack of feet trampling it. Unc had died the year before the takeover.

She used to bring him food once a week. Sometimes he was already frying meat over the pit. Sometimes he wasn't there, off hunting or fishing. She always waited for his return.

He'd died in his bed. She'd examined his face closely for signs of pain or grief, but he only looked gone. She wrapped him in his sheet and buried him deep in the woods. He'd be glad to feed the creatures in the ground.

Underneath a bright green, thick moss, the log they used to sit still looked solid. However, the one room cabin lay splayed on the ground under the battered, fallen roof. Spec dropped his head and yanked at the grass. He shivered once from nose to tail.

Clare dismounted and sat on the log. She let her mind drift to a wordless place and stared into space. The horse's enthusiastic chewing finally roused her. "Come on, Spec," she said. "Let's go look at the creek. You must be thirsty after the long climb." The little horse struggled to keep on eating, but Clare pulled his head. "You can eat a little more when we get back. I don't want you colicing on the rich grass."

Clare heard the stream before she saw it. Countless creeks ran through these mountains. This was one of the best: wide, deep in the middle, shallow on the sides. Less than a mile above this spot, it dropped straight down over rocks and shale, purifying the water so it was clean enough to drink without boiling. The tumbling water dug into the earth, producing a place fish loved. Spec dropped his nose and drank deeply.

Satisfied that Unc's favorite fishing hole hadn't dried up or changed course, Clare led the horse back to the clearing, let him graze for fifteen minutes, then swung into the saddle. She surveyed the mountains around her. No one hunted or fished this high up, the trek being too hard on foot and no ordinary vehicles could make the steep climb over rocks and into the trees. There would be deer and bear and fish aplenty. She patted Spec's neck. "Well, little guy," she said, "we'll either be back in one or two days or never again."

# CHAPTER TWENTY-EIGHT

**S**loan retrieved the banana bread for tomorrow's breakfast from the oven and wrapped it in plastic wrap. Next, she removed her apron and hung it on its hook. She looked at the clock. Past midnight. Rosie had already gone home.

Walking out the back door and around the house, she noticed an SUV parked at the curb in front of the house. It looked familiar. She ducked her head to see inside. Sonny sat behind the wheel. He leaned over and opened the passenger door.

Sloan cautiously pulled her seat belt across her lap and buckled it. What did Sonny know? Had word gotten back to the White House about her slip-up?

Sonny started the engine. "I called Blair House and told them I'd pick you up tonight."

"Why?"

"I thought you might like to talk."

"About?"

"Shimmer left tonight. For Coleton."

This was not what Sloan had expected to hear. She blinked back tears. "Without even telling me goodbye?"

"He couldn't. You know that." Sonny pulled into traffic. "We arranged a way for him to get out tonight and he had to take it."

Sloan said nothing.

"He's got to tell his contacts what's going on. And your folks." Sonny glanced into the rearview mirror, checking to see if anyone followed them.

"I didn't think he'd leave so soon."

"The sooner the better. People will need time to figure out what to do."

Sloan stared out the front window. "I told Mr. and Mrs. Whitbeck I knew where Rosemary was," she said, her tone as casual as if talking about what she made for dinner.

Sonny whipped his head in her direction. "*Seriously!?* What on God's green earth were you thinking? Tell me you're kidding."

"I'm not and I wasn't… thinking. He was being a real beast and I lost my temper. The words just jumped out of my mouth."

"Son-of-a-bitch! I can't believe it."

"He didn't believe it either. I mean, how could a lowly chef know anything top secret? Right?"

A horn blew and Sonny jerked the car back into the correct lane. "How do you know he didn't believe you?"

Sloan had her hand on the dash. "He said so."

Sonny shook his head. "Oh, in that case I'm sure he didn't. Because he said so. He wouldn't lie or anything like that."

"I've recruited his wife."

Sonny started drumming his forefinger on the steering wheel. "Really? And just how did you do that?"

"I told her I would make sure her daughter was safe if she helped us. Anyway, they think I'm from Nebraska."

"And why is that?"

"I told them I was."

"And why Nebraska, if I might ask?"

"It's far away and the only place I could think of. But then Whitbeck wanted to know which city in Nebraska, and I couldn't think of one, so I said

Billings and he said Billings is in Montana, so I had to change it to Montana. So, actually, they think I live in Montana."

Sonny again turned to stare at Sloan. "Nebraska. Billings. Montana. Where do you come up with this stuff?"

"It just pops into my head."

"Words fly out of your mouth. Ideas fly into your head. I don't think you make a very good spy."

"I don't. I should go back to Coleton."

A muscle along Sonny's jaw twitched. "If I thought for one minute you did all this so I'd send you back, you'd regret it for the rest of your life."

Sloan thought a moment and then a moment longer. Finally, she said, "I know there isn't anything I can say that would convince you that's not the case, but the truth is, it just happened. Things happen. We're not perfect."

They rode in silence. The traffic this time of night was light. Sonny slowed, pulled into a side street, and parked. "When did this conversation about Rosemary take place?"

Sloan felt tears threatening to escape. "Early afternoon."

"Mike came by tonight and swept the car. He's got this thing to detect bugs. It's clean. Not the house though. But you already know that." Sonny drew in a deep breath and exhaled slowly. "Mike didn't say anything about what you just told me, so I don't think the White House knows anything. It wouldn't do Whitbeck any good to give Diamond another person to torture. Not that he'd care what happens to you, but he sure doesn't want you revealing Rosemary's whereabouts to Diamond. He can't beat you into spilling your guts himself, with all those guards around watching him. I think we're okay. But drop Mrs. Whitbeck. She's a drunk and everything she says is probably a lie." He frowned. "You're not a drinker, are you?"

Sloan turned to him. "So, when can I go back?" she said, an edge in her voice.

"Listen, these few days are critical. Timing is everything. I want you to stay for at least three, maybe four days, then your job here is done."

"Right. After all, hell has broken loose and there's no way to get home."

Sloan turned and looked out the side window.

Sonny touched her seat. "We'll get you back. I promise. Do this a little longer. I don't need to tell you how important it is."

Sloan faced front. "You don't think Mary can help because she's a woman."

"I don't think she can help because she's a drunk."

"If she were a man, you wouldn't care about the drinking."

"That's not—look, I'm not going to argue with you about it." Sonny jerked the car into gear, made a U-turn, and sped toward his house.

As head chef in a high-end restaurant in New York, misogyny didn't play a part in Sloan's world. It was "Yes, chef." or out the door. Since she'd been back home, it had started to creep into her life. Now she wondered if this feeling had started with Shimmer. Come here. Don't go there. Do this. Do that. It made her sick to think about the possibility.

Following the fine example of Empress Maude, Whitbeck tied sheets together to make his escape. However, he either didn't know or dismissed the fact that not only did she use white sheets to drop out the castle window and land on the ground, but she also dressed in them making her invisible in the blizzard whirling around her as she made her way to freedom.

By pure luck, the sheets on Whitbeck's ancient four-poster bed were the ubiquitous gray of the 2020s and blended nicely with the outside of Blair House. He slithered down them till his feet touched the ground. A heavy cloud cover made the night dark and miserable, but not so dark it could obliterate the light from the streetlamps. It was 3:30 a.m.

Dressed in a gray suit with 6,000 dollars' worth of one-hundred-dollar bills folded into every pocket, Whitbeck felt not only liberated but vindicated. He'd gotten free while his guards played poker at the kitchen table.

Diamond had always hated the British because of their superior attitude. He loved them for the same reason. No one was classier, in his mind, than an English gentleman. Taking a page from Buckingham Palace's book, he posted sentinels across the street from Blair House. They didn't wear the fluffy fur hats or the red coats of the palace guards. They wore the drab, disappear-into-the-crowd attire of the Secret Service.

When one of the eight men saw the bushes in front of the president's guest house tremble and part, his excellent night vision sharpened. He whispered into the radio on the inside of his wrist. Out of the feckless bushes a man appeared. At first, he crouched, then he rose to his full height of six foot two.

"Go," said the guard with the keen eyesight.

The eight men flowed across the street and had Whitbeck shackled and contained in less than a minute.

$\mathbf{S}$loan was late for work the next day. The man assigned to drive her to the open markets had the car parked in the driveway and running. When she opened the vehicle's back door, he said, "You're late."

Sloan didn't respond.

"Well, have I got news for you."

The man had never spoken to Sloan before. Not to say hello or the irritating, "Have a nice day," when they parted. They had no bond that would account for this sudden familiarity.

"Mr. Whitbeck was captured last night," the driver said, not waiting for an answer.

"Captured? From where? He's already captured."

The driver pushed the button to open the gate. "He was caught trying to escape out the window. Using bed sheets." The man grinned and looked at Sloan in the rearview mirror.

She leaned back against the seat. "Well, well, well."

"He's surrounded by guards now. Up close and personal. Even in the bathroom."

"What's the mood in the house?"

"Oh, everyone is excited. It's pretty dull watching a man who just mopes around." The driver caught her eye in the mirror and grinned even deeper.

Sloan didn't return his smile. "I don't need much at the market today. We won't be long." What would Mary Whitbeck have to say about this?

Undaunted, the driver continued. "What's your name, by the way? We've never introduced ourselves."

"Sloan Rafferty."

"Jim Wilson, here. Nice to meet you." He tried again. "Everyone's walking on tiptoes. Lots of rumors going round."

Sloan leaned forward, her head close to Jim's. "Like what?"

"Some say Whitbeck is going to be taken to the White House. They want him to hand over his money, but so far, he won't." Jim raised his eyebrows. "There's talk of torture."

Sloan flew through the market, grabbing shrimp, zucchini, yellow squash, and new potatoes. She only filled two baskets and had them in the back of the SUV in fifteen minutes. She jumped in the back seat and said, "Home, James."

The look on Jim's face said he wasn't amused.

Back at Blair House, there was no sign of Mr. Whitbeck. Sloan found Mary sitting in the living room, grasping her hands. When she saw Sloan, she jerked to her feet. "Have you heard of my husband's sad attempt at escape?"

"Yes. And I've got to get to the White House right away. Don't ask me why."

Under the white hair, ravaged face and scrawny neck, the older woman's bones aligned themselves firmly in perfect posture. "Has the order of goose livers come in yet?"

Sloan blinked. "I'm not sure."

"It should have by now. Fetch it and the other ingredients to make foie gras. You do know how to make foie gras, don't you?"

Sloan nodded.

"I'll call the White House and tell them you're coming. Foie gras must be eaten fresh, or it loses its distinct flavor. Some people like it aged but not the president. He won't eat it if it's over four hours old. The former chef here always made it at the White House so Diamond would know it was fresh. Take some cans of caviar, too. If anyone says anything, you can imply it's a form of apology for last night's debacle. From me. Not Stirling. They'd never believe it came from Stirling."

"What's going to happen to your husband?"

Mary reached behind and took hold of the arm of her chair. She sank slowly to her seat. "He's not in shackles anymore, but he's always got a guard on either side of him. They don't just stand against the wall like they used to. They cleared a bathroom of everything but toilet paper, a bar of soap, and a towel. He's allowed to go in there to do his business in privacy with two men standing on the other side of the door." She sighed and stared at her shoes.

Neither spoke for a moment then Mary looked up at Sloan. She flicked a hand at the door. "Go on then. Someone will escort you across the street as soon as you've gathered what you need."

Wow, Sloan thought as she left the room. Surround that woman's husband with armed guards and she becomes a general.

Nearly sick with anticipation, Sloan walked into the White House kitchen. The staff had their heads bowed, concentrating on work. The head chef looked up as the door swung shut. It was not Randy, who seemed to have disappeared. This man was dark, boney with the kind of looks you wouldn't want to meet in a dark alley. The words "if looks could kill" slid through Sloan's mind. She made her foie gras—which basically she hated for humane reasons as well as the taste—heavy on the pepper with a splash of cognac. After putting the goose livers and other ingredients in the processor, she watched them turn into a disgusting goop. She could barely force herself to dig the pale, thick paste out of the bowl into a glass loaf pan. Wrapping it tightly in plastic wrap, she popped it into the fridge. She shifted her eyes toward the head chef. He was watching her. She side-eyed him, lifted her chin, dropped her apron on a hook and walked out the door.

There are 132 rooms in the public section of the White House, with six staircases to accommodate them. Sloan prayed Mike wasn't in the private quarters, painting some room bordello orange.

The Oval Office and the Situation Room were obviously off limits. That left 130 rooms to walk through without being suspected of anything. Sloan wished she had a can of paint and paintbrush.

Trying to look like she was just another staff member, she wandered through the Cross Hall, Green, Blue, Red Rooms, and the State Dining Room, all eerily empty except for the occasional housekeeper. Where was everyone? Thoughts of disaster made her stomach hurt.

She glanced into the famous East Room, expecting it to be empty. Three painters dressed in white were painting floor molding. Mike was on a ladder working on the crown molding over the doors leading to the lawn. They stood open to the fine day. Sloan walked past and let her hand glide across the ladder on her way outside. Mike looked down and saw her.

The yellow and peach roses were in full bloom. Pretending she had been sent to make a bouquet, Sloan reached out to pick some and stabbed herself on a thorn. "Shit," she said too loudly. Blood rolled down her finger.

"No one's allowed to touch those." Mike handed her a cloth and Sloan jumped sideways. "God, you scared me."

"Listen carefully. This has to be quick. I talked to Sonny for a minute before he had to go to the president. Everything's been moved up. Don't know the exact date, but it could be as early as tonight."

Sloan dropped the flowers. "I've got to get home. Now. To warn my family." Sloan looked around as if she could find a solution in the garden.

"Sonny understands. We don't have time to arrange things the way we normally do. I'll take you to Coleton."

"Okay, let's go."

Mike shook his head. "It doesn't work that way. I have to work till five. You know that."

Sloan began to turn in circles.

Mike grabbed her arm. "Now listen up. Go back to Blair House and find out what Whitbeck's going to do. That's your job. We must know if he's going to cave. At five-fifteen, say you're sick. They'll have you out of there damn quick. Nothing scares these idiots so much as hearing someone's sick even though they get boosted every five minutes. I'll be waiting for you."

Sloan didn't know how she was going to wait for five-fifteen to arrive. Concentrate on finding out about Whitbeck, she told herself, and do your job as though this is just another day. She forced herself to walk, not run, into the Blair House kitchen.

"Mrs. Whitbeck has gone back to bed," Rose said, not looking up from the pot she was stirring. She was still sulking because she hadn't been the first to tell Sloan about the daring escape attempt. "She's been asking for you. I've got her broth here."

"Don't scorch it." Sloan moved to the stove and turned off the burner. "Roast me a few leaves of spinach, will you."

"And why are you so late getting back?"

"I made the foie gras."

"Did you now? It don't take that long to make the stuff."

Sloan snapped. "Maybe I flirted a little with one of the line cooks."

"No need to bite my head off." Rose turned away from the stove, her back to Sloan.

As soon as the spinach leaves crisped, Sloan put them on a plate and salted them. "Does the broth already have rum in it?"

"A little."

Sloan put the plate and a bowl of the broth on a tray and pushed through the kitchen door with her hip.

Mary Whitbeck wasn't in bed but sitting in the overstuffed chair by the window. Sloan noticed the straight back and clear eyes. Only the woman's skin betrayed her, the color of the underbelly of a fish, death moving through her veins as hope slowly drained away. Sloan put the soup tray on the dressing table and crumbled the spinach leaves on top. She brought the broth with the green flecks to Mary, who peered inside the bowl. "What's that?"

"Some roasted spinach. You've got to eat more. You're starving to death. Think of your daughter and staying well for her."

"Believe me, she's all I think about."

"Here's a spoon. There's rum in it but not too much." Sloan sat on the edge of the bed.

Mary picked up the spoon, dipped it in the broth and brought it to her lips. Her hand was shaking. Sloan followed the movements of that trembling hand, knowing how slender the woman's hold on life was. How could she not tell this suffering soul she had seen her daughter less than a week ago? Alone in this God almighty world, Mary Whitbeck had only Rosemary. But Sloan couldn't think of how she would explain where she saw her. It would have to be some place nearer than Montana and no way would the girl be here in DC. She thought of her mother and John and Colleen. Who knew what would happen to them in the crossfire of the Nationalists as they charged the mountain looking for Whitbeck's daughter? There could be *no* link between Sloan and Coleton.

Mary put her spoon on the tray and raised her eyes to Sloan's. "Where was it you said you were from?"

"Billings, Montana."

"I thought you said Nebraska."

"Really? Huh."

Mary looked faintly puzzled. "I must have remembered it wrong. He called me *darling*."

"What?"

"In the night, I heard doors opening and shutting. Then I heard men's voices. I don't sleep well anymore… without the rum. I went downstairs and the entrance hall was filled with men. Stirling was handcuffed and two men held his arms. He looked at me. He looked right at my face and said, 'May I hug my wife?' It's been years since he really looked at me… especially in the face. They walked him over to me and uncuffed him. He put his arms around me. Imagine. He hugged me and whispered, 'Darling, don't let Diamond get near our daughter.' Then they tried to pull him away, but he held me a few more seconds. 'If I crack, they won't care about her. Find her and take her away.' Then they cuffed him again and led him out of the room. I haven't seen him since."

"Will he give Diamond the money? It sounds like he might." The last word creaked as Sloan's throat tightened. She gulped involuntarily.

Mary looked lost. "I don't know. He might."

Sloan wondered if Mary could hear her heart pounding. "Have you heard anything? From the guards or the staff?" She unclenched her fists and slid her hands under her thighs.

"No one talks to me."

"Did you overhear anything?"

Mary frowned. "You told me Rosemary was safe. Were you lying?"

"No."

"How would you know? She must be where you're from. That means she's in Billings, Montana, or maybe closer like... like where you went to school. How else would you know she's safe? Do you talk to the people where she is? You must be careful. The phones are bugged."

Sloan cleared her throat. "I use a burner phone."

Mary's eyebrows drew together. "*Tell me where she is.*" The woman clutched the arms of the chair to push herself up but lost her grip and flopped onto the cushions.

"The fewer people who know where your daughter is, the better."

"I'm her mother!"

"I know. But you wouldn't be able to see her anyway, and Diamond might... you know."

"Waterboard me?" Mary raised a wry eyebrow.

Sloan smiled bitterly. "If your husband doesn't cooperate, they might do just that."

"I have heard the staff talking. The guards. I've heard they're sending troops to the place where we had our horse farm. Somewhere in the Allegheny Mountains. Near the Western Maryland border. It's very isolated. Private. That's where I last saw her. She didn't come to DC with us. She just vanished." Mary stopped and stared in front of her for a moment. "Diamond's people have been monitoring all the roads out of that region... you know how it is today, video cameras everywhere. There's no record of her leaving. So, the president thinks she's still there and he's sending in troops and heat sensitive drones."

"That's ridiculous. They can't cover every back road leaving those mountains. People could use ATVs. Not use roads at all."

"They have to get gas, food… shelter."

"There's the underground for that."

Mary looked at Sloan as though she hoped the young woman could somehow fix the terrible facts. "I want to die."

"Stop that kind of talk. It doesn't do any good." The words came out harsher than Sloan had meant them to.

"Just promise me she's safe. I won't ask you how you know." Mary smiled. "Sometimes I picture her in England, in the Cotswolds… it's so beautiful there… riding her horses with lots of friends."

"Finish your soup. Later, I'll bring you cognac poached shrimp and parsley potatoes." Sloan stood, went to Mary, and put a hand on her shoulder. "Your daughter's safe," she said. "Now eat."

She'd never felt so despicable.

# CHAPTER THIRTY

**M**ike picked Sloan up at five-thirty sharp. He delivered her to Sonny at six. "I won't come in," he said. "I'll be back in half an hour, hour at the most."

Sloan opened the front door to see Sonny trotting down the stairs. She could hear Lena in the kitchen.

He took her elbow and guided her outside and onto the sidewalk. "This has to be quick. Long gaps in my conversational flow are suspicious. Mike will take you as far as Warrenton, where you will switch to another driver. I just arranged it."

Sloan didn't have the patience to ask how he'd managed it. Instead, she said, "Why are you sending me back now? I thought you needed me to tell you what Whitbeck was going to do."

"You need to be with your family."

"Why now all of a sudden?" Sloan managed to ask despite the fact she felt as though the wind had been kicked out of her.

"I can find out what's happening from Diamond. The way he clings, you'd think I was his priest."

"Mr. Whitbeck might be wavering. I talked to his wife." Sloan leveled her eyes at Sonny. Diamond's favorite Secret Service man. "She's not sure, but it's a possibility."

Sonny stopped walking and shoved his hands in his pockets. He looked at the sky as though reading the clouds. No metaphoric message displayed itself. No symbol of any kind gathered and shaped into anything of meaning. In the humid air of DC, the sullen clouds barely moved, an indistinct line bigger in the middle and tapering at the ends. Only the varying shades of dirty gray gave it any interest and not much of that. "If he caves, Diamond will stay in power for at least a few more years. Who knows what will happen to this country in that time." He looked down at Sloan. "At least his daughter won't be in danger any longer and your folks too. More or less. The government will continue rounding up people and taking their possessions." He hesitated. "Look, Sloan, I hate to tell you this. Diamond's talking about napalm."

Sloan underwent a sea change. Instead of becoming hysterical, a hard objective calm took over. At twenty-four, she had finally grown up. "When will this happen?"

"It depends on Whitbeck. If he agrees to turning over his money, it *won't* happen. If he doesn't, it could be very soon. Diamond's in a rage, hardly coherent. He decompensates more every day—every hour. It's gotten personal. And crazy."

Sloan turned toward Sonny's house and started walking.

He hurried to catch up. "I'm so sorry, Sloan."

"How will you get word to us if he decides to go ahead with it? The napalm, I mean."

Sonny reached in his pocket and pulled out a burner phone. He handed it to her. "Don't turn this on till you're well out in the countryside. Even burner phones can be tracked if you have three towers to ping off. Don't use it to call me or anyone. I will call you. It's still a risk but with what's going on at the White House, I doubt they'll be looking for you. That is if they *don't* know you told Whitbeck you knew where Rosemary was." He paused, giving Sloan a chance to respond. When she didn't, he said, "Tell Rose you decided to go home."

Sloan set her jaw and said nothing.

"Do you have reception where you live?"

"Sometimes. It's iffy."

"Get to Shimmer as soon as you can. He's got amazing resources."

They'd reached the house. Sloan walked into the kitchen. "Something smells good," she said.

Lena smiled then frowned. "How are you doing?"

"I'll be better once I talk to my mom."

"Of course."

While waiting for Mike, Sloan sat in the kitchen watching Lena cook. They talked recipes. Italian recipes. Sonny joined them and stood around looking uncomfortable.

When Mike arrived, Lena wiped her hands on her apron and hugged Sloan. She smelled of tarragon, oregano, and basil, bringing New York and all its wonders rushing back. Sonny put his arm around her and said, "May God be with you."

The girl who had just turned into a hard, cold, objective woman allowed herself to cry.

Apparently, the second leg of Sloan's journey home was to take place in a vehicle needing to be rebuilt from the ground up: new tires, new exhaust, new turn signals, new headlights, new windshield wipers. Mr. Smith—that's what he called himself—lived in the middle of a dense woods off a dirt road. His home consisted of a single-wide trailer with a garage attached. Mike barely got out of the car to introduce Sloan before he backed out of the gutted driveway and was gone.

Smith looked like he should be running a still and there was no reason to think he wasn't. A round-bellied man, with ham hock shoulders, dirty white t-shirt, and jeans that, unable to make the trip over his stomach, threatened to fall off.

"I've got a few things to do to the truck," he said.

Sloan knew about trucks from living with her mother. She thought this one might be a vintage Dodge, borrowing parts from other makes. The back wheel fender clearly didn't belong to the original vehicle. The bed had wood frames on the sides.

Dodge trucks were work horses and the old ones easy to repair. This wouldn't take long.

Smith removed a front tire and carried it to a corner of the garage and with his broad back to her, proceeded to work on it. The place was strewn with odd bits of this and that, but nothing you could use as a seat, even a precarious one. Finally, in the dark corner opposite where Smith worked, Sloan saw an old wire egg basket sitting on top of cardboard boxes. Climbing over a stack of crow bars, a shovel, a plastic box filled with objects so tangled and dirty they defied definition, a hose running loose threatening to trip her, tires, and a twisted bicycle frame, she grabbed the basket.

Sloan placed the egg basket next to the truck. The cross hatched wires hurt the instant she sat on them. She watched Mr. Smith and wondered how long it would take him to fix the tire. "How long have you lived here," she asked, for lack of anything else to do.

"Why're you asking?"

"Just wondering."

"Well, don't."

All righty then. It was going to be a long haul home.

The sun had disappeared, the only source of light now the proverbial naked bulb hanging from the peaked ceiling. Sloan studied the garage's framing. It looked hand made. Her mother and Annie had done a lot of construction as they grew their horse business. Some of it they did themselves. Sloan knew about plumbing a line, truing a corner, the importance of a solid roof. As she examined this one, she noticed the front corner sagged and the wood under it was splintered and darker than the rest. She looked at the hard packed dirt floor where a space between it and the wall showed the black night.

Mr. Smith returned to the truck with the presumably fixed tire and sat to put it on. When he finished, he walked around the front of the truck and removed the other tire and took it to the same corner. Sloan wanted desperately to ask him if all the tires needed to be changed but didn't dare.

What seemed like an hour passed. Whenever Sloan wanted to scream, she reminded herself that at twenty-four, she was a full-fledged adult.

After three tires were patched and the fourth replaced, Mr. Smith laid on the ground and began to do something to the tail pipe.

"May I use the restroom?" Sloan said.

"It's inside."

Glad to hear it, she almost said aloud. The door was unlocked and opened into the kitchen, a small space littered with dirty dishes and a large black plastic bag on the floor spilling fast food detritus and beer cans on the linoleum. The living room walls were made of fake wood paneling. Several more beer cans lay comfortably on the couch and a pair of sneakers stood sentry in front of it.

The bathroom wasn't filthy, but it wasn't clean either. Living in New York City, Sloan had become adept at hovering, and it served her well now.

When she returned to the garage, Mr. Smith had removed a headlight and was tinkering with wires. Sloan resumed sitting on the egg basket. Time became relative, turning this night into an eternity. She was dozing off when the door to the trailer opened and shut. Mr. Smith had gone inside. Sloan rubbed the sleep out of her eyes and resumed waiting. This time the waiting didn't last long.

"Are you ready," Mr. Smith said crossly, letting the door slam behind him.

Sloan almost laughed.

The roads to Coleton twisted and turned, looped around themselves, did switchbacks, all on back roads, often going deep into woods. Images from Law and Order flashed in Sloan's mind. Bodies dismembered, skin removed, women enslaved for days while villainous men had their way with them over and over. Only her trust in Mike and even more in Sonny kept her from leaping out of the truck.

# CHAPTER THIRTY-ONE

**L**uther woke to a silent house. He sat up, pushed the sheet off, and put his head in his hands. New York to Idaho, where he discovered his whole family was dead; Idaho to Coleton, where he was taken by the Nationalists; Coleton to Sloan's old home to find out she was in DC with a man called Shimmer. Shimmer. What kind of man called himself Shimmer? Probably a gay one. Luther lifted his head and looked at the liquor bottle. He'd only taken a few sips. That and the ride on Rusty's bike had put him to sleep in a matter of minutes.

He went into the kitchen and poured himself a glass of water, ate a biscuit, and walked outside. Not a soul in sight. He listened carefully. More silence, then a possible thump coming from the stable.

The familiar scent of large herbivores living together settled his nerves. A stall door opened and a skeleton holding a pitchfork walked into the aisle. Images of Nazi death camps formed in the young man's mind.

The person raised the pitchfork. "Give me a good reason not to run this through you."

"I'm Luther, Sloan's sous-chef when we were in New York… until we had to run for it, then I went back home to Idaho, where I found out my family was dead. I got the virus, but my neighbors saved me, and I took Amtrak to

Coleton because Sloan said if I ever needed to, to come here, but I got caught by the Nationalists and I had to stay with them at the Holiday Inn. But I had to warn Sloan that more troops are coming to search for Whitbeck's daughter and they're coming here. To take your mother's farm. We drove by it the other day. So, I escaped, and a boy with a motorcycle brought me here. His name is Rusty."

Reaching Luther, Colleen stood in front of him. He had never seen anyone so thin. He understood by the voice and delicate features she was a girl. A dark hue of hair covered her otherwise bald head.

"You say the Nationalists are coming here. When?"

"In a few days. Maybe four or five."

Colleen leaned the pitchfork against the stall door. "And you told this to Clare?"

"Of course."

"Huh."

Luther waited for more of a reaction, but none came until the woman said, "So, you worked with Sloan. What was that like?"

"Um. Great."

"I didn't hear you come in. When did you get here?"

"Just after dark."

"I must have been asleep. I sleep all the time now. Clare's not here. Neither is Sloan. Where did you sleep?"

"On the couch."

"I didn't see you when I went outside, but then I wasn't looking. And it was barely light."

They stood awkwardly looking at each other. Finally, Colleen said, "John's probably fishing. And Whitbeck's daughter, Rosemary, is probably in the shed with Jack."

"Whitbeck's daughter is here!?"

"Yeah." Colleen looked down and kicked at some stray sawdust. "I knew that girl would be trouble."

"Good God!"

"I know. But the Nationalists would be coming here to take the farm anyway, right?"

"That's right."

Colleen shrugged.

Luther couldn't believe how unemotional she seemed. Her voice didn't change at his news, nor did her expression.

She stepped around him. "Come on, you can help me throw hay to these horses."

A farm boy, Luther fell into the chore without having to think about it. So, this was where Sloan had grown up. And now she was in DC with a guy named Shimmer. He lifted his head. "How long do you think Sloan will be gone?"

"No idea."

"How did that guy get the name Shimmer?"

"He had the virus and it left him covered in tiny specks of gold."

Luther noticed the change in her voice. This man he already resented meant something to her. He broke open a bale with more force than necessary and the flakes burst everywhere. Colleen looked over at him. Covering his agitation, he said, "This is nice looking hay."

"It'll be gone by Christmas."

Luther turned at the sudden bitterness in her tone, but she wouldn't look at him. He started throwing flakes of hay into stalls. When he came to the next to last before the door, he stopped dead in his tracks and stared at Sloan's neatly made bed.

Colleen noticed him. "That's Sloan's bed. Didn't I tell you she sleeps in the barn?"

"Um, I think someone did." For some reason the tidy bed made him want to cry. Instead, he returned to feeding the horses then, following Colleen's lead, tossed soiled bedding into a wheelbarrow. Eyes on his task, he didn't see Rosemary come into the stables. When she said hello, he spun around to face a young woman with dark frizzy hair, huge brown eyes, narrow frame, and diffident manner. "Who are you?" she said, her voice barely above a whisper.

He had no interest in repeating what he had told Colleen. Fortunately, she spoke for him and gave Rosemary a summary of Luther's story. She left out the part about the ensuing manhunt. Watching her, Luther found it difficult to reconcile this tender child with the frenzy she was creating from here all the way to DC.

Rosemary walked down the aisle to a stall where a big chestnut horse stuck his head over the door. "Colleen," she said, "can I give him some more hay?" Of all the horses, Wilson Elliot the Third fared the worst. Unlike the mountain horses around him, who were bred with stamina and the ability to withstand hardship, his heavy-boned frame had dropped so much weight his ribs could be counted.

"Yeah, go ahead." Colleen stopped working and leaned on her pitchfork. "I don't know how we're going to get through the winter. If we last that long." She went to the next stall and stopped. "I think I know where Clare is. Spec is missing. She's probably gone up the mountain for some reason."

Luther heard what sounded like a truck coming up the driveway. He and Colleen looked at each other. Luther said, "Are you expecting someone?" A car door slammed and tires crunched as the vehicle turned to leave. He heard footsteps, a shadow spread on the dirt floor in front of the door, and there was Sloan looking straight at him. They stood as still as fence posts, eyes locked until Sloan walked up to him and laid her palm on the side of his face. "Ah," she said. "You've been sick."

# CHAPTER THIRTY-TWO

**S**loan, Luther, Colleen, and Rosemary sat at the kitchen table. Earlier that day, they'd made three trips in the truck to Pap's house, carrying essentials for an indefinite stay. The last trip they filled the bed with hay. Clare and John stayed to string barbed wire among the trees. The two of them would spend the night in the old house. Jack went to the Holler with bear meat to barter for buckets, more barbed wire, and ammunition.

Sloan had given the remaining three each a glass of water before sitting beside Luther. She cleared her throat. "Luther, tell them what you know about the Nationalists."

The young man was nearly quaking with fatigue but told the group the whole story from his capture to what he thought of as his midnight ride with Rusty. Next, Sloan told them about what she learned in DC. She tried to slip in the fact of the napalm as casually as possible.

Rosemary burst into tears. "Take me to the Holiday Inn. I want to turn myself in."

Luther said no way would he take her. Colleen pointed out he didn't have a truck and Clare wouldn't want him driving hers so unless they planned to walk, he couldn't get her there if he wanted to.

"They're coming for the farm anyway," he said. "To take Clare's land. So, no point in turning yourself in."

"But they won't go looking up the mountain because they'll already have me." Rosemary wiped her nose on her t-shirt.

"And they won't drop napalm," Colleen added.

Luther glanced at her before saying, "We're not sure about the napalm."

Sloan put her hand on the girl's shoulder. "My mother would kill us all if we turned you over. She's a proud and arrogant woman and wouldn't tolerate the Nationalists getting hold of you. What you can do is stop crying and go to bed. Tomorrow is going to be a long day."

When it was just the two of them, Luther and Sloan removed bear meat from the refrigerator. After cutting it into strips with a butcher knife, they hung these over the fire pit and sat next to it, keeping just enough flame to turn it into jerky. Being alone with Sloan, Luther couldn't stop talking. He described in detail how he steered his way through his time with the Nationalists. He marveled aloud at the abundance of food, the comfortable beds, the different personalities. "Henry, my roommate, was exceptionally nice to me. He persuaded the kitchen staff to make special dishes for me. I can't tolerate much fat because of the virus, so he'd bring me poached chicken and eggs. And Captain Riddick, well, as it turned out he is on our side, so he helped me escape. He's a saint in my eyes. But most of the others were pretty awful." Luther went on to describe the nightmare trip into the Bell. He followed this with a faltering description of driving past Clare's farm. He watched Sloan in the dim light of the coals.

Sloan listened and poked listlessly at the fire pit with a stick. Luther's steady voice was easy to relax into. As he spoke of his ride here on Rusty's bike, she nodded off then jerked awake. "You shouldn't have come here," she said as though waking from a dream.

Luther recoiled. "How can you say that?"

"You'd have been safer as a pseudo-Nationalist. Not here in this devil's brew."

"Oh. You're worried about my safety. For a minute there I thought… well, never mind. I had to come and warn you. Anyway, whatever happens I want it to happen with me near you."

Sloan leaned her head against his shoulder for three seconds before she rose abruptly to her feet. "I'm done in. If I don't go to bed now, I will fall asleep on these coals."

Luther looked up at her.

Sloan knew that look. "You can sleep in my mother's bed if you want. Has to be more comfortable than the couch."

Luther looked away. "That's all right, the couch is fine. I'd feel strange sleeping in your mom's bed."

How nice it was to slip into her tidy bed. Sloan folded the blanket at the end of the mattress. She plumped the pillow and laid on her back, eyes facing the rafters. What with the mad dash to Smith's home and their drive here, waiting to be assaulted any moment in the goriest way, followed by the three treks up the mountain, Sloan hadn't had time to ponder. Now she did. Visions from a documentary kept flashing in her mind. Napalm fire, red touched with snapping yellow, soaring above the jungle trees. Sonny saying, "You need to be with your family," at a time when her position at Blair House was the most vital. Her connection with Mary could give her information as to Whitbeck's frame of mind far sooner than Sonny or the president could find out.

And there was Luther, standing struck dumb in the stable she'd spent so much time in as a youth. Dear, sweet Luther with his open, honest face, straw-like hair, and new tan splotches, and realizing in an instant how much she loved him and knowing, even so, she didn't love him enough.

"You need to be with your family," Sonny'd said. There was only one reason he would say that. Tears leaked from Sloan's eyes into her ears and onto the mattress. She didn't sob or make any sound. Her stomach didn't tremble. Only the trickling salty water expressed her knowledge of what was to come.

What month was it? June? July? The crickets still madly rubbed their legs together and in addition to their urgent soprano, the cicadas' metallic sound filled the night. A horse sighed, ruffling its nostrils. Another stomped at a fly. Sloan closed her eyes. When she opened them a moment later, the black crown of curls over the stall door didn't surprise her. It was too dark to make out Shimmer's face, even with the speckles, but she'd know that ever-buoyant hair anywhere.

They woke entwined. She didn't remember how it began. At one point Shimmer put an arm across her and a hand on the small of her back and pulled her against him, lips against her ear, whispering her name over and over. She remembered the chime of boundaries breaking, sparks of lightning blazing through scars, dark energy transformed by wonder.

Sloan tipped her head to see their entangled brown and white limbs.

"Ah, you are awake. This is good. I did not want to have to wake you." Shimmer kissed her ear. "I believe the time was right, no? It was good to wait and long for a while. I felt the longing very strongly." He kissed her temple. "You are a fire ball dropping from heaven." He kissed her eyelids. "Echoes of thunder deep inside. Full-blooded wild woman on the outside." He kissed her mouth. "I do not deserve to breathe the same air. You have destroyed me. I can never make love to anyone else and not hate them because they are not you." He rolled over so he was on top. "You think I am making all this up, maybe I say this to all the girls, but believe me, I have never spoken this before." He kissed her ear again and held her tightly. "Now we must go. The news is not good. All of you must leave at once." He jumped up and pulled the sheet off the mattress. "You won't be sleeping here tonight, so no need to make your bed. Perhaps you can bring the mattress with you."

The two walked through the dawn's blue air to the fire pit. The scent of biscuits met them. Sloan couldn't help holding Shimmer's hand, but she dropped it when they came to the clearing. They found Clare lifting the iron skillet off the flames.

She looked up and showed no surprise at seeing Shimmer. "John's already taking more wire up the mountain. We'll take the horses next. Come, eat. Who knows when we'll have biscuits again."

Shimmer squatted next to her. "I put bags of salt, flour, and sugar on the kitchen table. The Nationalists will be here today. Maybe tomorrow. You should rouse the others."

Clare was looking at Sloan as though reading a map. She looked at Shimmer then back to Sloan then bent her head and overturned the biscuits onto a cloth on the ground. Sloan smelled bear grease.

Shimmer touched a biscuit gingerly, snatched back his hand. He blew several puffs of air on the pastry and yanked off a hunk. He took a cautious bite and nodded while puffing out his cheeks. He rose to his feet in an easy motion. "I will be going now. Do not waste time. You have no time for a leisurely breakfast." He smiled.

"Going? You're leaving? You just got here." Sloan who, still drunk from the night's unraveling had been sleepily watching the smoldering fire, jerked to attention.

Before Shimmer could answer, the kitchen door slammed, and Luther walked across the yard. When he reached the fire pit, he stared at the interloper. The fire's glow found Shimmer's spots, turning them to gold.

"I guess you're the guy they call Shimmer."

"And you are Luther. I have heard of you. The Nationalists are looking for you, and I think if they find you, they will tear you to pieces." Shimmer laughed and patted Luther's shoulder. "I am only joking and not such a funny joke, eh? Pay no attention to me. The Nationalists are far more interested in a certain girl. They have forgotten all about you. But now I must go. Am already late."

Hampered by Luther's presence, Sloan didn't move or demand that she go with her lover. That was the way she thought of him now. How could he walk away after such a night? But of course, he could. He should. There was no question of indulging in anything but survival.

"I will be back soon," he told her, his face suddenly clouded. "I will find you. You must not worry."

"Sloan, go wake Rosemary," Clare said, cutting off any revealing goodbyes.

# CHAPTER THIRTY-THREE

**S**loan watched Shimmer and her mother walk across the yard to where their trucks were parked. Shimmer lowered the tailgate and pulled two fifty-pound bags of corn to the back and slung one over his shoulder. Her mother hoisted the other and they transferred the bags to Clare's truck, covering them with a black plastic tarp. Clare stepped back a few paces as Shimmer climbed into the driver's seat. The only concession he made to the fact that he might not see Sloan or any of them again was to stare straight ahead before he looked down to turn on the engine. Clare didn't wave goodbye.

Sloan turned on her heel and went to the shed. She would not watch Shimmer as he drove away. A sharp knock on the door produced a rustling of fabric and hushed voices then a timid "What?" from Rosemary.

"Come on out. Clare wants to talk to you."

More rustling before Rosemary stepped squinting into the sunlight, her hair frizzier than ever. Jack came behind her, pulling on his t-shirt. It made Sloan physically sick to see the two of them this way.

Clare waited for everyone to reach her outside the kitchen door. She looked from one to the other, taking her time. "We're going up the mountain as soon as John's back."

Sloan looked past her mother's shoulder. John came out of the woods carrying his fishing basket.

"So, gather what you need or what you think you need. You'll carry it on your back. John, Colleen, and Luther will go in the truck. Me and Sloan will ride and pony the horses." Clare looked long and hard at Jack, who put his arm loosely around Rosemary, resting his hand on her shoulder.

"Rosemary and I ain't goin' up the mountain. We're going to my place in the Holler."

The air grew still. John, who had reached the group, put down his basket.

Sloan stared at the terrible tableau made up of a middle-aged man laying claim to a teenage girl. And then, like tumblers falling into place and the safe door opening, she saw the brilliance of the idea. Having passed through the fringes of the Holler, the Nationalists would sit in their vehicles, stopped by the solid, undeniable mass that lined the dirt road on both sides. They would take note of the still, silent men barely discernable from their surroundings, and the unblinking, deadly way they stared at these people who didn't belong there. The Nationalists would tell themselves or each other it was impossible for the daughter of a Whitbeck to end up in a place of such dissolution, such decadence, such determined disregard for humanity. But they each would know in their heart of hearts the real reason they did not move forward. No way would they venture onto such unhallowed ground.

Sloan looked at her mother, whose face held the inscrutable look she was so used to. No one spoke for an unbearable length of time until Clare finally nodded and said, "What do you want to take with you?"

"Bear jerky, vegetables, the fish lying in John's basket, and a blanket would be fine."

Clare nodded again and with that, turned her attention back to the rest of them. "Sloan, you're the smallest. You ride Spec and I'll ride Timber." The big gray was a retired steeplechaser Clare had been boarding until the owners disappeared and now he belonged to her. That left four, two training colts who'd also been abandoned, an old, home-bred mare, and Wilson. "I'll pony Wilson and Guinevere, Sloan, you take the others."

Rosemary covered her mouth with her hand.

"You can't take him to the Holler," Clare said. "You know that. You can still come with us if you want." She flicked a glance at Jack, dismissing him.

Rosemary looked at the ground and shook her head.

"We want to travel light, so we don't leave much of a trail. We've already been to Pap's so much, any fool could follow it, but still."

Fifteen minutes later, John turned the truck toward the mountain with Clare, Sloan, and the four riderless horses following behind him. Sloan hadn't missed her old home in the frenetic world of New York City's restaurant scene. Now a rock settled in her chest so heavy it didn't allow for the lightness of tears. She didn't look over her shoulder as they turned on the path; she looked at her mother, whose indefatigable face cleaved the air as she rode away.

No one spoke. Ponying the four horses made progress slow. The sun rose scarlet over the mountains, announcing a day of heat, bugs, and sweat. To Sloan, the sound of the horse's hooves striking rocks sounded like bells announcing their journey. They stumbled forward, concentrating on keeping the ponied horses from getting tangled or fighting each other. Sloan lost track of time, fought the urge to dwell on Shimmer. If she never saw him again, she would have last night when he healed her affliction. A fly buzzed by her ear, and the horses shook their heads, fighting off others. Shimmer, she thought, Shimmer, and without realizing it she repeated the word silently with the rhythm of the horse's hooves.

A sound rang out, so foreign, so jarring in this world of trees, rocks and animals, Sloan jumped away from it. Spec leaped in the opposite direction, causing the ponied horses to rear. One of them pulled back, broke its halter, and dashed ahead. Any rider who hadn't been riding before she walked would have been unseated, but Sloan not only stayed put, she pulled the phone out of her pocket.

Clare stopped and watched her daughter. Sloan looked up from the burner phone. "That's Sonny, the president's Secret Service man. He texted me that the 'meeting' is going to happen at dawn tomorrow. Drones and helicopters might be sent ahead."

For the second time, Sloan saw her mother waver; confusion—even disbelief—covered her face. Sloan realized this was the first time their situation really hit home for her. Clare had gone through all the preparations she could think of without feeling true terror or loss.

The truck came to a halt as the runaway horse passed it. John stepped down and went to Clare, who bent her head and told him the news. She straightened and settled into her saddle, lost in thought. Suspended, they rested on the mountain.

The party didn't go to Pap's as had been planned. John drove the truck as far as he could then hid it in the woods. Clare put Colleen on Timber. John rode one of the training colts bareback, using the halter and lead strap as a bridle. Luther, along with Clare, chose to walk the rest of the way. The runaway returned to the group as Sloan knew he would. They picked their way higher and higher until they reached Unc's small clearing.

Clare sat on the log to catch her breath. Luther sat next to her, head in his hands. The others stood in front of them looking lost.

Clare drew a deep breath. "Hobble Spec and Timber. Turn the rest loose. There's a creek nearby. We'll just have to wait and see what happens tomorrow. Maybe two of us can sneak to Pap's for some supplies. Maybe not." She rose to her feet and stretched. "Take Spec and Timber to get a drink. I've got jerky in my pack. It'll be a cold camp tonight."

No one moved except Colleen, who dismounted and lay down on lush grass and looked into the sun-faded blue sky. "It's nice here. As good a place as any to die."

Clare nudged her with a booted foot. "It don't do no good to talk like that."

# CHAPTER THIRTY-FOUR

**E**xcept for Wilson and Guinevere, the freed horses disappeared into the woods, exploring. The big, once-magnificent chestnut stayed in the clearing, his teeth pulling on the grass so greedily he tore some out by the roots.

"He'll eat it all," said Colleen.

"He needs it most," said Clare.

They'd all been to the creek for a drink and to fill the plastic bottles they'd brought with them. The others had fallen under her mother's spell of optimism. Sloan knew they had left too many supplies at Pap's, that they'd most likely be here in the high, light air just below the apex of the mountain for a long time. She also knew they didn't need to worry about survival as long as the Nationalists didn't find them. The woods would provide everything necessary: shelter, food, and water. A campfire, on the other hand, could be risky. The thought of eating bear jerky or raw fish made her stomach turn over. Even the greasy biscuits wrapped in a towel in her mother's pack repelled her.

Clare and John sat close together on the log; Colleen had selected her spot for a bed, where she dozed. Sloan laid opposite her, and she too found it hard to keep her eyes open.

John drew tiny figure eights in the small patch of rotted wood at his feet.

"So, Luther, if the Nationalists arrived at dawn, do you have any idea how long they will be at the farm?"

Luther looked at him, surprised. "No. None at all. They'll see we've left pretty quick, but will they then start a search?" He paused to think. "I'm pretty sure they'll search the surrounding area now that I think about it. They want that girl damn bad." He paused again. "There's this Captain Riddick. The guy who helped me escape. I'm pretty sure he's with us, but you never know. He could be setting us up. I think he's from around here. He'll know to look up the mountain. He'll find the path we took to Pap's immediately if he wants to. Don't know if he'll figure to go farther."

"We'll need to know that," Clare said.

"I'll go as lookout," Luther volunteered.

Clare watched him quietly. "You don't know these mountains."

"I know enough to get to Pap's. That's where they'll go first."

"There's a good chance they won't go farther." Clare leaned against John.

Sloan opened her eyes enough to read her mother's face. She was as at home here as any human could be. Her self-confidence had returned. Sloan could see it in the relaxed set of her jaw, the smooth lines of her cheeks, her quiet eyes. This probably wasn't a good thing, but Sloan couldn't worry about that now. Her eyes closed and didn't open again until a rabbit, caught by an owl, screamed in the moonlit night. She propped herself up on an elbow. Everyone was asleep. Her head pounded. She rolled onto her hands and knees and crawled as far as she could before throwing up. She dragged herself back to the clearing, slumped on the ground, and fell back asleep.

The shapes of the trees were just visible when Luther gently shook Sloan's shoulder. He put his palm on her forehead. "You're burning up."

Her eyes burned, and it felt like she had an axe in her head. Clare held a bottle of water to her lips, but she pushed it away and drifted into a twilight sleep.

"She won't drink until she's so thirsty she can't stand it." Luther moved the sticky hair out of her face. He took off his shirt and laid it lightly over her shoulders. "She's burning up now, but she'll get the chills soon." He and

Clare looked at each other. John walked over and sat between them. "It's dawn. The fireworks are about to start. Did you see that chopper just a few minutes ago?"

Both Clare and Luther nodded. "We don't need to do nothin," Clare said. "Not for a while. Best to just stay here as quiet as we can." The four loose horses had come back to the clearing in the night and nibbled grass. "We'd better hobble them, so they don't return to the farm. Be a dead giveaway to look farther up." She pulled a rag out of a jean pocket, poured water over it, and placed it on Sloan's forehead.

"If she's been to the White House, she's been vaccinated for sure," Luther said. "She won't get so sick."

Colleen and Sloan slept while the others led the horses to the creek for water. After that it became a waiting game until John said, "I think I'll go for a walk."

Luther stood up. "I'm going with you."

John looked at Clare, who nodded. "I'm not leaving these girls."

The men did not take the path and without John, Luther would have been lost. They moved so cautiously only a trained woodsman would have heard them. Zigzagging in a broken line, they moved from tree to tree. Deep enough in the woods neither could see where the sun rose in the sky. They had only their sense of time to know how far into the morning they were when they looked down at Pap's place.

Luther came to stand beside John. "I don't see anyone, do you?"

"Not yet." John hunkered down, his back against a tree, and Luther did the same. His thighs trembled from the effort of moving downward with stealth. He pulled off his pack and sat cross-legged. Neither spoke, absorbed in their own thoughts until Luther said, "Do you really think they will come here?"

"We've all but given them a map from Valley Farm to Pap's with all that carryin' stuff up here. Depends on who they are. Anybody from these mountains will know to climb higher, but if it's just Coleton folks or imports, they might not think of it."

The air was already hot and heavy. Pap's place could have been a painting:

resolute, long ago abandoned, a sad scar on the pristine and wild mountain. Luther looked at John's profile. "You don't seem nervous."

John smiled. "Don't I? Well, I assure you I am. It's just there are so many variables it's hard to know what to fear." He shifted his weight. "Except for napalm. I have a righteous fear of napalm. Clear and fierce." John pushed himself upright. "The problem is those hay bales. Any country boy will know it's this year's first cutting. That and the way we've stacked our supplies in one room."

Luther looked up. "Are you thinking of going down there?"

"We must. Like I said, local Nationalists will know to look farther than Valley Farm."

When they reached Pap's farm, John took hold of the back of Luther's arm. "You go in the house and start spreading things around. Break down that pile of supplies. Throw things outside. You got a knife? Split open the mattresses. Throw some into the destroyed part of the house. You know what I'm saying. It should look as though abandoned years ago."

"What are you going to do?"

"Try to make that hay look old."

Luther walked up the stairs to the kitchen and into the house. He found himself tiptoeing, afraid any extra weight would bring the whole place tumbling down and flatten him. He stood gazing out of the part of the house not there. Tall grass and weeds thrust up-right from their dew-soaked stems. Untamed foliage all but covered the driveway. A buzzard hung lazily in the sky, his wings at least three feet long. Luther turned and put a foot on the first stair to the bedrooms. It held him. He made his cautious way to the second-floor bathroom and closet storage place over the kitchen. They had piled the supplies there because it seemed the driest spot in the house. He filled his backpack one third of the way with ammunition. He tossed pots and pans and tools out of various windows. He picked up a blanket for Sloan and stuffed it in his pack. Ripping open three small bundles of clothes, he kicked them with his boots throughout the house. Two truckloads of stuff they mostly didn't need. Clare's foolishness surprised him. Dragging a bedframe and mattress to the destroyed part of the house, he shoved them out and down to the first floor where they landed with a soft thump on the rotting boards. He knew this was no time for nostalgia, that haste was needed instead. Even so, he couldn't help standing still. This was where Sloan was born and raised. He never in his wildest imagination would have guessed it. She had seemed so New York. Direct, no sugar coating anything. No please could you pass me the porterhouse so I can season it. It was, *Porterhouse, now.* And if that didn't work, it became, *Bring me the goddamn porterhouse, now!* At top decibel.

It occurred to Luther as he stood thinking of Sloan that in many ways the major cities in the world and these mountains bred the same characteristics in people. Both cultures showed extreme loyalty to friends and family. Sloan's folks had taken him in without question once they knew he had been her sous-chef. Yet they could walk right past deviant behavior without looking, the words, "mind your own business" in their DNA. You could hide in these hills, unlike the flat land he spent his youth on, where farmers watched their neighbors with the eyes of hawks, judging, looking for weakness to exploit or at least enjoy.

He needed to keep moving. Yet in this wreck of a house, he felt part of Sloan's world. He could drink her in. He pictured her hair freed from the chef's bandana, picking up sun here in the wild and bouncing it back.

He was going to marry that girl, Shimmer be damned. He knew the type. Ramblers, never staying put, unable to form real relationships no matter how charming they were. Actually, he didn't know the type, having grown up where farms were passed generation to generation. But he'd seen enough movies. He let the fact he would marry her settle in, stayed staring into her world, refusing to rush the moment. His gaze grew soft and easy then suddenly sharpened. In the distance, did he see the sun glance off a black surface? He watched. Nothing. He glared through the morning haze of a summer's sun. Still nothing. Luther turned away and kicked and threw items around randomly, hurrying to get the job done.

# CHAPTER THIRTY-FIVE

**C**olleen soaked the bottom of the extra shirt she'd brought and held it to Sloan's lips. Her friend tossed her head and pushed Colleen's hand away. She leaned over and kissed Sloan's forehead. "She's way too hot. We've got to bring her temperature down." She ran her hand over her own head where the hair produced only a shadow.

Clare laid the back of her fingers along her daughter's cheek. "We'll take her to the creek. Are you strong enough?"

Putting Sloan's arms around their shoulders, they unceremoniously dragged her through the woods. When they reached the water's edge, Clare wanted to pull Sloan in straight away, but Colleen stopped her. She studied the fast, clear water. "Look there," she said. "See those two boulders. I'll wedge myself between them and hold Sloan on my lap. The rocks will keep me in place against the current."

Colleen waded to the middle of the stream, gasped as, holding onto the rocks, she lowered herself shoulder deep. She had to maneuver her boney hips to fit. She held out her arms.

Clare picked Sloan up, one arm under her knees, the other under her head. She nearly ran to Colleen to lower her daughter into the cold creek.

Sloan exploded, screaming, arms and legs striking, kicking, spraying water around her until it became an opaque froth. Colleen managed to wrap her arms around her and held on. Once Sloan was still enough, Clare cupped her hands and ladled the icy water onto her head. Eventually, Sloan went limp and, semi-conscious, laid her head on her friend's shoulder. Colleen added her tears to the roiling stream.

After twenty minutes, Clare stopped anointing her daughter. She laid down in the water on her back and held firm against the current before sitting up and shaking water out of her hair. She kissed Sloan's forehead again. "Bless these mountains, this creek, and all around it. She's sweating."

"How can you tell?"

"She tastes salty."

Colleen laughed.

Back at the clearing, Sloan fell into a deep slumber. Colleen laid her wet shirt over Sloan, who moaned but didn't fight.

Clare held her daughter's hand. "Luther said it won't be so bad cause she's had the vaccine."

Colleen stretched out on the ground close to Sloan but not touching, careful to keep her own body heat from adding to the fever.

Twice they had to repeat the trip to the stream. Twice sleep took her over when they brought Sloan back. As her temperature rose for the third time, she opened her eyes and looked at her mother. The whites had taken on a yellow hue. Clare looked into Colleen's face to see if she'd noticed.

She had. "I'm not sure how much more we can shock her body."

As Sloan grew warmer and warmer, Collen took all the extra clothes they'd brought, one pair of jeans and shirt each, and carried them to the creek to soak. When she returned, she laid them over Sloan. She leaned against Clare and slowly let her head slide into her lap. They remained like this until time became heavy, a malignant force surrounding them.

At the sound of a stem breaking deep in the wood, Clare turned her head. She did not call out or give voice to her thoughts about John and Luther.

Colleen closed her eyes.

# CHAPTER THIRTY-SIX

Luther couldn't think of anything more he could do to disguise their attempt at making Pap's place livable. He'd picked up an extra knife, tea bags, a few nails and stuffed them in his pockets. Eager to get back to Sloan, he walked outside, laid his pack against the house, and walked toward the stable to check on John.

The bullet hit him squarely between the shoulder blades. His arms flew out to the sides, spread like an eagle in full flight. He sank slowly to his knees and before his torso fell, whether reflexively or with purpose, he turned his head to the side. He landed stretched out on the earth as though embracing it, a brilliant red abstract slowly covering his back.

Henry walked up to him and kicked his side. "I trusted you." He kicked Luther again. "I thought we were friends." He was about to keep on kicking him when Riddick put a hand on his shoulder. "No need for that, son."

Slater joined them. "Do you think he was alone or with that witch's bunch?"

"I don't see them taking him on," Riddick said. "People like them don't take to strangers. He probably just come across this place and squatted here for a bit."

A car engine coughed and roared. The sound of chassis scraping rocks followed as two SUVs made their way along the road to Pap's place. Slater had parked his vehicle on the side of the road and he, Henry, and Riddick walked up the driveway.

Slater looked around at the house and stable. "What do you think? Any chance that girl is hiding here?"

"No way. She'd never stay here by herself."

"What about that witch? You think her and her coven are hiding out here?"

Riddick hesitated, gazing as though assessing the situation. "Doesn't look like it."

"Someone's been here. You can tell by the torn-up path. As good a place as any to hide out."

"I don't see it. More likely Clare and her gang have gone to live with someone they know. People here are clannish if you hadn't noticed. They might take in a helpless girl, though."

Slater squinted at the other captain. "You think? That girl's got to be somewhere in these hills. Diamond's convinced of that. Maybe she moved in with that witch. How perfect." He smirked then turned to Henry. "Go check out that fencing over there behind the stable. See if it looks new. Riddick, you look through the house. Careful you don't fall to your death."

Riddick picked his way from room to room, skirting the destroyed corner with only a brief glance down. It would take a certain knowledge to find evidence that Clare's family had been here, and he didn't think Slater possessed it. He tore a sheet in half and in half again, dragged the pieces through some dirt collected in a corner, and tossed them in a closet.

In the kitchen, he looked through the cupboards and under the sink. Satisfied, he went outside to the pump. Flecks of rust lay like confetti around the base.

The other two SUVs had arrived and were parked in the driveway. Ten recruits stood around Luther's body, looking hopelessly young in their brand-new crisp uniforms. Slater put his cupped hands to his mouth and called from an open stall door in the front of the stable. "You men, stop gaping and start going over this entire area. I want to know about any signs someone has been here recently. That means the woods, too."

Riddick watched the men as they spread out, checking to see if any looked local. If they were, they'd have a certain way of walking, a different set to their shoulders than those brought here. They all looked like outsiders to him. He stopped watching them and walked around the pump, pushing telltale red flakes into the dirt. If you looked at the pump, you could see where the rust had fallen away from the handle. Nothing to be done about it without drawing attention.

Before ambling to the stable, he lifted his binoculars and pointed them just below the crest, a place he'd only heard of in rumors, a wild man's home. He made sure to catch the sunlight. He knew he wouldn't see any signs of life, but there was a chance someone keeping watch would notice the reflection striking off the glass.

Inside the stable, Slater was staring at some hay scattered around the wind-swept dirty floor. "What do you think? Does this look suspicious to you? Why would there be hay in here?"

Riddick recognized instantly it was this year's first cut. "Could be lots of reasons. Deer have obviously been at it." He took a chance. "It's old. The old man who owned the place before he died may have left it here. More likely someone just used this abandoned stable to store extra hay and for some reason didn't come back to get it. You know how it is these days."

Slater knocked away a cobweb. "You know this is another world. Something from *Deliverance*. Why would anyone live in this godforsaken hole."

"Oh, it's not forsaken. Families have lived here since it was settled. Some folks have never even been to Coleton."

"You're kidding." Slater turned and walked away. "Personally, I can't wait to get reassigned. It's like living in the dark ages." Outside he stood, feet spread, hands on his hips. "At least we found this weasel. I never did trust the guy. You could see it in his face. Didn't have the stomach. Now we have to load him up, take him back, and arrange to bury him." He patted his shirt pocket, reached in, and brought out a cigarette. He inhaled deeply and blew smoke out his nose.

"Where do they do it? Bury them?"

"Don't know. We just load 'em into a refrigerator truck and off they go. Some mass grave somewhere, I guess."

"Why even bother? Just leave him here. The bears will clean him up."

Slater squinted in Riddick's direction. "Seriously? I can't believe you just said that. What about the paperwork? He needs to be accounted for."

"Do you really think with this manhunt going on and the big fuss about finding the girl, anyone's going to notice a missing recruit?"

Slater sighed. "The brass will be mad as hell if we don't find her."

"There's still a whole mountain to explore. Personally, I think she's long gone."

Slater swept his eyes over the valley, up the mountain to the summit. "It's like looking for a needle in a haystack. Why don't they just torture the guy until he confesses?"

"Confesses to what? Where his money is? It's offshore in banks that need retina prints to get to it. It's hard to drag a tortured man into a bank like that and then hold him up so some mysterious thing can scan his retina."

"How do you know it's offshore?"

"Just sayin."

"Diamond doesn't think that girl is long gone. He's convinced she's in these mountains."

"Diamond doesn't know these mountains."

"Our local Nationalists do."

"True." Riddick put a hand on one of the poles supporting the shed roof. "Suit yourself. Load him up and take him back or leave him here. I'm sure as hell not ever getting into the truck he's carried back in. Just sayin.' You can never really get rid of the blood stink."

"Maybe some of the other troops have had better luck."

"Tell me, Slater, since you hate it so much, why did you want her farm?"

"Cause she's a witch. You told me that. Remember?"

"People say things, you know. Just to say 'em. Doesn't mean it's true."

Slater swung his arm to encompass all the mountains softened into gentle outlines by age. "Get rid of that old barn and it could be nice. It's kind of picturesque, don't you think? Might want it as a vacation house. Get away from the world. Keep some horses just for the fun of it."

"How does that work?"

"What work?"

"How do you get the deed? Who signs the contract? Who notarizes it?"

"Are you fucking kidding me?"

"No."

Slater tossed his cigarette on the dirt floor and rubbed it in with his boot then lit another one. "You may have noticed times have changed. Some bigwigs or some captain wants it, they just move in. I just hope she comes back before it goes to someone else."

"Why's that?"

"Why's what?"

"Why do you want her to come back?"

"Why do you think? I've never done a witch."

Riddick looked his companion up and down. "You shouldn't be smoking around this dried-up hay." He glanced toward the ceiling. "And this dried-out old building."

Slater blew the whistle hanging around his neck and men came out of the woods, across the pastures, up the driveway. They gathered around their captains. Slater let them wait then said, "Did you see anything suspicious?"

Blank faces looked at him except for Henry, who said, "There's something about the strands of barbed wire. The wire looks old but the nails attaching it to the trees look new to me, and some of the trees, their bark looks recently chipped."

Slater slowly nodded. "Okay, we'll have to take a look at it. The rest of you? Anything? Anything at all?"

"Sir, no Sir."

Slater looked at the recruit with barely concealed contempt. "Don't overdo it, soldier. My ass can take only so much kissing." He called out four names. "You stay. The rest of you can go. You four and Henry and my fellow captain here will look around some more."

The other men trotted to the SUVs like schoolboys let out of school.

Henry cleared his throat. "What about Peter, Captain? We just going to leave him here?"

A buzzard swooped over Luther's body, kept going then closed his wings and settled on the pump, his ancient, calculating eyes on the men in front of the stable. Slater stared right back at him as though the two knew each other. "Riddick will decide about the body," he said, still looking at the bird. He reached in his pocket for another cigarette as he started for the pasture behind the stable. "Let's go look at the wire."

## CHAPTER THIRTY-SEVEN

**W**hat John saw when he slipped into Unc's clearing, tempered, for a moment, the anguish of seeing Luther murdered. Colleen and Clare lay on either side of Sloan, their arms around her. He could hear her teeth chattering. Clare looked over her shoulder. "She's sick."

John reached them and put his hand on Colleen's shoulder. "Let me take your place."

"I'm fine," Colleen said without looking at him.

"You're almost as cold as she is." He held out his hand and Colleen allowed her brother to pull her to her feet.

John kneeled and was about to stretch out when Clare put up a hand, palm out. "You'll get sick."

He looked at her in disbelief. "And you won't."

"I'm her mother."

John ignored the implication and settled his body as close to Sloan's as he could.

Sloan slapped his face. Hard. Her eyes and mouth flew open. "Get off me." She brought her knees up and kicked him with both feet.

John pushed himself away. "I'm sorry. I forgot. I should have known better."

Clare gathered her daughter in her arms, started to say something to John but changed her mind. She looked toward the place where he had stepped out of the woods then turned back to him, her face a question.

He shook his head once.

Clare closed her eyes. Sloan wrapped her arms around her mother's neck and began to whimper. Clare pulled her tighter. "She's having nightmares."

"How sick is she?"

"She's been vaccinated. Luther said it would help. Her fever has broke."

At Luther's name, John's face went slack.

Clare held and rocked Sloan until she stopped shivering and slipped into a fitful sleep. John removed his shirt and laid it across her as Clare eased her onto the ground.

"Where's Luther?" Colleen said, her tone angry.

John motioned the two of them away so Sloan wouldn't hear their voices and wake. He told them what he'd seen.

Colleen sank to the ground and rested her head on her knees. When Clare touched her, she shrugged her off, scrunched into a fetal position.

Clare shifted her weight from one leg to the other. "Do you think the Nationalists are coming here?"

"I don't know. It's possible. One of us should go over there, where you can see down the mountain without being seen. I'll go first."

"John… I'm sorry you had to see that. I'm sorry for Luther. He was a nice boy."

The next morning, Sloan's fever was gone and so were her chills. Colleen held a bottle of water to her lips. "Just sip it." Sloan tried to tilt it up so she could gulp.

Clare came back from her turn as lookout and carefully jiggled John awake. They ate biscuits and jerky for breakfast before John left to take his turn.

The sun was high overhead when Sloan woke for good. She sat up and looked at her arms and down the rest of her body. "I'm yellow," she said.

"It won't last, not all of it." Collen smiled. "At least you've still got your hair."

Sloan pulled on a shirt and jeans and looked around for her mother, who was asleep a few yards away. "I've had the most horrible nightmares. They were terrifying fever dreams."

"Tell me about it. You nearly knocked all three of us out with your thrashing."

"Three?"

"Clare, John, and me."

Sloan held still and silent for a moment. "Where's Luther?"

"They shot him."

"Who? Where?"

"The Nationalists at Pap's place. Clare and John have been keeping watch to see if they're coming up the mountain. So far, they haven't."

Sloan bent her head into her hands, but she was too dehydrated to cry. "He was so sweet. He was the best of us, you know." She looked at Colleen, imploring this worn-out, jaded sister of hers to believe her, to understand what the world had lost.

Colleen nodded. "You knew him and if you say so, it must be true. Your mother's awake."

After hearing Sloan's dream, Clare brought her to Unc's fallen down cabin and sat her on the log. Without going into graphic detail, she told her as simply and honestly as she could of the time the government took her away and put her in foster care; gave her to a family no eight-year-old girl should ever come across, let alone live with. Vile things happened in that house, manifested themselves in the rape of Clare's daughter over and over until her brain grew a protective coat of armor and shut down the synapses of memory.

Clare stroked her daughter's hair. "You knew what happened. Even was able to tell the police. But after a while, you started to forget. We never talked about it. Some said we should. Some horseshit about repressed memories. I hoped you'd never remember."

Sloan stared straight ahead for a moment. "I never could, um, you know, have sex. With anyone. I thought I never would. I'd just freak out when it came to the nitty-gritty. I actually ran away. Even if I really liked the guy, no matter how great he was, I just couldn't. Until our last night at home. With

Shimmer. It felt like we should have done it the first day we met. It felt like we should do it for the rest of our lives."

Clare nodded.

"If I never see him again, I'll never stop loving him. I can't imagine anyone else for me."

"I could see it in your face. And I'm glad." Clare stared into the middle distance. "I didn't want you to remember, but now that you have, I think it's good if it lets you be with someone. We all need that kind of connection. That boy will come back. He's too wily to get caught."

Sloan thought about her mother's new religion and the way she and John "prayed."

"Did those horrible dreams come because of what Shimmer and I did?"

"No, he opened a door, that's all. Good and bad can walk the same direction."

At dusk, they tried to have some kind of service for Luther. Clare had gone and come back from the lookout so they could all be present. Sloan started to describe him. "He looked so silly… so, um, cornfed." She drew a deep breath. "But he was really… a great sous-chef."

She said these last words in a rush. "He was always… right… um… there, knowing what… I needed." She shook her head. "I just can't." Sloan tried to regulate her breathing, which caused it to stop altogether. She gasped, hyperventilated, panic showing in her wide eyes, her shaking hands, one reaching for her chest as she struggled.

Clare slipped a backpack over her daughter's head and like a horse suddenly blinded, Sloan froze. Her breathing slowed, slowed some more, until she reached for the pack and pulled it away, remembering she was a twenty-four-year-old grown woman. She looked through the dark at John's silhouette. "Where is he? I mean his body?"

John hunkered down, sat on his haunches, and looked at Sloan. "I don't know, but I will go back tomorrow and try to find out."

"Great. Then both of you will be dead." Colleen dropped an arm around Sloan's neck. "Don't you worry, sister, my brother isn't going anywhere, even if I have to knock him out."

"You don't give me enough credit, Colleen. I can see without being seen."

"Right, just like a ghost."

"It's okay." Sloan slipped her hand in Colleen's. "If he doesn't go, I will. I need to know where he is."

No living creature can imitate the stillness of the dead. Seeing Luther's body on the ground between the stable and the house, John rested his forehead on the trunk of a tree, wrapped his arms around it to keep his knees from buckling.

He'd brought a sheet just in case, the only one in camp. Bottle flies covered Luther's back, others fought to get to the dark thick pool beneath him. John waved his hand over the young man's body. The flies rose sluggishly an inch or two before returning to their feast. This happened three times. "Get away, get away you motherfuckers," John screamed, spittle flying from his mouth. Ignoring his tears, sobs, and snot, he rolled Luther's body over. It had been one day, but the heat had done its work. John gagged, grabbed hold of Luther's shirt, and rolled him onto the sheet. Rolling, tucking, tying, he encased Luther in his shroud, leaving enough of the sheet for a handle. John then began to drag the body across the yard, past the stable and back pasture, across the path and into the darkness of the pines. Using the shovel he'd found in the stable, he started jabbing it in the earth.

The summer had turned beastly. John dug and dug, sweat blinding him. He gave up trying to wipe it away and shoved the pointed instrument into the ground by instinct. Sloan should be here, he thought. She was the one who could truly honor this man's life. He would bring her to this spot when the fear had died. It was the best he could do for now.

# CHAPTER THIRTY-EIGHT

The sun ascended from behind the mountain and cast navy-blue shadows from the trees into the clearing where Clare had spiked a fever. She spent the next two days lying with her arms around the same rocks Colleen had used when she was in the stream, head floating between them, the rest of her body under the water. When she began to shiver, she laid in a small patch of fierce sunlight until the chills passed. Barely lucid, she dragged herself back to the creek. She preferred to fight her battle against H26 alone, though the others begged her not to.

After two days, she was strong enough to return to the clearing and settled on her side, her left arm stretched so she could rest her head on her upper arm. She placed her right hand under her cheek. When one of the others dripped water into her mouth drop by slow drop, she didn't fight and forced herself to swallow. Gradually her sleep became less restless, her breathing less shallow. Only the thwack, thwack of helicopters flying lower and lower over the trees kept her from dropping into an eight-hour healing rest.

On the fifth day, Clare left the clearing while John was away on lookout and walked into the woods. She didn't carry a gun or bow. It was still too dangerous to start a fire to cook meat. She brought her pack instead. She made her fragile way through the forest until her strength failed her. She started to backtrack when a line of wild blackberries caught her eye. Clare gathered as many of the small, bitter fruit as she could and headed home. She didn't remember in her fever-drained state when the food had run out, but she hoped the berries would be a treat.

Even Colleen fell on them, popping them in her mouth and grinning as her gums turned blue.

John returned and sat on the log next to Clare, his arm around her, her head on his shoulder. "I think," John said, "it's time to start a fire."

Clare feebly shook her head against his neck. "Not yet."

"Except for me, you all are weak from the virus. You need food to build you back up. I'd rather die fighting than starving."

Colleen looked up from the berries in her hand. "What's that noise?"

# CHAPTER THIRTY-NINE

**S**himmer drove his truck as far as he could, swerved left and twined his way among the pines. Suddenly, he laughed. He braked and hit the wheel with the flat of his hand. "This is an amazing surprise, is it not. Imagine making just the right moves to end up here with Clare's truck."

He had to stop several yards back from it. Bound on three sides with trees, he couldn't have drawn alongside if he wanted to, which he didn't, two trucks being five times more visible than one.

He shifted gears and crept painstakingly forward, sometimes scraping the sides of his truck against rough bark. About half a mile beyond Clare's vehicle, he stopped and jumped out. He walked to the bed and lowered the tailgate and dragged out a travois, which he laid on the ground. He opened the passenger door and holding both her hands, helped Annie to the ground. Joint by joint, he lowered her onto the travois, gathered his backpack, and hooked the cradle straps onto his shoulders.

The going was terrible. Shimmer had no idea how long he put one foot in front of the other. He didn't stop to rest or give Annie water, knowing he might not be able to resume the awful climb.

When he dragged the travois into the clearing, all faces were staring at him. He staggered two more steps. "I brought you a surprise I think will please you."

Annie called out, "Are you there, Clare?"

What was she to do? She'd allowed all hope to die, buried it, refused to look for or at it, denied life to the most ancient and finest part of her soul. And then God or the universe, the sun, the earth turning on its axis, sparks and shows her the sin of despair.

The guilt of faith betrayed washed over Clare. But she was Clare Raffienne who had lost her parents before she knew anything, lost her beloved grandfather when she needed his wisdom most, lost and rescued her treasured daughter who bore wounds that would leave everlasting scars. She shoved the guilt aside. She caressed the knife-like bones in Annie's face, counted the fingers with no nails, circled the wrist between thumb and forefinger, smoothed her brittle hair. "I have berries," she said. "And water. Would you like some?" Arm around the yin to her yang, she helped Annie to the log.

Shimmer strode to Sloan, put the palms of his hand on either side of her face, and kissed her mouth then her ear. He wrapped his arms around her in a bear hug and swayed gently side to side. When he broke away, he moved his hands to her shoulders and stepped back, peering into her face. "Ah, you have had the plague." He ran a thumb over her right cheek, where a yellow, unevenly shaped oval with what looked like a small finger extending from the right side stood out against her white skin. "You are America," he said.

Sloan touched her cheek. Not having a mirror, she hadn't realized the virus had left her marked with a crude outline of the United States. Shimmer hugged her again and whispered, "You see. I keep my promises."

Sloan looked over at Annie. "Marshall?" she whispered.

Shimmer shook his head. "Come say hello."

"What happened to…?"

"Is best not to dwell on the dead. Annie is alive and think how happy your mother is for that."

Holding hands, Sloan and Shimmer walked over and kneeled before the two women. Annie looked like she'd been dropped from a great height. Sloan studied her misaligned bones pushing against skin striped with scars, her one knee the size of a cantaloupe, her fingers still raw from having their nails pulled off, and a foot still purple and blue, dark and shapeless.

"Annie can heal now she is with your mother. In fact, I can tell she has started," Shimmer said. "Her eyes shine." He rose, retrieved his backpack, and sat cross-legged, leaning against Sloan. "I have brought everyone other presents, though none so grand as you, Annie." He pulled three potatoes, two old apples, three cans of tuna, four cans of fruit cocktail, and a loaf of Wonder bread from his pack.

"Marshall's dead," Annie said flatly.

"I figured when I didn't see him. Do you want to tell us?"

"No."

Clare sorted through the food. She picked up a potato, letting it sit flat on her open hand to judge the weight. "It's all right to eat it raw."

John, who had been sitting on the other side of Annie, looked at Shimmer. "Did you pass by Pap's place?"

"Yes, of course. It is vacant. No one I know in Coleton is talking about it. The Nationalists have discovered people living on the Whitbeck estate. The McMannises, I am sure. I think they are looking for Rosemary there. The Nationalists, I mean. They are in for a surprise, yes." He laughed then looked around. "I am just noticing she is not here," he said, sounding alarmed.

Clare told him she'd gone into the Holler with Jack.

"This is clever idea. Perfect place. No one goes there without an invitation." He smiled then looked around again, his smile fading. "Where is the big boy with the blond hair?"

Sloan looked at her feet. "Dead."

"I see." He brought her hand to his lips and kissed it.

John stood and stretched his arms wide. "You heard the man. No one's at Pap's. They're all trying to figure out what to do with the McMannises. Good luck to them. I think it's time to build a fire. Let's roast those potatoes."

Twilight didn't arrive until after nine. They'd split the potatoes among them. The vitamin-rich carbs cast a spell, and they languished around the fire pit even though John had put it out. Colleen was asleep. Shimmer laid on his back, his head in Sloan's lap. They'd made a form of bedding from clothes and backpacks and propped Annie on it. Clare and John leaned against each other. The two deaths lingered, specter-like around them. By unspoken agreement, they kept their grief to themselves.

Shimmer, almost asleep, closed his eyes. Sloan noticed and marveled at how bright the setting sun had become: yellow mixed with orange, streaking from a stunning red base. Sparks and licks of flame leaped upward. "Jesus Christ," she shouted, jumping to her feet, rolling Shimmer on to his face. John was already on his feet. He grabbed Clare and pulled her upright. Shimmer recovered from being dumped, rose, and cupped a hand above his eyes, staring at the sky. "Napalm,'" he said simply. "I think we now know how the Nationalists are dealing with the McMannises."

Colleen slept on.

"Is it that far away?" Clare said. "It looks really far away."

"Yes," Shimmer answered with such certainty everyone believed him. "I must go to Coleton."

"No!"

"Sloan, we must know what is happening."

"Then I'm going with you."

"Not this time. You are still weak from being sick. You stay here."

"I'm going with you."

"No… you are not."

Sloan grabbed his shirt. "Yes, I am."

"Shimmer," John said. "Soon it will be dark. Why not wait till morning? Surely, they won't try to bomb anything else in the dark. Go in the morning."

"It is safer to drive in the dark."

"Not in these woods it's not."

Shimmer stared at John for a few moments. "True," he said. "I will leave at first light."

The night was endless. No one slept well. Sloan and Shimmer kept up a low grumble back and forth, obviously arguing. Finally, Colleen yelled, "Shut up." They disappeared into the woods.

The next morning, Sloan and Shimmer resolutely put knives, guns, and bullets into their backpacks. Neither said a word. Clare and John studiously ignored them. Finished packing, Shimmer took Sloan's pack and dropped it on the ground and wrapped his arms around her. "You must stay here. The others need you."

Sloan shoved him away. "Don't patronize me."

"All right. Come then. But if anything happens to you, I will never forgive you." He snatched her pack off the ground and shoved it at her. They were standing this way when suddenly something roared in the woods, rocks banging together hurtling down the mountain, tree limbs cracked like rifle shots. Rusty tore into the clearing and screeched to a halt. He jumped off the cycle and gasping and twitching, tried to talk. "I have news," he blurted.

Clare went to him and put her hand on his head to keep him still. "Breathe."

"President Diamond is dead. Someone shot him in the back of his head and in his back. In the bathroom. His fly was unbuttoned, and he fell across the toilet."

Sloan and Shimmer knew exactly who shot him. All innocence, Shimmer said, "No one could get that close to him. He is guarded by the best military men in the world. And they *love* him. He loves them. Very tight group. All loyalty and love."

Sloan touched his foot with hers. "So, you are misinformed," he finished.

"No, I'm not. Everyone is talking about it. Captain Riddick told me. The Holiday Inn is a madhouse."

Shimmer carefully inspected his fingernails. "No, much as I would like to believe what you are telling us, it simply cannot be true."

Standing perfectly still, Rusty faced down the naysayer. "Believe what you want. But President Diamond is dead as a doornail."

## CHAPTER FORTY
*ONE YEAR LATER*

Even though the Nationalists were no longer a unified force, Sloan and Shimmer stayed on the back roads, using the same strategy they had used before the assassination: back tracking, choosing circuitous routes, and traveling at night as much as possible. It took them six days to reach the rugged rocks of the Canadian Sheild Plateau.

Sonny and Lena lived in a pine forest near a town with the charmingly quixotic name of Flin Flon. Sonny was standing on the porch when they finally arrived. His military stance had not changed. He hugged Shimmer, shook Sloan's hand, and brought them inside a one-room house large enough to be called open concept instead of a one-room hut. Saskatchewan is hot in the summer, and that day the temperature was over ninety. Inside however, was cool and dim. Sloan noticed the kitchen was clean, but the appliances could have been twenty years old. The worn wooden floor was covered with a heavy braided rug. There were three braided rugs in all, giving definition to various spaces. The largest wood-burning stove Sloan had ever seen stood center stage. Behind it was a bed with small tables on either side and behind this a couch and three over-stuffed chairs. The cabin was filled with the scent of butter cooking and vegetables roasting.

Lena had lost weight, the softness in her face replaced by a knowing hardness.

Sonny put his arm around her shoulders. "I imagine you're full of questions, but my wife insists we eat first. She's made borscht especially for you, Shimmer." They all settled at the battered kitchen table while Lena ladled bowls of red soup. "We don't get many visitors," she said. "In fact, we don't get any except for our landlord and his family."

"This is wonderful," said Shimmer after his first spoonful. "We had it all the time growing up but nothing like this. Ours was mostly water."

After the soup came pierogies swimming in butter and filled with cheese and mushrooms along with small cabbage rolls stuffed with vegetables. Sloan had had plenty of pierogies before but none as good as these.

Shimmer ate seconds then thirds. At last, he sat back. "You spoil us. I thought all you would have is grizzly, snow bunnies, and caribou."

Sonny laughed. "It's really quite civilized here. There's a large Ukrainian population. These foods are common." He pushed back from the table and crossed his legs, his expression becoming serious. Without waiting for questions, he began a discourse that sounded to Sloan carefully thought out.

It had been easy, both emotionally and physically, to kill the president. "When he gave the order to waterboard Whitbeck, I alerted my contacts to be ready. Then he told me he was going to napalm the estate the following night. It was the gleeful way he said it that put me over the edge. He was wired, bouncing back and forth between fury and exaltation. He insisted I stay the night; said he'd never be able to get to sleep. Around one-thirty in the morning, he went into the bathroom to take a pee."

Lena reached over and took Sonny's hand.

"I put a silencer on my gun, and as the president unzipped his fly, I shot him in the back of the head and torso. I was worried the Secret Service guys outside the door would hear the shots even with the silencer. I didn't have a plan for that. I couldn't have shot them. I knew that much. I guess I hoped they didn't like Diamond any more than I did. I just didn't let myself think about it. Turned out they were asleep." Sonny laughed.

"The hard part was getting into Canada and the grueling relay from driver to driver on the way. I chose Flin Flon because it's so damn cold. Temperature drops below zero in November and doesn't budge until May." He sighed. "I figured no one would brave the bitter weather to find me."

"You killed him in the summer," Shimmer reminded him.

"DC was such a mess by then. Plots everywhere. I counted on the mixed loyalties to give me some time." Sonny let go of Lena's hand and finished his glass of wine. "Now it's your turn. What's it like down there? We don't get much news here."

"You are right," said Shimmer. "Everything was chaos in DC. People storming the capital. Riots in the streets. The generals sent in the Feds. What? Don't look so surprised. Diamond was not a popular guy with the military."

"What's happening now?"

"Still a mess in some places. The places where people didn't have jobs or couldn't make a living before Diamond put them to work still wage a disorganized war against the people who are glad the bastard is dead. But with no leader, they are like a snake with no head. The real National Guard is growing every day. Many volunteers. Even if at first they don't get paid."

"Any chance of a military state?"

"No, no. Big business would never allow it." Shimmer put more cabbage rolls on his plate. "I love America. The capitalists are not afraid of hard work or using the middle class to make monies. And Europe is thrilled to do business with us again." He shrugged. "There are still shortages everywhere while supply chains reform. You knew the Speaker of the House is acting president? They plan an election in 2030."

"No kidding. Do you think it will happen?"

Shimmer shrugged. "Is highly possible."

"And the virus?"

"Big pharma is working hard at pumping out vaccines as fast as they can." He rubbed his thumb and fingers together. "Always money in selling drugs to the people."

"Who's paying for it?"

"How would I know? Do you think I'm an accountant? I can tell you it will be the little people in the end."

Sonny stood up, went to the refrigerator, and brought back another bottle of wine. He looked at Shimmer who said, "One more glass of the good honest grape won't hurt my liver."

Sonny poured the wine. "And what about Rosemary? The eye of the storm."

"The ever-quiet eye of the storm." Sloan shook her head. "Strange girl. Her father came for her in an armored convoy. Three big, black, bulletproof SUVs four weeks after you murdered the president. She'd been living with this creep in a place no words can describe. Whitbeck showed up and whisked her away. She never looked back."

"How'd he find out where she was?"

"No idea. He just got word to us he was coming to get her. No explanation. My mom, with her usual arrogance, drove her truck to Jack's place and told Rosemary to get in, she would be returning to the farm so she could be reunited with her family and that was that.

"Haven't heard from her or her dad since," Sloan continued. "There's a rumor he's in Saudi Arabia." She turned to Lena. "What are you going to do next? Will you stay here?"

"God no," Sonny said before Lena could answer. "It's too damn cold." He looked at his wife. "No, we're leaving before the snow flies."

Sloan leaned toward Lena. "Come work with me. I love your cooking."

"What? You've opened a new restaurant? Where?"

"In the city. New York City."

Lena blushed again and smiled at Sonny. "Thanks, but I don't think so."

"New York is cold too," he said. "Anyway, I don't think we will be living in the US for a while."

Sloan felt a stir of anxiety. Half the country would vote for Sonny to be the new president. The other half thought he should be convicted of murder, and half of those thought he should be hung for treason. "Where will you go?"

"Somewhere warm," said Sonny.

"With tropical breezes," Lena added.

A month after the assassination, Clare and her family moved permanently to Pap's place. She would never again live next to a paved road.

Sloan, Shimmer, John, and Rusty helped break down the stable at Valley Farm and used the wood to rebuild Clare's old home. Colleen was still too weak and Annie too crippled to do anything but give advice.

Everyone had expected Rusty to fly down the mountain after he'd delivered his message, but he did not. He stayed, fidgeting and swaying, starting sentences, stopping, starting again, talking so fast no one could understand him. Attracted to Colleen's cool melancholy, he attached himself to her. They bickered constantly but these skirmishes brought color to Colleen's cheeks and focused Rusty enough to experience moments of motionless thought.

The able-bodied transported goods to their new home for two months before Valley Farm's closest neighbor—who lived seven miles away—bought the place. Annie considered the price sinfully low, especially with the five percent inflation. But prices were all over the place for everything. And selling was preferable to letting it stay empty. Besides, she realized she didn't mind cutting ties to the farm she once loved. She'd spent the best times of her youth at Clare's place.

Over the rest of the summer, Clare, with friends and family, restored the old house.

The stables were surprisingly sound and housed three training colts, all from people Clare had known her entire life. She and Annie would never do business with strangers again.

One evening in October when the light had the sharp, crisp shine of coming winter, the group sat in chairs or on the ground drinking beer and admiring how the house was shaping up. John dipped a hand in the ice-filled cooler, wiped off the moisture with his shirt, and handed it to Annie. They'd all been talking about bedroom arrangements. With Annie and Sloan back and Rusty and Shimmer moving in, they decided to add two or three rooms.

Clare reached in the cooler for another beer and held the bottle over her head so the light would catch it. She smiled. "Liquor is fine for medicinal reasons but there ain't nothing like an ice-cold beer." She took a swallow. "So, how many rooms? If we did three, they'd be awfully small."

Shimmer, who'd been sitting at Sloan's feet, looked up at her.

"Um," Sloan said.

Her mother turned to her.

"Ah…"

Clare stared at her daughter for a long moment. "You're leaving," she said.

"Yeah."

"Where to?"

"New York. To try and re-open Sally's Sauce."

"It's prob'ly the most dangerous place in the country."

"I will go with her," Shimmer said. "It will be all right. And if it doesn't work out, we will come back. I will come back no matter what." He grinned. "I love you peoples. So, I will come to see you. For a while. Is too quiet here to just stay."

As it turned out, New York City was now one of the safest places in the country. When he took over, Diamond had sent in his most hard-core Nationalists to control the left-wing liberals. With Diamond dead, those who had fled the city came back and, along with those who had stayed, smashed windows and burned down government buildings until the hard-core Nationalists who had never wanted to be there in the first place went back to Wyoming or Montana or wherever they had come from. The city went back to doing business. Sloan moved into an abandoned deli three doors down from the original Sally's Sauce. She cobbled together a workable kitchen and small dining room furnished with mismatched tables, chairs, silverware, and plates found in garage sales and thrift stores or on the street. The tablecloths were all made from pale cream 800 count Egyptian cotton sheets she found at the Salvation Army. They raised her spirits whenever she looked at them. The night she opened, she served to a full house from six to midnight. People brought their own wine. Shimmer tended bar and proved to be a good mixologist, as long as the drink was vodka on the rocks.

Some of her customers couldn't pay, but in this lawless land it didn't matter. She'd begged, borrowed, and stolen what she needed to get started. She would pay everyone back some day, and she was sure her customers would pay her back as well, one way or another.

Her new sous-chef, Blithe, was a petite blonde whose half-inch hair lay close to her head. The girl worked with cheerful efficiency. But she wasn't Luther. Sloan missed him every day and started every evening by silently telling him so.

It would be nice to say Sloan and Shimmer settled into a partnership and ran the new Sally's Sauce together. But this is not a Disney story. He continued to come and go as always. Sloan's heart ached every time he left and sang every time he returned. He would walk through the door, unannounced and unexpected, looking dangerous and slightly dirty. Two days later, he would be in the dining room, clean, his black curls almost tamed. The guests always asked for him, and when he was home, he'd go from table to table, making people smile and sometimes sharing their dessert.

When the holidays came around, the city bedecked and bejeweled itself with every decoration people could find or make. Christmas carols rang out everywhere as though shouting to the world, "the wicked king is dead."

Two days before Thanksgiving, Shimmer crawled into the bed behind the kitchen. He pulled Sloan next to him and kissed her neck. "I will be leaving tomorrow," he whispered.

"But it's Thanksgiving. I could use your help."

"I never understood this American holiday with its big turkeys. Plymouth is on the water, no. Why not serve fish and seafood? Were the forests so full of turkeys back then the pilgrims ignore the bounty of the sea?"

The forests and farmers were not full of turkeys in 2027. They were scarcer than hen's teeth. In fact, Sloan substituted old, rangy hens and roosters for the traditional over-sized bird. It took all her talents to turn the wrecks into something tender and tasty.

She also bought bushels of yellow perch, mussels, scallops, and shrimp.

She'd been putting money aside for the holidays since she'd opened. Plus, Shimmer put some under her pillow before he left. When Sloan asked him where he got it, he said, "Supply and demand, my love, supply and demand. I am, how you say, Robin Hood."

Sloan was back from the open markets by eight in the morning. Blithe had no place to go, so she stayed with Sloan and started shelling seafood at ten a.m.

Even those without reservations began pouring in at noon, and Sally's Sauce was full until closing time. By the end of the day, Sloan was serving only bread and gravy and the proverbial green bean casserole made from cans.

Once the dishes were done and the kitchen clean, she and Blithe sat on stools with a bottle of white wine Sloan had held back. She removed her bandana and shook out her hair. "I had no idea it would be so busy."

"People told me they couldn't find food in the grocery stores. They were super glad you were open."

"It's like a third world country."

"It *is* a third world country."

They regarded each other. Sloan pointed to Blithe's head. "Have you had the virus?"

Blithe ran her hand over her hair. "Yes, but I was lucky. And you? Or is that a birth mark?"

Sloan laughed. "I was lucky too."

Blithe hesitated, then said, "Do you worry people who aren't immune don't wear masks?"

"I should...."

"Nobody else does."

"Why do you think that is?"

"I don't know. Maybe because with Diamond dead and the Nationalists back in hiding, people are just done with being scared. It wouldn't do any good trying to make them. They'd just ignore you."

Sloan bobbed her foot up and down. "I guess we'll get to herd immunity at some point." She poured more wine in their glasses. "How are you still awake? You must be exhausted."

"Not yet. It will hit me when the wine does."

Sloan went to the cash register and pulled out fifty dollars and handed it to her sous-chef. "I couldn't have done this without you. I wish it could be more. I think I lost money tonight."

Blithe handed her back the fifty.

"No, no. That's not what I meant. Just promise me you'll come back."

"Course I will."

Three days before Christmas, Sloan started shopping for Christmas dinner. Long Island ducks were plentiful, goose from Canada, apples and cranberries from upstate New York. Potatoes were hard to find, but after going store to store in Brooklyn, she found what she hoped was enough.

She rose at six Christmas day to check and make sure she had everything she needed. She started peeling apples for the pies. When the pies were in the oven, she started on the potatoes and put them in water so they wouldn't turn brown. She popped a stray slice of apple into her mouth. In her opinion, New York state apples were second to none.

She expected Blithe to be back from an underground run for mustard any minute so didn't look up when the bell over the door jingled. Shimmer walked in and dropped his backpack on the floor. Snow dusted his denim jacket.

"So, I guess it's snowing," was all Sloan managed to say. She thought she might cry.

He shrugged and smiled then walked around the table and wrapped his arms around her. He smelled of snow, the cold and the city. Sloan buried her face in his curls.

When she stepped back, her brows knitted together. "You're tan." His spots showed more clearly than ever.

"It's pretty here when it snows. We will have a white Christmas."

"Are you staying?"

"For a while."

"Where did you get your tan… if I may ask."

"Ko Lipe."

"Ko Lipe. Where the hell is that?"

"Some place warm. With tropical breezes."

Sloan watched him. "I see."

"I'm going back, and I want you to come with me. I have been missing you so much it hurts."

"When will you leave?"

"In a few days."

"It's the holidays."

"No one goes to restaurants during the holidays. Especially New Year's Eve. They will make merry in clubs. Besides, New York is filled with cold winds and ice in the winter."

Sloan looked at his dark desert face, his lovely mouth, and his eyes so brown they were almost black. A line from a Bob Dylan song went through her mind. *"It doesn't take a weatherman to know which way the wind blows."* Warmth. Tropical breezes. A sign on the door of Sally's Sauce saying CLOSED.

"Did you know," she said, "if you don't eat pork on New Year's Day, you will have bad luck for the rest of the year. Luckily, I know a guy. Not too far from the city. Has a pig farm. And an apple orchard. I thought I'd serve pork shoulder, my famous applesauce and, of course, the dish that started it all. Spaghetti and Cheese."

*THE END*

# About the Author

E. Compton Lee began her writing career as a freelance writer of nature and human-interest articles for magazines such as *Mother Earth News, Practical Horseman, American Country and Horseman*.

Her first novel, *Native*, takes place in the backwoods of Appalachia, and portrays a woman struggling to overcome misogyny and bigotry to find her place in the cutthroat world of the horse industry.

*My Name Is Sloan*, a companion to *Native*, tells of a mother fighting to rescue her daughter from foster care. She is helped by good people handcuffed by bureaucracy and the blindness that takes place in agencies meant to help children.

Born and raised in the Hudson River Valley, she left this region at the age of eighteen and embarked upon a journey which immersed her in a multitude of cultures. The knowledge gained from those experiences is what is used when she writes her novels.

E. Compton Lee lived in the Allegheny Mountains of Pennsylvania and western Maryland for fifteen years, where she worked as a therapist and ran a horse business. She currently lives in Williamsburg, Virginia, where she writes full time.